Janene Loucks

2 MINUTES: Revealed

ISBN: 0615928978
ISBN 13: 9780615928975

Two down, one to go…

Acknowledgments

I SURROUND MYSELF WITH those who add something wonderful to my life, not suck the living air out of me. My family, my children, my husband, and my friends helped create who I became and continue to allow me to grow into who I want to become; a better me.

By Janene Loucks

Chapter 1

"MY DEAREST GWEN...there's something I need to tell you that I should have told you years ago." I take a deep breath. "I didn't write the books. I took credit for something I didn't do and profited from it all these years." There, I've said it. "I wanted to tell you, and I tried to a thousand times, but I always chickened out, like a chump. I wanted to be a somebody so bad that I didn't care at what cost. One day this book showed up on my computer, and I have no idea where it came from, but it promised me everything I've ever wanted: money, fame, you." I start to choke up. "Every day of my life I wished to be someone else, someone who didn't look the way I did. I wanted someone to love me, someone to kiss every day. I wanted to wake up and look in the mirror and not see a new black eye or a split lip. I was so tired of being hated for the way I looked...I was desperate. When this book showed up, I thought my prayers were finally being answered. After all those years thinking God hated me, I felt vindicated for everything I endured; all the pain and gut-wrenching torture I had felt before was now going away. When you came into my life, I felt like a kid in a candy store. For the very first time, I knew what a woman felt like, how a kiss tasted. It truly felt like my heart was healing that day you came to my apartment. But then it seemed like everything started happening so quickly for me. Money started rolling in, people wanted to know me instead of hurt me...after twenty-eight years I was finally being treated like a person instead of a monster." I run my hands through my hair and start to pace back and forth. I look up at the sky as the clouds start to move in. I know it's going to start raining, but I need to tell her everything, right here, right now. "As ludicrous as it sounds, I had started to forget that I didn't even write the books. It wasn't hard, considering the first book was about my past, but when the second book showed up—promising me even more fame and money—I didn't care where it came from. In fact, I didn't even read it. I had no idea what was to come, of anyone or anything. All I knew was my life was going to be even better, so the hell with everything else!" My throat is getting so dry; I hope I can do this. Please don't hate me, Gwen. "You know, taking credit for the books and enjoying the profits from them wasn't the worst part. The books foretold the future and I ignored it. I knew people were going to die, but I didn't care. When I found out the Lavetti brothers were being killed off, I had a rush of adrenaline like you wouldn't believe! I thought: This is it! Vengeance is mine! I really thought I had some kind of power to make things happen, but as time went on, I realized that what I was doing wasn't right, and I had no way of stopping it. Every day my conscience was growing stronger, and every day that passed, I knew it was an opportunity I had missed to tell you about it. Four Lavetti brothers have been killed, and there are rumors going around that I am the one who killed them. I don't remember anything, Gwen, I swear, but I have a feeling they are right. I've woken up before with bloody clothes on and it wasn't my blood. Ruth had even mentioned she saw me start the fire that burned my mom's house down. I'm scared, Gwen, and I don't know what to do. When that last book showed up, I was going to delete it, but then you came home and I forgot. I wasn't going to make that book happen because I knew it would have caused your death. When I found out you were the one who did hit Send, I wanted to kill myself. How was I to tell the mother of my unborn child that she will die after she gives birth to our son?" I feel the raindrops fall on my skin. The clouds have now made their way above us, casting a shadow across the headstones. I kneel down in front of her grave. "I am so sorry, Gwen. All I ask is for your forgiveness, and to give me strength to take care of our son. I will always love you."

As I lay the orange lilies on her grave, I begin to sob uncontrollably. My heart feels as though it's going to pop out of my chest. I can't breathe. At this point I would rather die right here with my beloved, but the thought of my son starts to calm me down. I just lie there on the grass, allowing the rain to cleanse me of my sins. I close my eyes and take it all in. Memories start to flood my heart as the rain seems to be stopping. The sun is coming out; I can feel the light on my face. I open my eyes and turn my head toward her. In my grogginess, I feel like she's lying next to me, holding my hand, and I smile. I continue to lie there for a while, even though the wet grass has soaked through my clothes, but I don't care. It is at that moment that I find peace.

As I slowly stand up, I can feel the blood rushing to my head. I lean forward with my hands on my knees and take a few deep breaths. As I look down at my feet, I see the rain has made a muddy mess of things. When I rise back up I hear rustling of leaves or something behind me. I turn around just as the silhouette starts running away. "Hey!" I yell at him, but he doesn't turn around. I grab my jacket and run after him; well, try to at least. The muddy grass has made it difficult to gain speed, so I don't take my eyes off him as I try to maintain traction. I am almost to the parking lot when I see a green truck drive away. "Damn it! Who the hell was that?" I try to catch my breath, and then suddenly it hits me. "Oh shit! Whoever that was just heard my secret about the books, and that I might've killed the Lavettis! Fuck!" I get in my car and drive away. "What the hell am I going to do?" As I pull up to the house, I can't help reliving what just happened. "Wait a minute! Maybe he didn't hear anything! I could be worrying for nothing! Man, I am way too paranoid for daytime."

I pull into the garage just as Cheryl is walking in. "How did it go? You okay?" she asks.

"Yeah. It's never easy going there, but today, I don't know...it felt different to me. I finally felt peace for the first time. Maybe it was the rain."

Cheryl gets a look at the drenched rat standing before her. "Oh, Michael! Didn't anyone ever tell you to get out of the rain! You are soaked! Get in that house so I can wash these!"

"Yes, ma'am. How's Hunter?" I ask.

"Sleeping like an angel, but he should be getting up here soon. His cold seems to be subsiding, but his cough medicine still knocks him out. I guarantee, once you open his bedroom door and the aroma from the kitchen permeates his nostrils, he will bounce out of that bed so quick! That boy loves to eat, just like his daddy!" She smiles and pats my back.

We both walk to the house. "Cheryl," I say, stopping her before we go inside, "I don't think I could have done this without you. Thank you for being here for us. You are an angel." I start to tear up, but then I clear my throat. "What's for dinner?"

Cheryl just looks at me. "Meatloaf—and you're welcome." She smiles and then walks into the house.

I stand back, dreading this part every time. Walking in this house makes me relive that first day I came home without her. It feels like yesterday, even though it's been three years. When I walk through the door I can hear little footsteps running down the stairs, and immediately my sorrow turns to joy.

Hunter comes running over to me. "Daddy! I'm all better now!" He hugs me.

"I can see that, buddy! Are you hungry? Cheryl made meatloaf!" I tell him.

"Yeah!" he screams, and then he starts to run around the kitchen table. "Yeah! Yeah!" he continues, until he bites it going around the corner. He starts to cry when he figures out what just happened.

"Hey, buddy, are you okay? Maybe you shouldn't be running so fast," I explain to him, but he just wants to cry and wipe his nose on my sleeve. Good thing I haven't changed out of these wet clothes yet. Washer, here we come. After I clean him up and put him in his chair, he miraculously is all better. Funny how kids heal so quickly when there's food in front of them. I make my way upstairs to put some clean clothes on. I glance at our Italy photo. I sit down on the bed and lose track of time. I start reminiscing about our trip to Italy. It was the best two weeks of our lives. We went everywhere we could, not stopping to really enjoy the little things. We ate way too much, stuffing ourselves full of pasta, bread, and the best pastries you could possibly find. I am so thankful we were able to make that trip and have pictures to relive it, considering...

Before we left on that vacation, Angelique came to town and helped Gwen open the store. The grand opening was so amazing. Hundreds of people showed up and nearly bought out the entire store! Their online business was flourishing as well. Gwen did end up being the model for the brochures, although she was hesitant because she was pregnant. In the few short months Gwen was with us, her business was ridiculously busy. Angelique ended up renting an apartment in town, since Gwen was way too busy to run it herself. After Gwen died, I sold the business back to Angelique, with a promise that she would continue to use Gwen's image as the good luck charm she truly was. She agreed. The business is still there, doing as well as ever. I drive by every so often just so I can relive the happiest time of my life. Of course, I usually end up crying...I could possibly be an emotional cutter.

Memory lane is soon cut short as Cheryl comes in and asks me, "Are you going to eat?"

"Yeah, I'll be down in a minute. I just got caught up in...you know." I look back at the pictures and Cheryl's eyes follow.

"Michael, you have to stop this. It's not healthy to continue living in the past. You have a beautiful little boy downstairs asking where Daddy is. Come on, let's go." She smiles as she throws me a clean shirt.

If you have ever wondered what goes through a three-year-old's mind when there is food and no adults around—well, let me just paint that picture for you. Apparently, white is not on his color palette. The wall is now speckled with a lovely shade of meatloaf, and the floor—well, let's just say he has a knack for giving a smooth surface a new texture. But, the cherry on top of this man-made landfill has to be the globule of mashed potatoes and beets that he fruitfully precast into a torpedo and then hurled at least fifteen feet across the room, spraying the glass patio door.

"Hunter Lance Bali! What have you done?" My voice is, as it should be, ticked off.

"Daddy, look!" He points to the door. "Boogeyman!"

"What are you talking about? There is no boogeyman. We have talked about this, right?" I grab the rag and start cleaning up.

"No boogeyman! I scared him away, like a big boy!" He is quite pleased with himself.

"Wait, you saw a man at the door?" I walk over to it.

"Uh-huh! He ran away, Daddy!" Hunter continues to eat what's left on his plate.

"What the fu—?" I say under my breath as I open the door. I look out over the yard and around the garage. I walk back to the door and notice there's fresh mud on the steps. "Who in the hell was here?" I ask myself. Then I remember the cemetery today. It was muddy and someone was there, watching me. I go inside and decide not to tell Cheryl about it, not just yet. If this guy heard what I think he heard, I have to play this out strategically.

Chapter 2

I AM AWAKENED BY the smell of pancakes and bacon, two of the greatest smells ever invented. I begin to rub my eyes to wake myself up when I feel legs kick me. I look over and there's Hunter, starting to squirm himself awake. He must have climbed into my bed in the middle of the night. I watch him fight to wake up, until his eyes pop open and look around. When he notices me looking at him, he starts to laugh. When he sits up, I start to laugh, as it looks like squirrels have found a new home in his hair.

"Man, you need your hair cut!" I tell him as I ruffle his hair even more.

"No cut! Pancakes!" he yells, and crawls out of bed.

I can hear him going down the stairs and singing to himself; he is a happy little boy. I pray he remains like this, considering his face looks like mine. I was hoping it would've skipped a generation, but alas, no. He hasn't noticed it yet when he looks in the mirror, and I dread when that day comes. At least he will have someone to help him through this, unlike myself; I had to do it alone.

After I brush my teeth I head downstairs. The aromatic blessings called pancakes are sitting there, in a tall stack surrounded by bacon, their enchanting comrade, just waiting for me to dive in headfirst; so I do. My little munchkin is already hard at work with his sustenance.

I completely forget to say good morning to Cheryl. As she brings over more pancakes to the table, I manage to make room between bites to say, "Morning! These are just great!"

"Well, good morning to you! I've decided to make tacos for dinner tonight, so I made a list of things I need at the store. Do you think you can go for me? I noticed there's a lot of mud on the steps outside and I would like to clean it off, along with the outside windows," she explains.

"No problem," I reply.

Shortly after Gwen died, Cheryl came to live with us full time. I don't think I would have made it this far if she hadn't been here. Who knew she would turn out to be my rock? I owe her a great deal, and Hunter loves her, too.

"Okay, big guy, let's get you cleaned up. Into the bath we go!" Cheryl takes Hunter upstairs as he vehemently denies he needs one.

"Thanks, Cheryl. I will clean up down here." I smile at her, then I finish my plate full of heaven. My enjoyment is cut short by the telephone. "Hello?" I answer.

"Michael Bali?" the deep voice asks.

"Yes, can I help you?" I respond.

"Michael, this is Detective Manning. I was handling your mother's case from Spring Grove. Sorry to bother you, but we've just come across some information, and it's important that I speak with you about it." He sounds serious.

Okay, in my head right now, I am freaking out. Maybe that guy went to the police and told them what he heard me say? Wait, why would that same detective be calling me about this? *Calm down, Michael, stop sounding so fucking paranoid!*

"What's going on?" I ask.

"Well, as you know, almost four years ago Dave Lavetti made bail but skipped town, and we haven't been able to find him since. Now, before he left, he started talking up a storm to his cell mate about you," he starts explaining.

"About me? That doesn't sound good. Maybe he didn't like my books?" I try to laugh, but it comes across fake because it is.

"I wish it was, but I'm afraid it's more serious than that. It seems Mr. Lavetti had it in for you. He told his cell mate that when he gets out of there, he will find you and kill you. Now, most inmates talk the big talk only because they are angry they got caught, but I'm afraid this was different. That's why I am contacting you today." His voice has changed.

"Should I be worried here? I mean, you are kinda freaking me out here. What the hell did he say?" Now my voice has changed.

"Mr. Bali, he had started talking about his boys and how you took them from him, and now it's your turn to feel that kind of pain. He said if you ever had children that he would find them and kill them. Lately, we've had a few calls from people saying they've seen him around, but none of them have panned out, until this morning. Mrs. Lavetti took over the gas station after her husband went to jail, and she knew we were looking for him and Marty. She's been very cooperative with the police and, in fact, is quite scared of her husband. She wants him in jail just as much as we do, so when she called to let us know that Marty had just left the gas station, and that he threatened her if she told anyone she saw him—well, needless to say, she's terrified. She mentioned he looked quite tan, like he just came back from somewhere warm, maybe Mexico. There was a man in the cab of the truck, but she never got close enough to look in. Now, she can attest to what the cell mate had told us. When we brought her in for questioning after Mr. Lavetti didn't show up for his hearing, she started telling us the same things we heard from the cell mate."

"Wait, this doesn't make sense. He wasn't married. His wife died a long time ago," I tell him.

"It seems he remarried just a few months before he went to jail. She's a young gal, too, in her thirties. She came over from Germany, some kind of mail-order-bride thing. She's more scared for her sons than anything."

"Her sons? Wait…are you telling me that she had Dave Lavetti's kids? How old are they?" I am so distraught.

"Well, let's see…I have it written down here somewhere. Oh, she said her boys were three years old," he tells me.

"The same as mine," I mutter under my breath. "Um, do you know their names?"

"Luke and Andy," he replies.

Holy mother of fuck! He names his sons after my brothers! I can't believe this is happening, again!

"Mr. Bali, we just want you to be aware of your surroundings. Please let us know if you see anyone strange or anything out of the ordinary. This man is dangerous!" he exclaims.

"Thank you, I will. Oh, by the way, what color of truck were they in? I mean, maybe I should be on the lookout for that, too?" Well played, Columbo.

"Good idea. It was a green truck. Call us if you need anything." He hangs up.

I drop my head down in despair. "It's happening again. It's starting all over. It was them at the cemetery! Now, the last thing I want to do is cause any suspicion against myself, considering what I've possibly done." I begin to mumble, forgetting I'm not the only one in the house.

"What was that? Were you talking to me?" Cheryl asks as she starts to put things away from breakfast.

I notice she is doing exactly what I said I would do. "Cheryl, I'm sorry. I got a phone call and I forgot." I start helping her.

"Is everything all right?" she asks. "You look a little peaked."

"Yeah, everything is fine, just fine. Where's Hunter?" I look around.

"Oh, he wanted to dress himself this morning, so I gave him some privacy. I can't imagine what he'll come up with!" she laughs.

"I'd better go check on him." I head upstairs.

When I get close enough, I can hear him humming, so I quietly walk up to the door. I look into his room where he has started building something from Legos. I watch silently so he doesn't know I'm there. I often do this kind of thing so that I know he is comfortable playing alone. His humming becomes louder, but I can't quite make out what it is until my memory kicks in. He is humming the same lullaby Gwen was humming in the bathtub that fateful day. During her entire pregnancy, she would hum this beautiful song, whether she was working or sick, it didn't matter. She was so splendidly blissful being pregnant. She would have made the greatest mom in the world. As I continue to watch Hunter play, I start to reminisce about those last months with her.

She wasn't too sure about the name I came up with for our son. "I just think Hunter means just that, a hunter! I was thinking more along the lines of Julien or Chandler," she tells me.

"Julien, Really? No, my son will not have a name that is rooted with estrogen. Chandler? As in Chandler Bing? Hey, I'm a huge Friends *fan, too, but come on! The reason I wanted to name him Hunter is because my favorite writer's name is Hunter. I wanted to start writing because of him, so it's like I'm honoring his spirit in a way. Please?" I try to beg, but I just come off like a pathetic loser.*

"Fine, Hunter it is! You really are a big baby, you realize that, right?" Gwen starts to walk away, but I grab her from behind and hug her. I can still smell her hair.

"Daddy, come on and play!" Hunter grabs my hand and walks me into his room. It's decorated in greens and blues, and there are trains everywhere.

"Okay, buddy. I liked that song you were humming. Did you hear it someplace?" I just look at him in amazement that he's mine.

"I don't know," he says.

"Well, did you know that Mommy would hum that same song when she was here?" I ask him.

He looks up at me and says, "Mommy did?" Then he walks over to her picture and points to it. "Mommy there."

"That's right. That is your beautiful mommy, always watching over us, just like an angel would."

Hunter begins tearing down what he'd just built and I just watch him, smiling. I look back at Gwen's picture and begin to relive that last month she was pregnant.

"Son of a bitch!" she yells as she pushes on her tummy. "Holy Mother of God, that hurt! Your son really likes my ribs!" She tries to stand up from the bed, but needs a little help from me, so I push her. "Thanks, dear, you are such a help," she sneers.

"Where are you going?" I ask her.

"I have to pee, again," she snaps.

Man, who knew that being pregnant could bring out the inner Satan in her? "I'm sorry, honey. I will rub your feet when you come back, okay?" I try to sound like I'm not scared of her.

Before she comes back in the room, I hear, "Are you kidding me?" She wobbles back in.

"What's wrong?" I ask her.

"I just stepped on the scale and I've gained eleven more pounds this month! This month! I'm a blimp!" She sits on the bed; her eyes are filling up with tears. "Do I look ugly to you? You'd tell me, right?" Her sullen face looks at me as if I hold the secret to her happiness. How do I approach this one?

"Gwen, I find you even more beautiful because you are carrying our child, what we created out of pure love. If you weren't gaining weight I would be worried! I won't even begin to try and understand what it feels like having someone grow inside you, but what I can say is...your ass is getting huge!" I make my eyes totally wide, which makes me start to laugh. Then she slugs me, hard.

"Hey, I have an idea! Let's go get some ice cream, and then we will watch a scary movie. How's that for a romantic evening?" I brush the hair out of her face and kiss her cheek. She smiles and says okay. As I start to walk out the bedroom door, I turn around and tell her, "But you only get one scoop, blubber butt!" The next thing I know, she's hurling a book at my head. Contact. Ouch.

"Hey, watch this, Daddy! I can make my nose do this!" He starts to flare out his nostrils.

"Hey, I can do that, too. Watch Daddy!" I begin to flare my nostrils back at him. Together we flare; like father, like son. I'm so proud. "I have to go to the store. Do you want to come with me or stay here with Auntie Cheryl?"

I like to give him some decision making, makes him feel important.

"Stay wif Cheryl," he states matter-of-factly.

I lean down and kiss his head. "Okay, buddy, be good!"

Going into the garage used to make me giddy, but ever since that motherfucker, Marty, took my Mustang—man, I just get pissed more than anything. Don't get me wrong, I still love my other girls, but that yellow one, man, ticks me off. I could go buy another one, but I need to start changing my life in order to be a great father, and buying sports cars "just because" isn't the way to start. I decided to keep Gwen's Range Rover instead of selling it. It feels like she's still with me when I drive it; plus, it's a lot safer for me to drive Hunter around than my other beauties. I might even start to sell my other cars, maybe move away, who knows. This whole new shit about Dave and Marty being back in town just might make that happen.

I pull into the grocery store just as a downpour starts. I make a run for it, but I am not fast enough; the rain has washed half the ink off the list. "Damn it!" I mutter. I start down each aisle thinking that it may trigger my memory. I grab some cereal, syrup, cough medicine, soap...at this point I'm just throwing anything in my cart. The last time I went grocery shopping was...three years ago. By the time I am done, my cart is full of random crap and I have no idea what I'm buying. When I get home, Cheryl stands there watching in amusement while I bring in bag after bag after bag.

"Hey, Michael, did you forget the list or something?" she smirks.

I look at her. "How'd ya guess? I figured if I fill this cart up with arbitrary items from every aisle in the store, my odds are pretty good that I will get everything on your list." I bring in the last three bags. "There! That should hold us over!" I grab a Gatorade and some jerky, find the most comfortable chair in the house, sit down, and begin to read my *People* magazine. Don't judge me.

A few minutes later, I hear laughing in the kitchen. I fold over the corner so I don't lose my place, and start walking in the direction of what was laughter but now has turned into an uncontrollable belly laugh. "What's going on?" I ask. Cheryl has tears running down her cheeks and, if I'm not mistaken, is doing the potty dance.

"Oh my gosh, this is too funny! Michael, can't you do anything right?" She wipes the tears from her now red face.

"What?" I stand there looking like an idiot when I know, according to Laughy Taffy over here, I did something wrong.

"You bought all this food and didn't get one thing on my list! Was this your way of never having to go grocery shopping?" She continues to put away the four hundred dollars' worth of what I would call a noteworthy and handsome pile of provisions. Doomsday Preppers got nothing on me!

"Why did you buy tampons?" she asks me, holding up the pink box.

Oh, I don't even know why. "For you?" I shrug my shoulders and smile wearily.

"Oh, honey, that boat sank years ago! Well, since we don't have anything for tacos, like I planned, how about spaghetti and meatballs?"

Chapter 3

AFTER DINNER, I return to the living room where my waiting *People* magazine calls for me. The sun has gone down and the lights have come on outside. I stare out the window for a while, watching the world nestle down under its nightfall blanket, when something catches my eye—something or someone. I move closer to the window, squinting my eyes, trying to see what it is. Just then the motion lights come on; I jump back as it gives me a fright. I run to the front door and throw it open like a madman, hoping to scare the bejesus out of whomever. I step out onto the front porch, looking left, then right. I yell out, "Who's there?" but no one answers. My heart starts beating rapidly. I remember the same feeling years back, when Marty started this same bullshit. "Marty! I bet it's him again!" I mumble under my breath. I continue to walk around the house, looking at the ground for muddy footprints. I then go into the garage, all the while wishing I had a bat or something in case I do come across someone. Instead, I have my *People* magazine in hand; at least I roll it up. The garage seems secure, so I drop my magazine and grab a shovel, then head back out to the yard. This is the only time I wish my lawn wasn't so damn huge. I wipe off the beads of sweat that have now formed over my brow. Step by slow step, I manage to make it around the house to the other side without tripping. I have to keep wiping my hands on my jeans, as the shovel starts to slip through my damp fingers. "Come on, muthafuckers, come out, come out, wherever you are," I whisper into the dark air.

A dog starts barking next door like he's just seen something. I run in that direction, hoping to catch a glimpse of something important. The dog's bark is louder and more furious; he's fighting with someone. The closer I get, the more I can hear his growling. Then I hear him yelp.

"Oh shit! That didn't sound good." I make it to the fence just in time to see white sneakers run off in the dark. I'm out of breath, but I climb over the fence to check out the dog. To my horror, he has been stabbed repeatedly. I start to yell for someone to come out of the house. I can't believe no one heard him barking the way he did! I run over to the back door and start pounding on it. "Hey, your dog is hurt! Anyone home here? Your dog is badly hurt!" I yell, but no one seems to be home. "Fucking great." I bow my head and walk back to where the injured dog lies. I kneel down to see if he's still alive. For a moment, I think I feel a pulse, faint as it is. I tell him he'll be all right and I start to stroke his head. I remember I have my phone on me, so I dial 911 and tell them what I saw, and that the dog doesn't look like he'll make it. I know there is nothing I can do, since moving him could make it worse; I have no way of knowing how many times he's been stabbed. So, under the moonlit sky I lie there, holding his paw in my hand while I hum Gwen's lullaby to him. I don't care how long I am going to be there, nobody deserves to die alone. I watch his eyes glaze over for what will be the last time. He dies there in my arms an hour later. The cops show up just minutes later. When they see what has happened, they all start to tear up. It seems German shepherds are used quite frequently as police dogs. Funny thing is, German shepherds are the one breed that scares the shit out of me. I run like the wind every time I see one. Tonight, I am thankful; I felt no wind.

After I tell the police everything I saw, the owners of the dog come home. I didn't even own the dog, but I feel just as distraught as they do after they find out what happened. I offer my condolences and then make my way back home, my clothing drenched in blood.

Cheryl is waiting on the porch, furious that she didn't know where I was, until she sees me.

"Oh my God, what the hell happened? Are you hurt?" Her eyes widen the closer I get.

I look at her, defeated. "I thought I saw someone outside, so I went to go look. As I was walking around the yard, I heard the neighbor's dog barking furiously, like he was fighting with something or someone. Right when I looked over the fence, I saw the whites of shoes disappear in the dark...and there was the dog, stabbed multiple times and just lying there. I stayed with him until the police came. That's why my clothes are bloody. I am so tired. How's Hunter?" I start to walk up the steps, wearily.

"He's fine and in bed. That poor dog! Come on inside." She opens the door and I follow her in. "Just leave those clothes in the bathroom. I will take care of them tomorrow," she tells me.

I walk despairingly up the stairs, trying to hold in the tears I so want to let out. I walk into the bathroom and look at myself in the mirror. I break down and fall to the floor; I didn't realize how much blood he'd lost. Whoever did this, may they rot in hell. My tears turn into anger, then back into tears. I lean against the bathtub, feeling the cold marble on my back. The last time I was on this floor was that night with Gwen. I crawl into the tub, fully clothed. I curl up, laying my head against the cool agate, and just let it all out. I cry for a couple hours that night; I actually cry myself to sleep, still in the bathtub, still fully clothed and devastated. That night I wrestle with myself over what happened. I know I saw someone out there, but whom? I have nightmares all night. One makes me jerk around so much that I smack my head on the faucet; now I'm awake. It takes me a minute to comprehend where I am, since it's dark out and only the glow of the moon has lit a small porthole of light. I rub my eyes and stand up, only to notice my bloodstained clothes. I quickly take them off and leave them on the bathroom floor. I climb into bed, hoping to fall asleep quickly so I don't have to keep replaying what happened. I sleep for another six hours—success.

That morning shows its ugly ass to me in the form of rain and thunder. I hate rain and thunder, it still freaks me out. I can remember when I was a kid and these horrible thunderstorms would blanket the town, with the loudest cracking of lightning and huge thunderbolts that, I swear, were close enough to torch the two hairs off my balls. My mom and Ruth would sit on the porch just watching in amazement while I hid away in my room, too scared to make it to the bathroom in time, but not too young to do my own laundry. There were times that I had to sleep on towels because I would wet the bed after a storm. I'm glad I don't do that anymore, to say the least, but I'm still freaked the fuck out.

According to the elbow jab at my groin, Hunter feels the same way. He wakes up to the sound of my pain. "Daddy, I scared!" he says.

As I put my eyes back in their sockets, I look over at him. "It's okay, buddy, I don't like them either. What do you want to do today?"

"Let's go to the park! I want to go down the slide!" He climbs out of bed and tells me to get ready to go.

"Well, wait, Hunter, it's raining out. Let's wait for a while, maybe it will clear up for us!" I climb out of bed, all the while trying to hide my discomfort with a pillow.

"No! Let's go now!" Hunter demands.

"Hunter, I said we will wait. Now, let's go eat some breakfast. Auntie Cheryl probably misses your morning kiss, and I need coffee. I think I even saw some Pop-Tarts downstairs waiting for you!" I tell him as I put the pillow down and walk into the bathroom.

"Pop-Tarts! Yeah!" he yells, and out the door he goes.

My bloody clothes are still on the floor, so I move them over with my foot. I stand in front of the mirror, leaning over the sink. I just stare at my face, wondering what kind of man I've become to have a maniac after me again. Will it ever end for me? I start to brush my teeth, still contemplating my next move. I'm seriously thinking about moving away, somewhere on the West Coast, maybe. The farther the better sounds best to me. I lean down to spit and when I stand back up, Cheryl is standing there.

"Oh! Damn!" I spit again and then wipe my mouth. "You scared the shit out of me!"

"Oh, sorry, I thought you heard me. I was yelling that your breakfast is ready." She picks up the bloody clothes and starts to walk out.

"Hey, Cheryl, you know, can you just throw those away, please? I don't really want to remember last night," I tell her.

She looks down at the clothes. "You bet. How are you doing, anyway?"

"It felt like I was fighting some demons all night, but all in all, I'm good. Do we have Pop-Tarts?" I smile at her.

"I am quite sure that you picked up a few boxes on your last shopping trip. If not, then you can eat the smoked oysters or the canned trout that you seemed so fond of." She raises one eyebrow at me.

"Ick, I bought that?" My body shivers.

"Yep." She walks out.

Just as I spit out the last of the toothpaste, a huge crack of thunder comes down and scares the living shit out of me. The lights in the house start flickering, and I can hear my son yelling at the top of his lungs that we are all going to die. Hey, as long as I get my Pop-Tarts, I'm good.

I saunter downstairs, trying not to look as freaked out as I am on the inside, when there's a knock at the door. "I'll get it!" I yell to Cheryl, and open the door. "Dad, what the hell—er, I mean, what are you doing here?" I proclaim, then hug him.

"Hey, son, thought I'd surprise you! Now, where's that grandson of mine?" he asks as he strolls by, bag in hand. I wonder how long he's going to stay, because that "weekend bag" looks like it can fit a few of them in there.

"Dad...did you come alone? Mitch and Winnie didn't want to come with you?" I ask him.

"No. Honestly, son, Winnie and I haven't been getting along too great lately. After Gwen passed away, I wanted to move here, closer to you and Hunter. I tried to explain to her that it would be a gift to be able to see you and Hunter every day, considering the time I lost with you. On the one hand, she understands my needs, but on the other, she doesn't want me to forget Mitch. She somehow believes that I want to relive all the days I missed out on with you through Hunter. You know, maybe she's right. Maybe the guilt I still have weighs too heavily on me to forget. Now, I want them both here with me, but I'm not sure if that's going to happen, son," he explains as he puts his big bag down.

"Oh, Dad, I'm sorry to hear that, but we are fine. Plus, Cheryl has moved in now, so Hunter is very well taken care of. I don't want you to move here and lose your family. Trust me; now that I've lost Gwen, who was my whole life, I know how important family truly is. You can't lose your wife and son over this, Dad. I won't allow it." My voice is stern but soft.

"You don't want me here, Michael? Is that what you are saying to me?" He sounds angry.

"No, Dad, that's not what I am saying. Look, you are obviously still angry with Winnie over this, and I'm not going to get in the way of your marriage. I appreciate you wanting to be here for us, but not at this cost. And to be quite honest with you, I am thinking about moving away, possibly to the West Coast," I tell him.

"What? Moving? You can't move! Why, I just got you back in my life, and now Hunter...that's just not right, son."

"Not right? How can you say that? Do you have any idea how hard it is to wake up every day in this house without the love of my life? Everywhere I go in this town reminds me of her, Dad! I can't even drive down the street without one of her friends waving at me! I can't do it anymore, Dad, it hurts too much. I want Hunter to grow up in a place where his father isn't sad to go to the park because that's where Mommy loved to run, or we can't go to Baskin-Robbins because that's where Mommy's favorite ice cream is. I thought I could move on, but I can't! My life feels like it stopped that day I buried my wife, and I can't get past it. I want to enjoy my son and our lives together, but it will not happen if I am still here, in this house." I take a deep breath and then let it out. I have no idea how I truly feel until I hear myself say it.

"Son, I'm sorry you are hurting so bad. Maybe just moving to another neighborhood instead of another state? I don't want you to make a huge mistake by running away, like I did," he answers.

"Like you did? Don't you mean like you are? You ran away from me and Mom a long time ago, and now you are doing the same thing to Winnie and Mitch! You are a hypocrite, Dad! You want to be the almighty one who has shed his sins, but it's not all true, is it? You are running away from your responsibilities! What is happening to you? What is really going on, Dad, and don't you dare lie to me." I feel like I'm the parent and he's the child.

My father, the minister, just looks at me. He looks down and kind of breathes out while shaking his head. He starts to look at the pictures on the wall, then walks over to the mantel where I have a picture of me, Gwen, and Hunter, taken just minutes before she passed away. He smiles and taps the picture with his index finger. "This is a good picture. I remember the day—"

I interrupt him. "Dad, stop doing this. Now, what the hell is going on?"

He looks at the ground. "She kicked me out. My wife kicked me out of my own house because I started drinking again."

"What? Why? Dad...what are you thinking?" I am utterly pissed.

"I don't know, son, I just cracked. I've lived without sinning for so long that I think I underestimated my own coping abilities. Lately, I haven't been able to listen to my parishioners with an open heart. I began judging them, something I know is wrong, but I couldn't help it. I started drinking so I could sleep at night. My conscience was growing a conscience, and I didn't know what else to do. Suddenly, I was drinking every night, then every morning. I thought I hid it well, until Winnie found my bottle tucked away between my Bible and another bottle." He starts to grin.

"This isn't fucking funny, Dad! You need help, and you need it today! You have to stop this! There is no way you are staying here, either. I am not helping a drunk. I have enough to deal with. I can't do this. You have to go—now." I pick up his bag and walk to the door. "Let's go. I'm not kidding, Dad." I open the front door and nearly step on a dead raccoon. "Son of a bitch, what the hell is this?" I put his bag down and just gaze at the grotesque animal on my front porch. I look around to see if anyone is out there, then I notice bloody footprints down the stairs of my porch.

My dad comes out, and the first thing he says is, "Think this is the same guy we chased before?"

I look back at him. "I don't know, Dad. Things have started happening again, and that's another reason why I want to move. I have to protect my son, no matter what. Don't touch anything until I take some pictures, okay?" I head into the house to grab my phone; luckily, Cheryl has kept Hunter busy in the kitchen once she heard the yelling.

"Everything okay, Michael? Is your dad still here?" she asks.

"For now. Um…can you keep Hunter away from the porch for a while? I need to…um…get rid of something, and I don't want him to see it," I tell her as I grab my phone and head toward the front door.

"What's going on?" she starts in on me. "Do you need help with—"

I stop her and hold up my hand. "Stop, Cheryl. Just please keep him away, okay?" I get a trash bag from under the sink, along with some bleach, gloves, and a few towels. On my way to the dead carcass on my porch, my mind wanders back to the day I opened that box and found a dead squirrel. Everything is happening again, but why? I stop in my tracks. "The book! I don't remember reading any of this before!" I mutter as I continue to the porch. "Maybe I should read it again. What if I missed something before Gwen…?"

"Read what?" my dad asks. "What do you need to read again?"

"Oh, nothing, Dad, but as soon as I take these pictures, I need you to help me clean this up before Hunter sees anything, okay?" I start snapping photo after photo, making sure to get every bloody footstep. My mind is racing nonstop with memories flooding my brain. I begin to look around to see if anything else is out of place, all the while muttering to myself about the last book. "I can't remember anything about a raccoon, though." I start to look up at the trees and under the porch. "It didn't say anything about a raccoon."

"Okay, son, what's going on? You've been muttering to yourself about not reading this in the book. What book?" he asks me, before shoving the dead raccoon in the bag.

"Trust me, Dad, you don't want to open that can of worms. Let's just get this cleaned up," I tell him as I begin the bleaching process. Thank God for gloves.

I call the cops and tell them what I found. Considering the history I have with them and the Lavettis, they take this seriously, and with Dave still on the run, they believe it has everything to do with him. They take away the evidence and ask me to send them the photos. Once again they tell me to keep a lookout for anyone suspicious. Now my dad is curious, and even more informed than I want him to be. I guess he should know what's been going on. In between the loud cracks of thunder and the downpour of rain, I put my hand on my father's shoulder and we go inside. After a good hour, my father is now informed of everything, except my secret. I know I should tell him, and now's as good a time as any, considering he's become a sinner once again; he can't use this against me. Just as I am going to tell him, I hear Cheryl yell for me, but it's not a normal yell. She sounds scared. My dad and I run into the kitchen to find her by the phone and white as a ghost.

"What is it, Cheryl?" I ask her.

"The phone...the phone rang and..." She takes a deep breath and starts to tremble.

"What about the phone? Who called?" my dad asks her.

"I don't know who it was, but the voice on the other end told me that we are all going to die, including Hunter!" She starts to cry.

"Where is Hunter?" I start to look around for him. "Cheryl, where is my son?" I start to panic.

My dad comforts Cheryl as I start to run around the house calling his name. "Hunter, where are you, buddy? Come on, answer me." I look in closets and in the bedrooms; I can't find him. I run back to the kitchen. "Cheryl, where is my son?"

"I don't know. He was here a minute ago, then he heard thunder and took off. I started after him, but that's when the phone rang." She puts her hand over her mouth. "Whoever that was said Hunter's name."

We all fan out and start looking for him. "Hunter, come on out! Everything is fine, storm is gone!" I yell, hoping my voice doesn't give away my paranoia.

Cheryl calls out to him, too, then my dad. We scour the entire house, finding nothing but little dust devils in the corners. I run into my room, then into my bathroom, when I hear the soft humming of a certain lullaby. I quietly walk into the closet, following the low purr of a three-year-old boy. I crouch down and look behind Gwen's clothes; I still don't have the heart to remove them. There he is, my scared little boy, humming away while covering his ears. That's why he couldn't hear us yelling for him.

I touch his arm and he looks up. "Daddy, the thunder was scaring me!" He jumps in my arms. My heart is pounding so fast and so loud I think for sure he will hear it, but he doesn't. He just curls up in my hug and holds on like there is no tomorrow. I hold him back just as tight.

Chapter 4

I BRING HIM DOWNSTAIRS so he can see his grandpa. I walk into the kitchen and say, "Hey, buddy, look who's here to see you!"

He turns around and his eyes widen. "Grandpa!" He wriggles out of my arms and runs to my dad, who snatches him up like a big bear.

"How's my big guy? You have grown so much! What are you eating?" He laughs and twirls him around.

"Pop-Tarts!" Hunter exclaims.

"Pop-Tarts? That's what you've been eating? Wow, I should start eating those, too! Maybe I'll start growing as much as you have!"

My dad is kind and genuine. I start to feel bad about what I said to him. After we all calm down about what has transpired, I ask Cheryl if the voice sounded familiar.

"No, I've never heard it before; at least I don't think so. All I know is that it scared the shit out of me, and I remember a couple years ago when we got that dead squirrel in the mail. Is it starting all over again, Michael?" she asks me as she blows her nose.

"I hope not, Cheryl, but anything's possible. Look, I already told Dad what's been going on, and now it looks like I need to tell you, too. Dave and Marty Lavetti have been missing ever since he was bailed out of jail a couple years ago. Lately, there have been sightings of them, and the police think he might be after me—again. You should know, Cheryl, that earlier Dad and I found a dead raccoon on the porch. That's why I didn't want you or Hunter out there. I think this phone call has made this whole thing even more real. Cheryl, I think you should go stay with your sister for a while. I can handle things here. Plus, my dad is going to visit for a spell." I look over at him and he smiles.

Cheryl reluctantly agrees, but then asks if she can take Hunter, too. "At least for a couple weeks. That way, you and your dad can have more time to figure this out, without having to watch a three-year-old."

"That's a good idea, Cheryl, thanks for offering," I tell her.

"I'll start packing our bags now." She gets up and then turns around. "Be careful, you two. I will be on pins and needles until things chill out." She heads upstairs to pack, Hunter following close behind.

I look at my dad, wondering how he feels about this. I kinda feel like Starsky and Hutch right now, even though we haven't schemed, or even have a plan of what to do next. I'm not even sure if we should do anything. I mean, what the hell can we do? "Dad, did you want some coffee or tea? I'm sure you know by now we don't—and never will—have alcohol here." I raise my eyebrow at him.

He smirks, "Probably a good idea—no, a great idea, son. Coffee sounds just perfect."

"I'll go brew a fresh pot. I want to talk to you about something, and I need you to keep it between us, Dad." I take the carafe to the sink and start to fill it with water. I look out the window and notice the rain has finally stopped. "You know, Dad, when I went to visit Mom just before her house burnt down, she was standing at the sink filling her carafe just like I am now. She started daydreaming about her daughter and ended up burning herself with the hot water. I think it was raining that day, too." I finish filling it and pour the water into the machine. "Did you know she loved her vodka and made great pancakes?" I scoop the coffee into the filter, close the lid, and then turn it on.

"Son, where are you going with this?" he asks as he taps his fingers on the table.

"I don't know, making small talk, I guess. Now, Dad, what I have to tell you is not going to be easy for me, and you have to promise you won't tell anybody—not Winnie, or even another minister—about this!" I cross my arms and wait for him to promise me.

"Um…okay, but what can possibly be so secretive? You haven't killed anyone, have you?" He laughs, but then stops as he sees that I am not laughing with him. "Michael? Have you killed someone?" He stands up.

I take a deep breath. "Dad, I don't know, but I think I may have. Please sit down. I need to explain this to you from the beginning. Did you want cream or sugar?" I ask him.

"Just black, please." He just stares at me until I sit down in front of him. "Michael Lance Bali, just what the hell is going on?"

My stomach feels like it's in knots, and my heart is pounding with the force of bass drum. This will be the first time I will be admitting to everything: the books, the possible murders, Gwen. Talking to a headstone really doesn't count. I rub my chin, then my eyes. I put my hands on top of my head, then lean back in my chair, contemplating if I'm doing the right thing.

"Does this have anything to do with you wanting to move away, Michael?" He takes a sip of coffee.

I look down, then up at him. "Yep. Well, partly. Everything is true with what I've told you before about how hard it's been on me. Man, Dad, this is really hard." I take a sip of my coffee, but it doesn't calm me down. Why would I think that a caffeinated beverage would calm me down? "Are you hungry?"

"I could eat a sandwich," he tells me, "if it'll help you spill the beans."

I make us both a sandwich, and grab some chips and a box of Pop-Tarts. "Pop-Tarts?" He raises both eyebrows this time.

"Oh, yeah, I don't even know why I grabbed those. Lately, they've been the calming force with this family." As I start to pick the box back up, my dad grabs my hand.

"It's been years since I've had these, so let's just leave them here." He smiles, then takes a bite of his turkey sandwich. I decide to wait to talk until we've eaten. After

I divulge the truth, maybe it won't feel so sickening to me on a full stomach. Here's to hoping! We both finish our food, quietly, until Hunter comes barreling down the stairs and into his grandpa's arms.

"Hey, are you eating my Pop-Tarts, Grandpa?" He scrambles out of his arms and onto the table so he can reach the box.

"I haven't just yet, but I was thinking about it. I remember you telling me that's how you got big!" He starts to tickle Hunter's belly. Hunter laughs so hard, he forgets that he's on Grandpa's lap, and the next thing I hear is, "Son of a whopperdigger!" Grandpa got his nuts kicked in by a size-five Nike. I start to laugh, even though I've been there—too many times, in fact.

"What's wrong, Grandpa? You sick?" Hunter asks, after he successfully grabs the Pop-Tarts box.

"You can say that." My dad doesn't look so hot.

"You okay, Dad?" I can't help but laugh, even though I try to hide it. I suck at hiding.

"Oh, yeah, dandy. I think I'll go to the bathroom."

He gets up rather slowly and walks like a miser to the nearest latrine. I can't help but laugh; it is a nice break from what is turning into a life changer, for the both of us. I clean up the table after Hunter eats a sandwich and his damn Pop-Tarts. I tell him to go help Cheryl pack for a big trip. He scoots off at the same time Dad returns; at least he's walking better.

"So...how are things down under?" I smile at him.

"Back in their upright positions, thank you," he remarks rather smart-alecky. I can appreciate that. "Now, let's get back to that talk." He sits down, enjoying his coffee once more.

"Maybe we should hold off until they leave. This isn't a conversation I want anyone to hear, Dad," I explain to him. "Let's watch a movie or something."

"Hey, I just thought of something! I never read your last book! Do you have a copy lying around?" he inquires. "I know it's been a couple years, but I only started reading your other two books last year. Mitch finally gave them up. It's like he was treating them like gold or something. I have to admit, your books are quite dark, but very intriguing. I can see why they are best sellers! Now, let's take a gander at book three, huh?" He rubs his hands together like he's making a fire.

The last thing I want to think about is book three. It makes me sick to even think about people reading it word for word when my sweet Gwen dies. I realize that her name isn't used, but it still hurts just the same. I know, and soon my dad will know, the truth about the existence of these books. God, I dread this.

"Yeah, Dad, I know I have a copy somewhere in my office, but let's do something else. Hunter and Cheryl will be leaving soon, so let's think of something we all can do, okay?" Maybe that will detour him from it for a while.

"That sounds good. What shall it be, bowling or miniature golf?" His suggestions are forthcoming.

We head out for a fun-filled night of bowling and pizza. I've limited the places Hunter can go, since he doesn't look like other kids. I know what it's like to be stared at and made fun of. I pray that his ability not to see "ugly" lasts for a very long time. I also get butterflies in my stomach every time we are going someplace new. I don't want some little asshole to say something mean to him. I might just allow a beating to happen.

That next morning, Cheryl and Hunter pile in her car and head out to her sister's house, about eight hours away. I trust her implicitly with my son, even when driving long distances. I explain to Hunter that he's going on an adventure, and when he gets back there will be a big surprise for him. We hug and say our good-byes. I thank Cheryl for everything and wish her happy trails. I buckle Hunter in his car seat, making sure he has his Cheerios and juice. "I love you buddy! I always will! Be a good boy for Cheryl, okay? I'll see you soon!" I hug him again, and this time I start to tear up. My dad notices, and he tries to intervene so Hunter won't see.

"Hey, you know what? I ate some Pop-Tarts this morning and I think I grew! You are right about those things! They do make you a big kid! Thanks, Hunter, for sharing with me! I love you!"

"Bye! Bye, Daddy!" He waves and is in seventh heaven, considering Cheerios are his movie food—cue the DVD.

I can feel my father staring at me. I know he's waiting for me to continue our conversation. I turn around and yep, there he is, arms crossed.

"You ready now, son?"

"No, but I have to be." We walk inside; he puts his hand on my shoulder like he's walking me to the electric chair. Right now, that might not be a bad alternative. We sit down in the living room, but before I start spilling my secrets, I ask him not to judge me, and say that this is harder than he thinks it is.

"Well, all right then, go on. I am listening and not judging," he tells me.

I start to fidget, trying to get comfortable for the most uncomfortable conversation I think I've ever had.

"Okay, Dad, it all started when I was twenty-eight years old. My life was shit, totally worthless. I had nothing and no one, and I really didn't care if I woke up again. One day this book showed up on my computer. I have no idea where it came from or who sent it. I began reading it and it was about my life, details that only I would know—but again, I didn't write it. The last chapter is what really shook me up. Dad, the night before I received this book, I was walking home and was jumped by John Lavetti. He was yelling about how much he hated me. He put his hands around my throat; he was trying to kill me. I don't remember anything after that, I blacked out. The next morning I was back in my apartment, clothes ripped and covered in blood, but it wasn't my blood! I looked at myself in the mirror and there were handprints around my neck. My knuckles were bloody, but I had no idea what had happened. The last chapter of this book talked about a maniac killing a man and ripping his arms off. I think that might have been...me...Dad."

I stop to take a breath. My hands are sweating profusely, and I feel like I could throw up at any minute. I look at my dad and wonder if he thinks I'm a loony bird already, but I don't ask. I don't think I even want to know the answer. He just nods as if it's okay for me to continue, so I do.

"Anyway, the last paragraph of the book told me if I wanted fame and fortune, all I needed to do was hit Send and I would be known the world over as a great author. It's all I've ever wanted, Dad. At first I thought it was a joke, but then I thought, what the hell, what could go wrong? I mean, after all, I just read my life story, even though I didn't write it. So I did it, I hit Send. Things started happening for me, Dad. I met Gwen, and money started rolling in. It was amazing, and I didn't think badly about it at all. I didn't tell anyone about this, even Gwen, and she was my first interview! How ironic is that? Anyway, a couple years passed and suddenly book two showed up the exact same way. I started to read some of it, but then turned to the last page. I wanted to see if that same paragraph was there, like in the first book. There it was, saying the same thing as before, but this time if I hit Send, my life would be even greater and I would make even more money. I didn't even care what the book was about! I became so greedy that I didn't even finish the story, I just hit Send. Well, come to find out, the Lavettis were being killed off one by one, and I happened to be there when it happened, even though I didn't remember any of it. I don't remember hurting anyone, let alone killing someone!"

I stop again and run my hands through my hair. I sit back in the chair, looking up at the ceiling, wishing to be anywhere else but here. All I can hear is my dad's breathing; he hasn't said anything at all. I slowly start to look in his direction, but he looks calm, hasn't changed positions yet, nor has he even cleared his throat. I continue telling him about everything, including Ruth saying she saw me burn the house down with T. J. Lavetti inside. I go on and on, about Mom and the cemetery, and finding out she had a child with Dave Lavetti that died at birth. I told him about her having to go to the mental institution, and Dave leaving drugs for her to take so she could kill herself. I proceed with the Blue Bonnet box, and how I knew whoever wore that hat was going to die, and it turned out to be Trudy. I look at the clock and only one hour has passed since I started this confession. I know I can't stop now, so I continue to tell him about Dave going to jail, and his sons, who later confessed to killing my brothers, being found dead shortly after I arrived back in town.

"Dad, the night they died I had dreamed how they perished. The next morning I woke up, once again with my clothes ripped and bloody. I don't know what happens to me. I must black out, then go and commit these heinous crimes, but make it home in time that no one is the wiser! I was staying with Ruth at the time, and she didn't even know I had left in the middle of the night! Dad, that's four of the Lavetti brothers dead. The last book showed up the same way. I read this one, and there was no way I was going to do anything but delete this book. It foretold the future of my life. It said if I hit Send on this one, the last of the Lavetti brothers would die, but also my wife. It also said this would be my only chance at having children. There was no way I would give Gwen up for anything, Dad! Gwen happened to be out of town, but surprised me by coming home early. I heard her come through the door, and I was so elated she was home that I forgot all about the third book. I ran downstairs, so happy that she was back. She told me she wanted to take a bath, so I made her favorite snack and was on my way to give it to her, when I remembered I hadn't deleted the book yet. I went into my office and there was a present sitting next to my computer. I opened it, and there was a positive pregnancy stick inside. I couldn't believe what I was seeing. According to the book, I would have to hit Send for this to happen, and since the other books were true, why wouldn't this one be? Then I heard my computer 'quip.' I looked over and it was flashing 'published.' Dad, Gwen hit Send—she was the one who got the book published, not me!"

I stop talking as tears are flooding my eyes. My body is in agony as I recall those last moments with my beloved. I stand up and yell, "This wasn't supposed to happen! We were happy." I fall to the ground. "Why did this happen? Why didn't I stop it? It's my fault she's dead, Dad!" I tip my head back and scream, "She's dead because of me!" I cover my face in defeat.

My father runs over and tries to comfort me, but it doesn't work. I have become a shell of a man. The flow of insurmountable tears soaks my shirt. I can't even look at my father, considering what I've just told him. I'm surprised he can even touch me without burning himself, as I am cloaked in sin. My breathing is shallow, and my hands are starting to stiffen up. The only word I can get out is *pills*, and I pray my dad knows what that means. He runs to my bathroom, thinking any bottle of prescription anything has to be it. Thank God he finds them, and returns with water in hand. I know I have to calm myself down so I can swallow the pills. I concentrate on my breathing to slow it enough that I won't choke on the water. I look up at my dad as he tries to give me my pills; his eyes are filled with tears.

"Michael, hold on. Everything will be all right. Just calm down, son, calm down. I'm here and I love you." Finally I am able to swallow my medication. My dad just keeps me in his arms, rocking me back and forth. "Michael, you're doing great! Just think of Hunter and how much he loves you, and the great life you two will have. He needs you, Michael. Calm down, son. I'm here. I'm here."

Chapter 5

I FEEL SOMETHING COOL on my forehead. I open my eyes and see my dad holding a washcloth to my face.

"You back now?" he asks with a smile.

For a moment I don't remember what happened, but only for a moment. I do remember, all too well; I just confessed my secret to my own father. I can't believe I actually did it. "Yeah, Dad, I'm good." I slowly sit up, clearing my throat and trying to focus my eyes. They are still swollen from the tears.

"How do you feel?" he asks.

I just look at the floor and smirk, "Embarrassed, ashamed, to say the least. But the real question is how you feel, now that you know the truth."

He kinda makes that *humph* sound. "I'm still taking it all in, Michael."

I stand up, rubbing my eyes. "Dad, I don't want you to..." I start but don't finish.

"I know...I know, Michael. What can I say? You're my son and I will stand behind you, no matter what." He hugs me and pats my back. "What do we do now?" he asks me.

I kinda laugh and shrug my shoulders. "I have no idea, Dad. You hungry?"

"I could eat something, but let's go out. We've been cooped up here too long. I could use a good steak right now, maybe some green beans and a baked potato, loaded!" He pats down his shirt, looking for his wallet.

"Steak sounds great, but so does cheesecake." I locate his wallet and hand it to him. "Think they'd look at me strangely if I order both at once?"

"Not if I order the same thing!" He smiles. "Come on, now, I'm starving!"

I grab a jacket from the closet, checking the pockets for my keys. "Hmm...my keys aren't here. I might have left them upstairs. I'll be back."

I dart out of the room and up the staircase, almost tripping over my feet. I start to think about how well he took that whole thing. I really expected him to freak out or tell me he can't keep a secret like this since he's a man of the cloth. I underestimated him. I find my keys on my dresser, then head back down to find my father standing there, rubbing his chin like he's thinking about something.

"Ready?" I ask him.

"Michael, I do have a question. You said in the third book it foretells the future, right? What does it say about me? Did you know I would start drinking again?" he asks.

"Dad, honestly, the only thing it said was our family would fight so badly that it would break up. Now that I think about it, the last book didn't reveal a lot like the other two did. In fact, I don't even think the events are happening in order. From what I remember, Marty was supposed to die before Gwen and I knew he was still around," I explain.

"Okay, I have another question. If you know what's going to happen because the book tells you what's going to happen, how is it that you haven't been arrested yet, if the books say you killed those men? Wouldn't that implicate you?" he asks.

"Well, it doesn't actually say I did it. All the names have been changed for just that reason. Dad, if I really did kill four people, what does that make me? Am I really the evil monster everyone said I was?" My heart sinks as I hear myself ask that question out loud.

"Was there anything in the books that didn't pan out? Has everything come true so far?"

I shake my head in confusion. "Dad, I don't know. I guess I haven't made a checklist. What's with the questions? What are you saying? That I dreamed up this stuff?" My voice starts to sound angry. "Because believe me, Dad, dreaming Gwen would die after she gave birth to our son is not something I wished for!"

"No, son, that's not what I'm saying at all. I'm just trying to decipher this whole mess with a new set of eyes. Have you thought that maybe things have happened because it was fate? Maybe you believed so much in what you were reading that you made those things happen?" He starts to rub his hands together. "Just hear me out here. You said yourself that you black out and don't remember things you've done. Maybe you did write these things during one of your blackouts?"

"No, no, Dad, it's not possible. You are forgetting the whole publishing thing. Let's say I did write them, how did they become published? See, there's no way I could have done it. Plus, I can't see into the future. Can you?" I ask him.

"No, I can't. It was just a thought, Michael. Come on, let's go eat."

We head out to the steak house and have an awesome meal. The steak is perfect and the cheesecake is delish. My father is right; no one even looks at us. Even though we are home pretty early, we both seem to be exhausted. I lock down the house while my father unpacks his big bag.

"Are you going to call Winnie and tell her you're here?" I ask him.

"I already did, although I had to leave a message. I knew she wouldn't answer my call, but that's okay. I understand where she's coming from. I told her if she wants to talk she can call any time of day, and that I will be here for a while helping you out while Cheryl and Hunter are gone. I did apologize to her for drinking again, and I promised to never touch the stuff again. I do mean it, Michael. I just wanted you to know." He hugs me and I happily hug him back. "Do you think I can read the third book?" he asks. "You could say my interest in it has now been piqued."

"You still want to, after all this?" I can't believe he's asking.

"Maybe I can help figure stuff out, now that I know about it. Together, maybe we can stop it," he tells me.

"Stop what, Dad? Gwen was taken from me, and that was the only thing I would have changed. I couldn't care less about that bastard Marty being killed off! Wait! Marty! The only thing left from the book is Marty's death! After that, then it's done. I don't have to live like this anymore! Oh my God! I didn't even think about that!" I suddenly feel a cold breeze come over me. I look around, thinking maybe I left a door open. "Did you feel that?" I ask my dad.

"Feel what, son?" he responds.

"That cold feeling like someone opened a door? No?" I start to walk around the house, making sure I didn't forget an open window or something. I stand at the back door looking outside, when I feel the hairs on the back of my neck rise up. I turn around expecting to see my dad, but there isn't anyone there. I call out, "Dad? Where are you?"

"Upstairs," he calls down. "Why? Do you need something?"

"No, I just...never mind." God, please don't let me lose it now. I give the house the once-over again, and then head upstairs. I find my dad in my office. "Whatcha lookin' for, Pops?"

"I would like to read the book, son. May I?" He stops looking and looks back at me.

"Sure, top shelf on the left-hand side," I tell him. While I watch him get the book down I feel those hairs on my neck rise up again. I quickly turn around, but nothing's there—again. I grab the back of my head. "What the fuck?" I whisper.

"What's that, son?" my dad asks me as he closes the door to my bookcase. "Son?" He looks at me because I don't answer. "Michael?" He walks over to me and touches my arm. I jump.

"Huh?"

"What's going on with you? You okay? Looks like you've seen a ghost!" He just looks at me and waits for a response, but I don't say anything. "Well, I'm off to bed, see you in the morning." He pats my shoulder and retires to his room.

I just look around, wondering if I did see a ghost, or at least felt one. I walk back to my room and close the door. I look around as if something should be there, but what? I finally realize I am being paranoid, probably because another living person knows my secret and it's now out there. I take a couple sleeping pills, then crawl into bed. I stare at the ceiling waiting for them to kick in. My mind starts to wander, and soon I am in thrall to my past and reliving the day I married Gwen. I fall asleep, soothed by the thoughts of the woman I loved.

There it is again. The morning sun has decided to pierce through my curtains and beeline it toward my eyes, causing me to wake up—something I'm not that fond of. Although I'm not a fan of mornings, it's kinda nice not to feel an elbow smash against my face. He may be small, but that kid has a right hook like nobody's business, which may come in handy later on. I jump in the shower and get ready in hopes I can beat my dad to the kitchen, and start making breakfast before he does. The one thing I both love and hate about this house is all the windows. On the one hand, you don't even have to turn the lights on, considering how much sun comes through. But on the other hand, walking around with my ass hanging out isn't an option, either. The closer I get to the kitchen, the stronger the smell of coffee. "Damn, he beat me to it!" I tell myself. I walk around the corner to find my dad sitting there, book in hand. It looks like he's almost done with it already.

"Morning, son. I made some coffee, although it might be close to empty." He smiles and takes a sip of his.

"How long have you been up?" I ask as I pour a quarter cup of coffee for myself. I take a seat next to him.

"Oh, a couple hours, I suppose. I've been reading this book and I can't put it down!" He starts thumbing through the pages. "See, almost done."

I already know what the book says, so I'm not excited to relive any part of it. I know he'll want to discuss what he's read so far, and it's too early in the morning for me to be rational. "Pancakes and eggs sound good?" Hopefully that will keep his words at bay, at least for now. I get up and walk to the fridge.

"Sounds great. I've been reading this and—"

I stop him. "Dad, I don't want to talk about it right now, okay? Trust me, there's plenty of time, but not now." I take the eggs out of the fridge and nearly drop them. I didn't know how I would feel about my dad actually knowing, but now that he does, I have a feeling he's going to be irritatingly scrupulous.

He puts his hands up. "Okay, okay...questions later, pancakes now." He folds over the page and then closes the book. "Can I help?"

"How about making another pot of coffee?"

"I can do that." He takes the pot and fills it with water. "I wanted to tell you that Winnie called me last night."

"Oh, yeah? That's good, right?" I break the eggs into the bowl.

"Yeah. I mean, we talked, but nothing was resolved. She still is adamant that I've gone down the wrong path and haven't found my way back yet. I tried to explain to her that I've changed, but she doesn't believe me yet. The conversation ended with us arguing again." He sounds defeated.

"Well, Dad, she'll forgive you. I wouldn't worry too much about it." I try to sound positive, but I immediately start to recall what the book said, and I know that's what he is thinking about, too. "I hope you like scrambled." I start talking like Julia Child. "Now, you take the egg and throw it up in the air, wait for it to come down and splatter all over the floor, then you take a spoon and drop it in the bowl. No one will ever know the difference!" I hear him laugh, although it might have been a pitying one.

"I know what you're trying to do, and I appreciate it, but you and I both know what's inevitable. That book...I can't get past it. After we eat I am going to finish it, then you and I can discuss what we need to. How about I make the pancakes?" My dad looks terribly somber.

I hand him the batter. "Hit it."

After a very filling breakfast, my dad picks up the book and continues reading. I clean up, then take the trash out. The day is turning out to be sunny, quite a difference from the rain and cold we've had lately. I look up at the sky. "Come on, vitamin D, show me some love." I just stand there with my face nearly vertical with the sky. I can hear birds chirping and dogs barking. I love this neighborhood. I turn to go inside, when the mailman honks his horn—*beep-beep*. I wave and say good morning.

"Hey, Michael, how have you been?" he asks while he hands me the mail.

"Pretty good, thanks for asking," I respond. I turn to leave, but he tells me there's one more and I have to sign for it. It looks like a normal letter, so I don't think anything of it. I sign away.

"Thanks, Michael, have a great day!" He smiles and waves.

I walk into the house, not even looking at the mail yet. I put it down on the table right inside the door, then go on my merry little way upstairs to check my e-mail. I've been lying low since Gwen's passing, so I can imagine how many e-mails I have. I log in, then get up to get a Gatorade while it loads. I begin to look at the pictures on my bookshelves, smiling at the history that stands before me.

My favorite picture was taken during a weekend trip to New York. It was the first time Gwen had been there, so she wanted to see the Statue of Liberty. On our way to the dock, there were people dressed as Lady

Liberty in the park, and, for the right price, you could have your picture taken with them. I talked Gwen into standing next to one so I could take her picture. Now, keep in mind, these people act as "statues" and really don't move unless the situation calls for scaring the shit out of someone. While Gwen was standing there and smiling next to a "statue," a very hairy naked man came up from behind and photobombed the picture. I laughed so hard I think I pissed my pants. When the statue guy saw what the naked guy did, he started yelling in true New York style, things like, "Yo, man, what the fuck?" and "You gotta be fucking kidding me, you dumb son of a bitch! Get the fuck outta here!" Gwen had her hand over her mouth, her eyes wide open. She leaned over to me and said, "Oh my God! I saw his thingy!" She started to giggle like an idiot, and I was on the ground, laughing my ass off. I love that picture, and every time I look at it, it makes me miss her more.

As I take a drink of my Gatorade, my computer tells me it's ready by the lovely *bleep* sound. I sit down and it shows I have 582 e-mails. "Holy shit!" I whisper out loud. I begin to scroll through them, deleting the ones I couldn't care less about. I notice a few from Dawnna, my agent. They all mimic each other: "What are your plans for your next book?" and "Let me know when you are ready for me to edit." I don't have the heart to tell her I won't be "writing" any more. I know that profiting from those books was wrong, but I am thankful that I made enough so I can take care of Hunter's future.

An hour has passed when my dad walks into my office. "I'm done with it." He holds up the book.

I don't even look up at him. "Yeah, and what do you think?" I continue typing.

He sits down across from me. "You know, it dawned on me while I was reading the last chapter: why do you think this book has to happen? I mean, if it's true and you did kill those men, why can't you stop it now? Nothing is making you do it—maybe all you need is accountability, and that's what I bring you. No one knew about this before, so there was nothing stopping you. Now there is: me."

I stop typing and look up at him. "That's a good theory, Dad, but...you keep forgetting one thing. So far, everything has come true! Marty dying is the only thing that hasn't happened yet. I don't see a way around it." I lean back in my chair and put my hands on top of my head.

"Not true. That's not the last thing that happens. You are forgetting that the family fights and we don't talk anymore. I can't let that happen, Michael." He starts tapping his fingers on the cover.

"Oh, so you're going to take some kind of stance against this and what—become who? John Wayne?" I smile.

"John Wayne? How old do you think I am?" he laughs.

I lean forward. "Dad, the book doesn't say you and I start fighting, it just says the family. You do realize that at this very moment, you are fighting with family? Your wife...it's already begun." I stand up to stretch my back. "Face it, Dad, I'm screwed. I figure the only way I can go on with my life is if I move away, far away, and start over. I don't have any other options here, Dad." I walk over and look out the window. "I appreciate what you're trying to do, and trust me, I am scared. I am so terrified that I am going to wake up one morning with my clothes ripped and bloody again—and what if Hunter sees me?" I drop my head and begin to shake it back and forth. "I don't know what to do, Dad."

He gets up and stands next to me; looking out at the lawn, he begins telling me how he met Winnie. The way he remembers little details, like what she was wearing on their first date and how she sounds when she laughs really hard. He tells me about her surviving breast cancer, and how she lost all her hair but his love never wavered. He thought she was even more beautiful without hair because God was allowing him to see all of her. When he stops talking I look over at him; he is wiping away tears.

"Let me tell you something, there's nothing in this world that could stop me from loving my wife. There's also nothing in that book that would make me want to leave my wife. I believe in the written word, Michael, but not this one." He holds up the book, then throws it on the floor. "Come on, let's get out of here."

My dad's little speech makes me feel better about this whole thing. On our way to the door, I notice the mail I haven't opened yet. "Oh, hold up, Dad. Let me look at this stuff first." I pick up the mail and start sorting. "Bill,

bill, credit card app, letter, letter, credit card app—hmm, what's this one?" I open the one I signed for. I notice a strange smell coming from the envelope itself, but after I open it, the smell is pungent enough for my dad to notice, and he is at least six feet away.

"Holy cow, what is that smell?" he asks me, waving his hand in front of his face.

"I have no idea, but it's coming from this envelope. It's pretty damn rank, isn't it?" I take out the paper from inside and it's covered in red goo. "Oh, yuck, what the hell is this shit?" I lift up my hand so I can get a closer look. "Oh my God, it's blood! It's fucking blood, Dad!" I drop everything on the ground and beeline it to the kitchen to wash my hands, with bleach. "I can't believe this shit! Who in the hell would send me something like that? Fucking blood, really?" I start to scrub the shit out of my hands, nearly taking the skin off. I can hear my dad mumbling from the other room. "Dad, don't touch it, and just leave it there!" I yell to him as I finish de-skinning my hands. I go back into the entryway; my dad has picked up the letter with a tissue. "Dad, I told you to leave it alone! We don't know where the hell that blood came from. It could be infected with something!"

"There is a note still in the envelope!" My dad points to it on the floor; a corner of white paper is sticking out.

"Okay, let me go put some gloves on. Don't touch anything!" I run to the kitchen, and under the sink are some rubber gloves. I look rather dashing with bright yellow neoprene mittens that go all the way up to my elbows.

My father begins to laugh hysterically when he sees me. "Oh, wow...that's nice."

"Bite me, daddy-o." I lean down and pick up the manila envelope. I take out the white paper and immediately drop the envelope again. I open the note, dreading what I am about to read. I drop my head back when the first word I read is *Mikey*. The only person who ever called me that was Dave Lavetti, and I am about to read his chicken scratch. This is what it says:

Mikey,
    I believe there is some unfinished business between us.
    Now, I feel it's the right thing to do that you and Marty shake hands...and fight to the death.
    See you soon!
    P.S. Did you like your furry little gift?

"Dad, it's begun. This is proof...we can't stop it." I show him the letter, then walk back into the kitchen. I grab the bleach and a sponge, leaving my gloves on. I walk back to the "crime scene" and start cleaning up the blood where I dropped the envelope. "I can't believe this. I can't do this again..." I stop in midsentence. My dad stands there, not saying much. I know he finally understands what I've been saying all along. He kneels down, stopping my hand from scrubbing the floor.

"Son, it's time we came up with a plan," he tells me.

"A plan for what, Dad? As I see it, I have two choices: run or shake his hand." I continue cleaning the floor.

"Well, I've always believed when you greet someone you should shake his hand." His voice is firm.

I stop and look up at him. "What? You really want to plan how to kill Marty? Is that what you're saying?"

He smiles and walks away.

Chapter 6

I FOLLOW MY DAD into the study, wondering what kind of conversation is about to take place. "He can't be serious," I say to myself.

He sits down on the couch, face serious and calm as a cucumber. "Michael, we will need a pen and some paper." I just look at him, dumbfounded, but I oblige. I sit down on the couch and hand him the items, but he pushes them back to me. "Oh, no. I need you to write and I will talk." He seems rather stoic.

"Dad, what are you doing? I mean, you can't be serious with this!" I can't help but feel completely apprehensive, and my voice doesn't hide it.

"Let me tell you a story, Michael. Even though I wasn't around when you were growing up, I know what you went through. Having these faces…well…it's safe to say we've both had our fair share of beatings to last us a lifetime. I learned how to fight at a very young age, and I've honed my skills over the years. What I am about to tell you can't go any further than this room, understood?"

I don't think I've ever heard him this serious before. "Sure, Dad, but you are kinda freaking me out here." I convey my uneasiness through a series of head scratches and throat clearings.

"I've never told anyone about this before, and I wasn't sure I would ever tell you, until you came clean about your books. I know that was extremely hard for you, so understand, this is just as hard for me, okay?" He raises his eyebrows.

I clear my throat again. "Okay," is all I say. I have no idea what this man is about to say, but if he's comparing my secret to his, I don't even know if I want to know.

He takes a deep breath. "When I was fifteen, I had a huge crush on this girl named Melissa. She was so beautiful. I can even remember her favorite candy: butterscotch Life Savers. You know, she was the one girl who gave me the time of day? I helped her once with her English paper, and the next day she baked me brownies as a thank-you. Well, the word got around and her boyfriend, Jake, the biggest douchebag on the football team, wanted to pummel me. Now, up to then, the fights I got into were one-sided—their side. I never fought back, only because I didn't know how to and I was scared shitless. I was a scrawny freshman with a face only a mother could love, and that was even stretching it. Melissa was nice to everyone. She helped out with the special needs kids; she even volunteered to be an assistant counselor for incoming freshmen. That's how I met her; I was shoved in my locker that first day of school and got cut really bad from it. When I was in the nurse's office, Melissa came in and wanted to talk to me. She made me feel like I wasn't a freak or a monster. She didn't shy away once from me—in fact, she hugged me. That was the first time I even touched a girl. It turned out the guy that shoved me into the locker was her boyfriend, and when he found out that I told her it was him—well, he's had it in for me ever since. You could say he was my Lavetti brother." He stops to clear his throat again. I just stare and listen to him, like a kid when a librarian reads out loud. "Anyway, I had to deal with this asshole every day. If it wasn't a black eye, then apparently my nose needed rearranging. I started skipping school so much that they called my mom, and she flipped out on me, but it wasn't anything compared to what my dad did. Now, I won't go into detail about that. Let's just say his choice of weaponry was a belt, but not just any kind of belt—he rode broncos. I had to go back to school looking like I had been in a bad car accident, so that's what I told everyone. It was a lot less embarrassing to say that than to say my dad beat the shit out of me. Pity was the last thing I wanted. I was now on the revenge train, and I was headed straight for Jake's station. I had to plan it so concisely that no one would ever suspect it was me." He stands up and walks to the window.

"Had to plan what, Dad?" I ask.

He looks back at me and says, "His death, son."

I can't believe what I just heard. "His death? Are you telling me you killed him?"

My dad looks back outside. "It's starting to rain again."

"Dad, don't do this! You finish this story!" I yell at him.

He bows his head and turns back to me, then sits down. "I knew it had to take place at night and after a football game. That way, the whole thing could be chalked up to an accidental death. Jake liked to drink, everyone knew that, and he especially liked to drink after a win. Now, I knew the next game was Friday night, so that gave me three days to prepare. It was an away game, which made it even better. Jake liked to drive himself, and since he was one of the top players, the coach didn't say no to him. The game started at seven and wouldn't get over until ten. Earlier that day, I found out Melissa wasn't going to be there, since she was going out of town with her family. I know I couldn't have gone through with this if there had been even a small chance she would have been hurt. Lucky for me, Grandma had a birthday. Friday came and I was getting nervous about going through with this. Could I even do it? At lunchtime, Jake thought it would be a good idea to pour hot sauce down my pants, then shove my face into my bowl of chili. After I cleaned myself up, my anxiety seemed to have disappeared. I looked at myself in the mirror and said, 'No more.'

"The game was only five miles away from the school, thank God, since I couldn't drive yet. It didn't feel that far after I walked there. I guess my adrenaline was so amped up that it only felt like down the street. I waited and watched patiently as the clock ticked down to the two-minute warning. I started to make my way to Jake's car, looking around for anyone who could see me. He was so proud of his Jeep that he always parked it away from the crowd, usually next to a fence. I walked to the parking lot, looking for the blue-and-yellow Jeep. There was always a group of screaming girls around, waiting for the players so they could go party with them. I could see the scoreboard from where I was; the score showed we were winning by seven points. I made my way over to his car and placed a note on his windshield. Now, Jake was a player, and a very well-known one. I knew if I wrote a note to him and posed as a girl, asking him to meet me after the game, he would definitely come, especially if I left a seductive picture. I found a half-nude picture of a girl from the previous summer, when I had gone with my parents to see my dad's brother. He lived on the lake, and you could always find numerous girls running around half naked in their swimsuits. I was never invited to the parties they had at night, when the sky would light up with all the beach fires. The next morning I would comb the sands for shells and possibly money. That was how I ended up with the picture. Coming up with what to say on the note proved difficult for me, considering I didn't even know how a girl would talk, let alone ask for sex. My dad had *Playboy*s hidden under his bed, so I thought that was a good start for me. It sure helped when Miss August spoke of a crush she had on a teacher and shared the note she left him. A few changed words and names, and poof! A dirty little note was made." He stops talking. "Michael, I am really thirsty, let's get something to drink."

He walks out of the room before I stand up. I have become so enthralled with his story that it takes me a minute to come out of my trance. I follow my dad down the stairs.

"You can't just stop in the middle of the story! What happened? Did he meet you?" I feel crazy with anticipation. We continue to the kitchen.

"This seems to be where we always end up," my dad comments as he opens the fridge. He takes out some salami and cheese. "Hey, this looks good!"

"I am dying here, Dad! What happened?" I start to act like my son before he opens presents.

"Jeez, let me eat a little and get some water. I really didn't think you'd be that interested," he says as he fills his mouth with meat and cheese.

"Why wouldn't I be interested? You are telling me a story about...well...what sounds like a murder plot!" I take some of the cheese and eat it. I only let ten minutes pass before I can't stand it anymore. "Okay, old man, no more food until I hear the story!" I take the plate away and put it back in the fridge. "Now, let's go into the living room and finish this story!" I make sure he goes first so I can follow him. I grab another pad of paper and a pen from the phone desk before I leave the kitchen. We sit down on the couch. "Okay, you were saying?" I encourage him with hand movements.

"Okay, now, where was I? Oh, yeah, the dirty note. I can even remember what I wrote. I told him if he liked what he saw in the picture, to meet me in the park, by the picnic table, which was about a hundred feet from his car. I told him that I was into everything sexual, and I was turned on by football players and fucking in public places. I said not to tell anyone. I ended the note by asking him to wait until everyone was gone, and to bring the note with him so I would know he was the one I was looking at. That way, I would get the note back, and not have to worry about the evidence. I waited in the dark, watching everyone get in their cars and leave, one by one. Finally I could see the players coming out, high-fiving one another and yelling up a storm. The cheerleaders were there too, screaming like yetis. As the guys started getting on the bus I kept looking around for Jake. Every minute that passed my anger was getting deeper and deeper, until finally he was in sight. I watched him walk to his car and put his gear in the back. I lowered my body, making sure I was out of sight. I looked up, and the moon seemed to be a lot brighter than usual—then again, when was I ever out after dark? I could hear my heart beating. My breathing became shallow, and sweat began to cover my back, making my shirt stick to my body. I looked back at Jake right when he grabbed the note. I was too far away to see his facial expression, but I did see him look up and straight ahead. He was interested, I could tell. He looked around and waved to a few cars leaving. About five minutes passed and the parking lot had cleared, giving him the absolution he needed. I watched him lock his door and climb the fence. He headed straight for me. I took a blond wig from my backpack, put it on, then hid my bag under the bench. I stood there with my back turned to him, my hands on my hips. I could hear him move closer. I started to fling my head around so my wig flowed and glistened in the moonlight. He was only a few feet away when I heard, "So, I hear you like to fuck in public? Lucky for you, so do I!" I could feel his breath on my neck. He put his hands on my shoulders and said, "I like little sluts like you. Turn around." I heard him unzip his jeans. "Come on, now, don't be shy. I want to see those pretty little hands of yours while they are jacking me off." What he didn't know was that my pretty little hand had a pretty little set of brass knuckles around it. As I turned around, I told him, "No thanks, I don't fuck losers," and I punched him right in the face. He fell to the ground screaming in pain. I continued to beat the shit out of him. He didn't get one hit in. When I stood up, the moon's beams showed the red victory all over my hands. Jake moaned in agony as I kicked him in the groin several times. I grabbed my backpack and took out several bottles of alcohol. I opened them, but left two in my bag. I poured it all over him, including down his throat. He started to choke, but I covered his mouth so he had to swallow. He screamed when it hit the open wounds on his face. "Shut up!" I yelled at him. My hands were hurting so bad, I knew I couldn't hit him again without breaking them, so instead, I grabbed one of the bottles and hit him over the head with it. It shattered all over the place and he stopped moving. I leaned down and took his pulse. It was faint, but not for long. I took another bottle and hit his head again. One last groan and he was dead. It took all of six minutes, and my life changed forever. I killed a man, and I was smiling. I grabbed all my belongings and made sure everything was back in my bag, including the note. With my wig still on, I ran back to his car, took the other two bottles out of my bag, and broke the windows. I retrieved a pennant from my bag that I had taken from the opposing school and threw that under his car. Three minutes later I was running from the scene. I ducked into an alley and took off my clothes. I knew blood would create an issue for me, so I also had baby wipes in my bag. I wiped myself off and put clean clothes on. I didn't throw anything away that close to the crime scene—I put everything in my backpack. From the time I threw my first punch to my change of clothes, my watch showed it took thirteen minutes. Thirteen minutes, Michael, and my world stopped hurting me." He lets out a deep breath, like he just repented.

I don't even know what to think at this point. I lean down and put my hands on my head. "How did you get away with it? Why aren't you in jail?" I ask him, still with my head down.

"I covered my tracks very well. Before I left for the game, I told my parents I wasn't feeling well and was going to bed. My mom never checked on me if I told her I was sick—she was terrified of catching anything—so I knew that was a good alibi. The burn ban had been lifted, so I knew the public incinerator was working, and I just chucked my bag right in there. When the cops looked at the surveillance tapes from the school parking lot, they saw a blond girl trashing his car. Everyone they interviewed spoke about his drinking habits and his sleeping around, especially with girls from competing schools. Turned out, he was not very well liked, even by his own teammates. There were no leads, no suspects. The case went cold."

Chapter 7

HAT DID I just hear? Did my father just tell me fucking killed someone? I stand up and start to pace the room. I run my hands through my hair, and I start talking to myself.

"Michael, please sit down. I told you this to help you, not hurt you," he tells me.

I stop pacing and look at him. "Um, Dad? You just told me you killed someone and...I don't even..." I throw my hands up in the air and walk out of the room. My dad follows me.

"Michael, stop! I know this is a lot to take in, but it happened a long time ago! You of all people should understand where I was coming from! I felt like I didn't have a choice anymore. There was no one out there to help me, I was my only solution! You have no room to judge me, son, we are both killers!" he yells at me.

I stop in my tracks. I turn around to face him. "The difference is, Dad, you plotted your revenge! You knew exactly what you were going to do and you did it! I didn't do that! I have no idea if I really did kill anyone! Don't you dare compare me to you!" I yell back at him.

"Oh, Michael, we are exactly alike! You can deny it all you want, but we are cut from the same cloth! You are a killer, just like me!" His voice is getting louder.

"I am nothing like you! I don't want to kill anyone, Dad! I might think about it, but I would never intentionally do it! You—a minister, of all things—can sit here and, in specific detail, tell me about something so horrific, and just expect me to say, what? Oh, cool, Dad, can I be just like you and plan a murder like that one on Marty? Fuck you, Dad, and the horse you rode in on! Get out of my life! I mean it this time, get your shit and get out—now!" I run up the stairs to my office and slam the door. "Fuck!" I yell as loud as I can.

About ten minutes, later I hear the front door shut. I stay in my office for the next few hours, going over what I just heard and what I should do. I turn on my computer and check my e-mails; my mind needs to be elsewhere right now. I read a few fan letters asking me when my next book comes out. I respond with the typical response: "I always have something cooking; just keep an eye out." I finally respond to my agent, telling her I'm not writing for a while; I need a break. I look in my fridge for a Gatorade, but apparently I drank it all. I go downstairs to look in the pantry for some, and I find a note on the kitchen table. It's from my dad, and this is what is says:

My son,
I guess this is it. You have my word; I will not bother you again until you ask.
Please keep my secret, as I will keep yours, until the day I die.
I guess that book was right after all, we just should have been looking in the mirror.
Dad

I go into his room thinking he's full of shit. I open the closet and it's empty. He really left; he's actually gone. I sit down on his bed rereading his letter. "Looking in the mirror, what does that mean?" I ask myself as I tap my chin with my index finger. I look up when I realize what he is saying. "Oh shit! The fighting! The book said the family would break up over fighting, and we thought it was him and Winnie. Turns out it was us." I fall back on the bed and lie there, looking up at the ceiling. Time has stood still for me; I can hear the clock ticking. I have no idea how long I lie there, but it is long enough for the sun to go away. I get up and walk into the kitchen, turning all the lights on. I don't remember the last time I was in this house alone, Cheryl or Gwen was always here. It feels ominous and kinda scary. I make myself a peanut butter and jelly sandwich, and sit at the table. I turn the TV on and watch *The Golden Girls*. It was Gwen's favorite, but I never gave it a chance. I thought, *How can four old broads be funny?* Man, was I wrong! That Betty White is a hoot! Lucky for me there is a *Golden Girls* marathon on and it will continue until five tomorrow night. I finish my sandwich, then grab a bag of chips, another Gatorade, and head to my room. I turn the TV on so I can continue my marathon, when I remember I didn't lock down the house. I head back downstairs, locking the front door and turning on the porch light, even though I have motion sensors. I feel better when it's all lit up, especially now that I'm alone. The back door is already locked, and so is the side door. I leave a light on in the kitchen, then go back upstairs. I can hear the theme song start to play: "Thank you for being a friend..." Funny how I know all the words now. I start to sing it as I change into my night pants, then brush my teeth. I climb into my big bed, chips and Gatorade in hand. I have no idea how many episodes I watch before I fall asleep, but the hum of the TV is still on when the sun breaks through the curtains the next morning. I look at the clock: the bright red numbers show nine thirty. I rub my eyes to try and wake my sorry ass up. I feel like I didn't sleep at all, and I could easily go back to sleep if I allowed myself. So I do, and I sleep for three more hours. When I roll over and see the red numbers flash twelve thirty, it doesn't bother me at all. I fall asleep once again, this time until three forty-five. The only reason I get out of bed is hunger. I have been dreaming of a hamburger, fries, and a chocolate milkshake, and I know none of those things are in this house. I jump in the shower and get dressed in my New York Yankees sweatshirt. No matter where I end up living, the Yankees will always be on my chest. I decide to call Cheryl and see how things are going. It's been so quiet without them, and I miss Hunter's toys all over the floor. I almost miss tripping over them—almost. Apparently, they are out shopping and then off to dinner, so I leave a message. I know Hunter is having the time of his life, considering Cheryl and her sister treat him like a prince and he can do no wrong. Unfortunately, when he comes home I get to disengage his engaging attitude of me, me, me to no, no, hell no.

I have all my car keys in a bowl, and when I'm feeling frisky, I close my eyes and just pick out a set, and that's the car I am driving that day. Today is a frisky kind of day. I close my eyes and—ta-da! It's the 1969 Boss 429's lucky day! I slide onto that smooth leather seat, turn the key, and rev up that engine. I forgot how much I love that sound of pure unadulterated engine anger. I look through my CD collection to pick out the right "going to get me a hamburger" music. I've never been one to use an MP3, so people look at me strangely when they see me changing out a CD. Today feels like an Ozzy day, track four—"All aboard, ha-ha-ha-ha"—damn, I love me some Ozzy! As I back out of my garage, I'm already into my sweet air guitar riff, and just like that, I'm not alone anymore; the prince of darkness has awakened me. I want to speed off, but my neighborhood doesn't resemble a raceway park, so I eagerly wait for the speed limit to change from twenty to forty-five. My slow-but-ever-so-wanting-to-go-fast self takes in the sights. I wave to a few people I know. The trees are starting to bloom since spring has sprung, finally. The people on this street really take care of their lawns, their homes, and themselves. I can definitely tell once I've reached the outskirts of my neighborhood, when trash becomes part of the décor. I will miss it here, but I know it will be for the best if Hunter and I want to move forward, instead of me always living in the past. The hard part will be Cheryl. She's been in my life since Gwen and I moved here. It's going to be quite a challenge to get her to understand we need a fresh start and that she needs to stay behind. Maybe it won't be so hard if I find her another family to take care of in this same neighborhood. It's worth a try, at least. I pull onto the highway where finally I can speed up. I find it very difficult to listen to Ozzy and not go above fifty miles per hour. Track eight takes me to "No More Tears," which was Gwen's favorite.

I never thought she was an Ozzy fan, until that one day in July. It was so bloody hot that day, my ass kept sticking to the seat. I guess wearing jeans with holes everywhere wasn't the smartest thing to do, but I hadn't been to the tanning booth in a very long time, so my white legs were not going to be seen in public, even though the dark hair that covered them would serve quite efficiently in that respect. My arms held the same accountability when it came to hair. It was so long you could comb it; at least that's what Gwen would do. She would use her hand as a smoothing device and comb it down when I had what she referred to as "bed head." It used to irritate me, but then I started looking forward to it. Now that she's gone, I find myself doing it as part of my morning ritual: shower, shave, comb arm hair.

I pull into my favorite burger place; it's one of those roller-skating ones where the girls don their blades and glide to your car. I just love it. If you've ever seen that movie *Vacation* with Chevy Chase, that's me when she comes over with the tray of food and Clark tells her no, it's a new car, and takes the tray before she can hook it on his window; dead-on balls accurate, and a damn good movie. I chow down on my hamburger and fries; I didn't realize how hungry I am. As I sit back and relax with my shake, I notice a woman with her two children sitting at one of the tables outside, and she keeps looking at me. I figure she is a fan, until she packs up her kids rather quickly and gets into her truck—a dark green truck. "That can't be her, can it?" I ask myself as I try to get a better look at her. I can see her in the driver's seat, just sitting there with the motor running. She doesn't drive away; instead, she gets out of her truck and walks over to me, looking around as if she's making sure no one is watching. She comes to my window and asks me if I'm Michael Bali.

"Yes, I am. Do I know you?" I retort.

"No, you don't know me, but you know my husband, Dave Lavetti." Her voice breaks.

"You are his wife? I don't think you should be talking to me..." I pause, as I don't know her name.

"Lena, my name is Lena. I just want to warn you that you need to get out of here, as soon as you can." She continues to look around.

"Get out of where, exactly? As you can see, I'm done eating, so I will be taking off." I take a sip of my shake.

"No, I mean out of town, far away. You don't know what he is capable of. He and Marty have been planning something, but I don't know what. They come into town for supplies, then leave just as fast. The only thing I know is they are after you and your son. Please, leave town now!" She hurries back to her truck. She backs out of her spot and looks over her shoulder at me. She mouths, "Get out," and then drives off.

I sit there, stunned. What just happened? I don't know her, but should I believe her? I mean, maybe she's part of the whole plan and she's setting me up? I throw away my food garbage and the rest of my shake; somehow this conversation ruined my ice cream experience. I decide to take a different way home; maybe I might see... something. I don't know. I'm so glad Cheryl took Hunter with her for a while, at least that's one thing I don't have to worry about. With that thought, I call Cheryl again, hoping I can talk to her. The phone rings four times before she answers.

"Hello?"

"Cheryl, it's Michael. I tried to call earlier, but you were gone. How's my son?" I try to sound calm.

"He's just fine, Michael. What's wrong? You don't sound well. Has something happened?" Now I've made her nervous.

"No, well, yes, but nothing...I'll tell you about it later. How's Hunter?" I forget I asked her already.

"I told you, he's fine. Now, what's going on? Tell me now!" She's turned demanding.

"Okay, my dad and I are no longer going to be talking. It's a mutual thing, so he's gone back home. I just had a weird conversation with Dave Lavetti's wife, and she told me I needed to get out of town for the sake of me and my son. Um…I've never been alone in that house before so it's freaking me out, and I think there's a ghost in the house." I rattle that off pretty good.

"What the hell? Have you been drinking? Nothing you said makes any sense. Your dad isn't in your life anymore? What happened there?" she asks.

"You know, it's a very long story, but in short, there's just too much history there to forgive and forget." It's not completely a lie.

"Okay, what about Dave's wife?"

"I didn't know who she was until she came up to me and told me to leave town because her husband is planning on hurting me and my son."

"What? Hunter? Are you going to the police?" She's starting to freak out.

"No, it could be all hearsay. How do I know this is even true?"

"She mentioned your son, Michael! That's important enough for me!" she yells.

"Cheryl, I am pulling up to the house now. We'll talk about this later. Please tell Hunter I love him, and don't worry about anything. I will take care of everything, okay?"

I don't think my explanation helps her, since she just hangs up the phone without saying good-bye. I can't worry about that right now; I have more important things to think about, like those fucking Lavettis! I go into the house feeling like I need to punch something. In the last twenty-four hours, my dad tells me he killed someone, I break off my relationship with him forever, Lavetti's wife tells me to leave town since her husband wants to hurt me and my son, and now Cheryl hangs up on me after I tell her the truth! What the fuck? I throw my keys back in the bowl and plop down on the sofa. I look at my watch; it's five o'clock. "Damn it! I missed *The Golden Girls* marathon!" I sit there for a while, debating on what the hell to do now. The last thing I want to think about is the Lavettis, but I'm afraid there's no way around it. I know that fucker is out to get me and I should come up with a plan, but not one like my father's plan. I still can't believe he killed that guy! As I start wondering what I should do, the doorbell rings. I'm not expecting anyone, and considering the conversation I had earlier with Lena, I'm not too keen on door answering. Upon inspection through the peephole, it turns out it's my neighbors, the ones whose dog was killed. When I open the door, their little girl is standing there with a puppy in her hands.

Her dad extends his hand to me. "Michael, thank you for what you did that night for our dog Chauncey. We'd had him since he was a pup, and having that happen to him"—he has to stop to regain his composure—"well, thank you so much. Isabella here wanted to show you her new puppy! She named him Michael, after you."

I look down at Isabella, then kneel down to pet her dog. "That was very nice of you, Isabella, to name your puppy after me. I am very sorry about Chauncey," I tell her as I pet her dog.

"Thank you, Michael, for helping Chauncey. He was my friend and I cried a lot after he died, but when Daddy got me my new puppy, I stopped crying!" She smiles this wonderful grin and then giggles.

"I am very happy for you, Isabella, and thank you for showing me your new puppy!" I stand up and shake her dad's hand again. "Did they ever catch whoever did it?" I ask.

"No, sorry to say, you were the only one who saw anything that night. I did hear the neighbors at the end of the street had their house broken into a couple nights ago, had a few guns stolen. I don't know if it's connected or not, but they have security cameras that caught an image of someone—or someones, I should say. I heard it was two men, and one had a beard, but that's all I know," he tells me. "Hey, thanks again, Michael. See you around." They both smile and leave.

I close the door and immediately think of those asshole Lavettis. If it was them who broke into that house, it means they now have guns—not that they didn't before. I haven't seen either one of them in a couple years, so I have no idea if one of them has a beard or not, but I'm sure Mexico wasn't a place where they really cared about hygiene. But then again, it could have been anyone who broke into that house. What if they break into mine? I don't even own a gun! Okay, it's official—I am freaking out. I decide to take a very long and very hot shower, then eat a big-ass bowl of ice cream. I go upstairs to my bathroom to turn on some music...but what shall I listen to? I flip through my CDs trying to figure out what will ease my mind and tension. Metallica. Yep, that's the one! I turn on the shower, making sure the steam from the heat surrounds and covers my bathroom like a soft blanket. I get down on the floor and do fifty sit-ups before heading into the shower. I love to sweat; it's one of the best feelings for me. I stand up and look at myself in the mirror, tracing my fingers against my abs. Thank God I started working out years ago and kept up with it. I can only imagine the flab I would have around my belly. I wouldn't have a six-pack, but more of a pony keg. Metallica's "One" comes on and I turn that shit up. I walk into my shower, thankful that when we built it, we made it big enough to house a bench, four heads, and no door; it's sweeter than a platter full of tits. Once I hear that sweet guitar riff I immediately take the stance of my inner rocker and begin my solo air guitar concert, not to mention my ultrasmooth singing voice that used to melt Gwen's butter. I don't want to brag, but she had compared me to Barry White before. I'm just saying.

The steam is so thick I can barely see around me, and it feels awesome. I listen to at least five songs on that CD before I get out of the shower. I am a complete prune, to say the least. My dick has shriveled up to what one would call a swizzle stick. And my balls? Well, let's just call those Marcona almonds. I am one hot fella right now. Ow! As I grab my towel and begin to dry off, I notice something on my mirror. "Is that writing?" I examine it closer. The steam is so thick it's penetrated every corner of the bathroom and blanketed my bedroom, so my vision has been somewhat altered by the white haze. I am three feet away from the mirror when the symbols become letters and the letters turn into words.

Let's shake on it

Chapter 8

"**O**H MY GOD, he's here!" I tell myself as I quickly get dressed. I start looking around for him—under my bed, in my closet. I have always kept a bat under my bed, even when I was a kid, so I quickly run to get that. I stop so I can hear...I turn my ear towards the door. I squint my eyes, as it seemingly works when you want to hear something better, but I don't hear anything. I slowly get up from the side of the bed where I grabbed my bat, and I softly walk to the door. I stop again, listening for anything. I peek out the door, looking left, then right, then left again. I raise my head so I can see down the stairs, but to no avail. I see nothing. I slowly walk to the top of the stairs and look over the bannister down into the living room and kitchen; still nothing. I tiptoe down the stairs, bat in hand and ready to battle. I call out, "Whoever had the balls to come into my house, I am armed and ready to fuck up your world!" As I get closer to the bottom of the stairs, I jump off and make a loud noise when I land on the marble floor. "Ha!" I start to run around the house making the loudest sounds possible, hoping to scare them out if they are hiding. I run into the kitchen, then the pantry; the bathroom, then the dining room; the study, then the living room. That's when I notice it: the front door is wide open, and there's a note taped to the picture of all three of us the day Hunter was born. I slam the door and lock it before I read the note. A sick feeling comes over me as I start to walk toward the message, as I know it's not a standard greeting or an invite to the symphony. The writing is the same as the one I received earlier, and this one is just as creepy:

Nice house…how's the wife?

"Fuck! What the fuck do I do now?" I yell at the top of my lungs. I start to pace back and forth, running my hands through my hair. "Oh shit, oh shit, oh shit! What the hell should I do now?" I run upstairs into my office and look up locksmiths. I finally get ahold of one who will come out tonight and change my locks; there's no way I can sleep if I don't. I wait for the next two hours like you would if you are about to go under the knife, in complete distress and praying you come out of it alive. It takes three hours to change all the locks on my house, and I get the heavy-duty ones that require a code to get in.

"You know, the people who usually get these kinds of locks have something to hide, or they are paranoid," the locksmith tells me.

"Um, thanks, but I'm just being cautious. I have a son to think about, and too many people know who I am," I retort.

"Oh, I didn't mean to offend you or anything. I just brought it up because most people let their guards down after they install these kinds of locks, and that's the last thing they should do. Even though these are the best locks we have, if someone wants to get in, they will find a way. Thanks, Mr. Bali, have a nice evening." He gets into his gray-and-black box-looking truck and drives away, leaving me feeling nowhere near better.

"Damn it! Why did he have to say that? Here I was, thinking that changing the locks on my house would somehow make it easier for me to go to sleep, and now I have Mr. Helpy Helperton telling me it's not going to work! What?" I begin to pace the house once again and ask myself questions. "What if he's right? What if today is the last day of my life, and I didn't say good-bye to Hunter? What if I'm wrong, and it's not even the Lavettis doing this shit to me? What if it's some other goon who has it in for me? What happens if they find out where Hunter is, and they kidnap him and hold him for ransom? That's it! I am putting this house up for sale tomorrow! Thanks, locksmith guy, for turning my life upside down with those words: *they will find a way.*"

I run upstairs and try to find the number for the real estate lady who sold us this house. After half an hour of searching—and when I say searching, I mean tossing everything from the desk onto the floor and then getting on my hands and knees to look—I say, "Ha! Here it is! And Gwen would always say I needed to be more organized... phhhft." I pick up the phone to call, but notice it's after ten. "Damn it! I should probably wait until the morning... no...wait...this would be a big fucking sale for her! Ah, hell no!" I dial her number and it rings several times. "Come on, answer!" I am fidgeting beyond belief.

A soft and just-awakened voice springs to life. "Hello, this is Kathy."

"Kathy, hey, it's Michael Bali. You sold us a house a few years back. Sorry it's so late, but I am in need of your services again."

"Oh, yes, Mr. Bali, how are you? It's been a while! What can I do for you?" She yawns.

"I need to put my house up for sale as soon as possible—like, tomorrow." I sound way too eager.

"Oh, okay...let me see...I need to check my schedule, so can you give me a moment?" she asks.

"Oh, sure, go ahead," I respond. Suddenly, the *Jeopardy* theme song comes on in my head and I start tapping my foot to it. I look outside and notice how black it is. The moon doesn't seem like it wants to play much.

"Okay, thanks for waiting, Michael. I have an eleven available. Does that work out for you?" she asks.

"Yes, it does. Thanks so much, Kathy. Bye!"

After I hang up the phone a sad feeling comes over me. *I'm really leaving, this is it, and...* I can't even finish my own thought. I can feel tears welling up in my eyes. I start to walk around my house, touching the walls and the furniture. Each room I go into reminds me of a great memory with Gwen. When I walk into the kitchen, the first thought that comes to mind is Gwen's cooking ability. There wasn't any. Oh, don't get me wrong, there were a few dishes she knew how to make, but it turned a little scary when she "experimented."

To give you an idea of the type of dish I am referring to, allow me to introduce you to flambé à la Gwen. Picture it: our kitchen, 2009. Okay, I think I've had my fill of *The Golden Girls*, but I digress. Gwen wanted to set the mood one hot summer night, so she lit candles and dimmed the lights. She had been watching Julia Child earlier that day and thought, *I can make that dish!* She went to the store and picked up all the ingredients herself, then told Cheryl to take the night off so she wouldn't be tempted to ask for help. She prepared all the vegetables and the squid—yes, I said squid—per instructions. She thought we should start trying new foods, since we had moved into a neighborhood that stank of uppity. If we were asked to dinner by a neighbor, we didn't want to be the ones who looked down at the plate and asked what it was, or possibly upchucked after we took a bite of an unknown substance. This way, if we started trying new things, then we would know what we liked and didn't like beforehand. Well, I could have told her that I didn't like squid, and I didn't even have to try it first. Squid? Really?

She had prepared everything, down to the exact number of forks one should have. I sat down, waiting for this sight to behold from my lovely Gwen. When she appeared, icky fish in hand, it seemed as though a terrified look had come over my face, because her expression turned from "Doesn't this look wonderful?" to "What the hell is that face for?" I didn't realize I was in for a fire show right at the table! She carefully placed the pan down, making an almost Vanna White motion with her hands. "Behold, Michael, for I have whipped up a scrumptious main course, with the help of the late and great Julia Child. She called it octopus, but I have chosen a better name that represents not only the chef, but also my own stamp, if you will. I call it flambé à la Gwen."

I thought for sure I needed to clap, but I was entranced by the matches and the lighter. She proceeded to dump—and when I say dump, I do mean dump—half a bottle of cognac into the pan. We don't drink, so seeing her with the bottle was like watching a pony walk for the first time; you want to laugh, but at the same time it's so endearing. She saw my eyes widen as she put the half-poured bottle down on the table. "Oh, Michael, don't worry! I watched them do this a thousand times on the Internet! Relax!"

"Wait, honey, um, I think you poured way too much in! Now, I'm not the brightest bulb in the tanning bed, but I have only seen flambé done to desserts like bananas Foster or cherries jubilee. Are you sure about this?" I kinda sat back in my chair, not knowing what the hell to do. I look around and eye the fire extinguisher.

"No, you're right, it's mainly done on desserts. But I thought, why not? Here we go!" She lit the pan and...

WOOOOOOOOOOOOOOOOOFFFFFF! The flame was so huge it shot up nearly two feet.

Gwen screamed, "Ah! Oh my God! Michael, get the fire thingy!"

I had to allow my eyes to fall back into their sockets before I could stand up. I ran over and grabbed the extinguisher, and quickly put out the octopus. All I can say is thank God for accidental disasters. You should have seen the mess it caused; there was food everywhere, considering she dropped the pan. Baby carrots and shallots were dispersed evenly on the floor, table, and our shirts, and the octopus—oh, excuse me, flambé à la Gwen—made its debut on the floor. She immediately started crying, but not me—I was laughing. I was nearly pissing my pants before Gwen decided it was rather funny. There we were, both covered in cognac and onions, laughing it up like nobody's business. That night we ended up eating peanut butter and jelly sandwiches, potato chips, and milk. That's the kind of life we had, and I miss it every day.

Even though it is late at night, I walk into the backyard next. I always forget how beautiful the grounds are. I rarely sit outside on the porch, even though we have awesome patio furniture arranged around a fire pit. I brush off some leaves that have fallen onto the chair before I sit down; I inhale deeply and take it all in. The moon has glistening beams all over the place, revealing some shiny new objects in the grass. I stand up and walk over to whatever the hell they are. As I get closer, the shimmering entities become bullets. "What the hell?" I ask myself as I lean down to pick one up. "A bullet?

Where did this come from?" Then I notice another one a few steps away, and I pick that one up. As I start to look around, I am now aware that my entire lawn is covered with bullets. A mass of glistening silver is spread across my lawn; there has to be a thousand of them. "Oh my God!" I say out loud as I start walking around. I begin to sweat, knowing that this is a Lavetti at work. "That house that was broken into down the street had guns taken, and now...oh, damn, it's happening." I quickly glance around, wondering if I'm being watched. I can hear dogs barking in the background, some chatter among neighbors, but that's it. I go back inside, glancing behind me every few steps. I lock the door immediately and pick up the phone to call the police, when there's a knock at the front door. I hang up the phone and look at the clock: eleven thirty? Who the hell can that be? I begin to walk toward the door, heart pounding, hands sweating. I stop before I get there, calling out, "Who's there?" No one answers. I take another step and there's another knock, this time at the back door. I jump as I turn around. Now, I know being a man I should not be this jittery, but holy hell, this is freaking me out. I try to see if anyone is standing at the back door, considering it's made of glass, but all I see is my reflection. I can feel the blood racing through my veins; I don't know what to do. I sneak back into the kitchen and pick up the phone again to call the police. Why I sneak, I have no idea.

"Nine-one-one, what's your emergency?"

Wait, what is my emergency? Someone's at my door and I don't want to answer it? I don't know what to say!

"Nine-one-one, hello? What's your emergency?"

"Oh, yes, I have someone at my front and back doors knocking and I don't want to answer. I also found at least a thousand bullets strewn about my backyard," I tell her as I nearly piss myself.

"Did you say bullets, sir? Do you know where they came from?"

"No, I just went out there tonight and saw them. Look, can you send someone out here? There's someone at my door and it's nearly midnight!" I don't think I sound terribly angry, considering I am scared to death.

"Sir, we have a unit on its way. Just stay on the phone with me until they arrive, okay?" she asks me.

"Oh, okay. That was fast." I am impressed.

"We had a unit in your neighborhood already, so they should be there momentarily." She is quite calm. I'm about to die, and she's as calm as a cucumber.

There's a knock at the front door.

"Oh shit, someone just knocked! It sounds just like the first knock! I think those guys are back! What do I do? I am freaking the fuck out, lady!"

"Sir, it's the police. They are at your front door, and it's safe to answer it now. Have a good night." She hangs up.

I keep the phone to my ear, not really understanding what she just said. I slowly start walking to the front of the house. This time, the doorbell rings.

"Oh my God, oh my God, I'm going to die," I repeat as I walk closer to the door, phone still at my ear.

"Mr. Bali, are you in there? It's the police," the voice calls out.

I drop my head back as I let out an arduous sigh. I wipe my brow with the phone, then realize I still have the phone. I put it on the table and then open the front door. Thank God for the black and blue!

"Mr. Bali, what seems to be the trouble?" he asks me.

"Well, I was just in my backyard and the lawn was full of bullets—I mean thousands of them. Then I came inside and someone knocked on my front door. I was hesitant about answering, considering the time, and then I heard someone knock at my back door. That's when I called you," I retort, still sweating.

"Bullets? Can we see?"

"Sure," I respond. They follow me around the side of the house and to the backyard. "See," I tell them, pointing to the still-glistening array of bullets.

"Wow, I've never seen this before. Have you, Larry?"

"No, this is not normal. You said you just noticed this tonight? When was the last time you were out here?" he asks me.

"Oh, a long time. I rarely come out here," I tell them.

"So these could have been here awhile. Do you mind if we take some pictures, Mr. Bali?" he asks me.

"No, go right ahead."

He tells his partner to go get the camera from the car and take pictures of the house, including the backyard. When he leaves, the deputy looks at me.

"I am aware of the story, Mr. Bali."

"What story?" I have no idea what he's talking about. Did he read my books?

"Look, my partner is new, and he isn't aware of what's been transpiring with you."

"I honestly have no idea what you're talking about."

"We've had a few calls lately about you and what you've been doing. One of the calls was a woman telling us about a dead raccoon on your front porch. Another saw you with blood all over your clothes and a shovel in your hand. We've also had a couple calls just this week about very loud yelling coming from your house. One man said he heard someone yell that you are a killer. Can you explain these things, Mr. Bali?"

His voice terrifies me, even though I haven't done anything wrong. I become panicked and can feel an attack coming on.

"I'm sorry, officer, but I need to take my medication right now or we will be going to the hospital. Feel free to follow me into the house if you want."

"I will be fine right here, Mr. Bali."

I have to go around the house to the front door since I locked the back door. The other officer has been taking pictures of everything, including my cars. I don't stop to ask him why. I need my meds. I run upstairs and into my bathroom. My pills are usually on the countertop, but they aren't there. I look through my drawers and in my closet. "Where the hell are they?" I can feel my hands tightening; my vision is getting blurry. I make it into my office and open the top drawer. I find the bottle, but the lid is off. I sit down now that I'm dizzy. I flip it over so the pills can come out, but there's something blocking them.

I take out the piece of paper and unroll it. My anxiety hits a wall:

> Bullets, bullets, bullets...why so many bullets?
> Call the cops and your son finds out why...

"Oh no! No, no, no!" I take my pills and use what's left of my saliva to swallow them. I put my hands on my head. "Shit, the cops are already here! What the hell do I do?" I start to rock back and forth, praying my pills take effect soon. My hands aren't loosening up at all and my chest is tight. I look up and the room is now closing in on me. I have to get a grip and calm myself down. *Breathe, Michael, breathe.*

Chapter 9

"MR. BALI, WAKE up!" His voice is firm and demanding. My eyes slowly open, and in my daze I see a man standing over me.

"Huh?" My voice is groggy.

"You okay, Mr. Bali? You passed out in here. We were waiting outside and you didn't come back. You okay?" he asks.

I blink my eyes to help me wake up. "Yeah. I didn't get my pills in me fast enough." Right then I remember everything. I sit up in a hurry. "Um…I'm okay, officers, you can go now." I hope they didn't see the note. I try to look for it without them noticing my erratic behavior, but I can't find it. "Let me walk you guys out. I'm sure I've taken up plenty of your time." As I lead them to the door of my office, one of them turns around.

"Didn't you forget something, Mr. Bali?" he asks me.

I begin to feel faint. "Forget something? What?" I respond.

"You called us here, remember? The bullets in your backyard, the knocking at your doors? We need to take a report."

"Oh, you know what? When I came upstairs my phone was ringing, and it turns out it was a prank by a friend of mine. He thought it would be funny to screw with me. What a joker, huh?" I put my hands on my hips and begin to fake laugh. "So you see, it was all just a big misunderstanding, so no need for a report! Let's just forget this whole thing. I'm sorry for taking up your time." I lead them all the way to the front door.

"A misunderstanding, you say?" one of the officers asks.

"Yep, just a big stupid misunderstanding due to an asshole of a friend!" I continue my fake laugh. I open the door and walk them out. "Sorry again, guys! You're doing a great job, by the way! Have a great night!"

I shut the door and run back upstairs. "Note, note, note, where are you?" I say to myself as I search my desk. The sound of crunched paper comes from under my left foot as I take a step closer. I look down and there it is, on the floor. "Oh shit, thank God they didn't see it!" I hold the note close to my heart. "How in the hell am I going to find out if they know I called the cops? This isn't good." I look at the clock and it's two in the morning. I decide to go to bed, hoping the next couple hours bring me some sleep. I go to bed and lie there, motionless and looking up at the ceiling. I silently say a prayer for my son's safe return home to me and for those bastard Lavettis to leave me alone. I would have asked for death, but I don't think

God would have listened to me then. A feeling of serenity comes over me and I am able to fall asleep, at least for the next four or five hours.

I must have been running in my dreams, because I jerk myself awake and nearly fall off the bed. The sun is trying to peek through the clouds; it looks like rain again. I wearily get out of bed, cracking my back as I stand up. Even though I've only slept a couple hours, I feel quite rested. I get into the shower and take a quick one, considering the long one I took ended up with writing on my mirror. Since I am meeting with Kathy this morning, I should get dressed in something nice. I pick out dark blue jeans and a light blue button-up, no tie. The one thing I've always remembered when dressing is always match your belt with your shoes. Gwen was on my ass for years about that. I would give anything to hear her yell at me one more time. After I feel like I look presentable, I head downstairs to call Cheryl.

"Hi, Cheryl, it's Michael. Is Hunter around? I want to talk to him."

"Yep, he's right here." She puts him on the phone.

"Hewo, Daddy! Where are you?" he asks me.

"Hey, buddy! I'm at home and missing you a lot! Are you having fun with Cheryl?"

"Yeah, but I want to come home now. I miss my toys."

"I know. You can come home soon, just not today, okay?" God, I miss him.

"Okay, Daddy. I'm eating waffles so I'm going now." He drops the phone.

I hear Cheryl pick it up. "Sorry, he dropped it faster than I could grab it. What did you tell him?" she asks me. "He doesn't seem so happy."

"Well, he wants to come home and I told him not yet, but soon."

"Yeah, actually, I would like to know when we can come home." If she's tapping her foot, I can feel it.

"Well, that's something I wanted to talk to you about, Cheryl. I'm putting the house up for sale today." I cringe at her response.

"What? Are you kidding me? Why?" Yeah, she's mad.

"Cheryl, we need a fresh start and it won't happen here. I need to move away. Plus, you know, the whole thing with the Lavettis. I can't put Hunter in danger like this." I try to explain to her until she interrupts me.

"Where, exactly? Where are you thinking about moving to?"

"West Coast. There's a town called Spokane that I was thinking about. It's in Washington State."

"I see...Hunter, no! I have to go, Michael. Hunter just threw his waffle against the wall."

She hangs up before I can tell her good-bye, but I say it anyway. I hang up the phone and an incredible sinking feeling overwhelms me. I think since I finally said it out loud to someone else, about moving, it seems more real. I walk directly to the back door and open it. I walk out onto the deck; the bullets are still there, looking like they are asleep. As I turn around to go back inside, I see some kind of flower sticking out of the lamppost. I reach up and pluck the petal from it, and notice it's a Toad lily.

"What the hell? Are you kidding me? Are you fucking kidding me?" My outburst causes my neighbor to look over the fence and ask if I am okay. "Oh, I'm fine, Mr. Adams, thanks." I go back inside, slamming the door behind me. "I need to get the hell out of here—now. Who would put this here?" I rack my brain trying to come up with my own set of suspects. I doubt the cops will help me now, considering my nosy-ass neighbors have made me look like a murdering raccoon freak. Fuck, I can't call them anyway! I am completely on my own.

I make myself some coffee and wait for Kathy to show up. I sit on the front porch, rocking away on my hand-carved wooden rocking chair. Gwen bought me this for my thirty-third birthday. She even had the guy carve two threes and my initials on the back of it. It's the most beautiful chair ever, and I can't imagine being without it, even in Spokane. This bad boy is coming with. My watch shows straight up ten o'clock when Kathy pulls into the drive. I stand up and wave to greet her.

"Hi, Michael, it's good to see you again! The house looks beautiful, like I knew it would!" She takes her large briefcase out from the backseat. Her high heels dig into the gravel path as she walks to greet me.

I extend my hand. "Kathy, good to see you again! Thanks for coming on such short notice." I smile.

She looks as if she's seen a ghost the closer she gets to me. "Oh, I'm sorry for staring, but you've had something done to your face, haven't you? You look different from the last time I saw you!" she beams.

I tend to forget the surgery I had years before. "Oh, yeah. Funny how some things you forget, huh? Come inside, looks like it's going to rain again." I open the door for her and let her go in first.

"Will Gwen be joining us?"

She smiles as she puts her briefcase down on the floor. She looks around the place, grinning from ear to ear. I just stand there. I haven't had to tell anyone of Gwen's passing in a long time and it catches me off guard. Kathy looks back at me.

"Michael? Is Gwen joining us?" she asks again.

"Kathy...Gwen passed away about three years ago." I could curl up and die right now, easily.

She puts her hand over her mouth, her eyes wide open. "Oh my gosh, I am so sorry. I didn't know!" Her sincerity shows through her voice and her watery eyes.

"It's okay, Kathy. That is actually why I want to sell this house. There are too many memories here, and I am still having a very hard time with it. Let's sit down on the couch. It's a lot more comfortable than the kitchen chairs."

Kathy still has her hand over her mouth as she watches me with her eyes. "Michael, I feel so bad for saying that. I—"

I interrupt her. "Kathy, it's okay, you didn't know. Did you want some coffee?" I ask her. "I just made a fresh pot." She nods her head yes. "Cream, sugar?" I ask as I start to walk away.

"Oh...um...both, please. Thanks, Michael."

By the sound of her voice, I can tell this conversation about Gwen isn't over, and I really don't want to get into it. I successfully pour both of us some coffee without spilling it, but walking it over to her is the challenge. I make it two feet away from her and then it happens. I spill it all over the floor, but it also gets on her pants.

"Oh shit, Kathy, I am so sorry!"

"Oh…do you have something I can wipe this off with?" she asks.

I blankly stare at her, then it hits me. "Oh, yeah, let me get something!"

I run into the kitchen and wet down a towel. After she wipes down her pants you can still see the stain. I offer her a pair of Gwen's pants so I can put hers in the wash. She agrees, and I take her upstairs so she can pick out a pair. All these years and I haven't thrown away a thing of hers. When Kathy walks into the closet, she's quite impressed with Gwen's style.

"I don't know if I should, Michael. These things are just beautiful and I wouldn't feel right." She looks at me apologetically.

"No, it's fine, Kathy. They aren't getting any use just hanging there. I haven't even thought about throwing them away, but now maybe I should. I mean, not throw them away, but donate them to the women's shelter or something like that."

"Yeah, yeah, that's a great idea. In fact, I know the director of the downtown shelter. I can call her if you like, and they will come and pack it all up for you, too," she tells me.

"That actually might make it a little easier on me, not going through them. It's been three years, Kathy, and it feels like yesterday that she died."

"Michael, please tell me if I'm out of line, but how did she die?" She sits down on the little couch that separated my side from hers.

I stand there with my hands in my pockets. My face has turned ashen as I begin to relive the best and worst day of my life.

"Well, it was a Friday and we were watching a horror movie. Those were her favorite. When a scary part came up and she jumped, she thought she had peed her pants. But it turned out, her water broke. I started freaking out, knowing this was it, but then I remembered the book and..." I stop talking. I can't believe I almost told Kathy about my book. I try to recover. "Um...I remembered what the pregnancy book said about what you should do when the water breaks, and I knew we had to make it to the hospital, like, now. So we hightailed it to the hospital. Gwen was not really freaking out, but I was, so she started to calm me down. I couldn't help but think what was going to happen, and this might be the last time I saw her again." Shit, I've done it again, and Kathy catches on.

"Last time you saw her? Huh?"

Recover, Michael, recover.

"I meant the last time I would see her alone, before the baby came." I can feel the sweat forming and running down my back. "Well, we made it there in plenty of time. She had Hunter at two fifteen the next morning. He was perfect—although my genetic disfigurement was passed down to him, so he looks like me, before my surgery—but still perfect. Shortly after Gwen gave birth she started bleeding, and they couldn't stop it. She died at three ten, less than one hour after Hunter was born. There's a picture on the mantel downstairs of all three of us. I'm glad God gave her enough time to see and hold her son." I stand up and walk around a bit. Tears are always right there when I start to talk about it, especially when it's entirely my fault.

Kathy stands up. "Michael, oh my gosh, that is the saddest thing I've ever heard!" She comes over to hug me and I hug her back.

"Thanks, Kathy, but I'm fine. I think no matter how many times I tell that story, it's still raw for me. I didn't mean to upset you, I apologize for that. Tell you what, you change into some pants and I will be downstairs." I quickly leave. Honestly, it feels like I am cheating on Gwen, having Kathy in her closet.

As I shut the door, I feel the hairs on the back of my neck rise up. I turn around, but see nothing there. I rub the back of my neck and walk down the stairs, only to feel it again as I reach the last step. This time it feels like someone is breathing on me. I nearly fall off that last step when I turn around to see what it is. For the first time I think I see Gwen—or her apparition, at least. I feel like I'm going crazy. I want to see her again so badly that I might be dreaming I see her. "Lord, help me with this," I whisper as I walk into the living room. I walk over to the picture I was telling Kathy about. Gwen was so happy at that moment; it kills me to think about it. Kathy nearly gives me a fright when she comes up behind me and I don't hear her.

"That is a great picture of you three," she tells me.

I turn around after I jump, a little. "Oh, jeez, Kathy, you scared me. Hey, you found some pants, that's great! Let's talk about the house, okay? I'm kind of anxious to sell this place."

"I can see that. Have you decided where you are going to go?" she asks me as she starts taking papers out of her briefcase.

"Yes. Spokane, Washington. It would be great if you could also help with finding me a home there, too. Is that possible?"

"Oh, um...I am not licensed for that state, but I can sure make some calls for you. I actually know a few folks that live there. It's a nice city, and a lot different from Baltimore."

"That sounds perfect. I need a new outlook on everything, including where I live. Okay, let's talk numbers here."

We begin with walking around, and she takes some pictures of the house, making sure she gets all the little things that we had redone, like the closet and the master bath moldings.

"Gwen had a great eye, Michael. This house will sell, no problem," she tells me.

"Awesome, that's what I want to hear. Do you think I can get what I'm asking for?"

"There's a good shot you will, but this business is so volatile right now. I can guarantee you will get offers, though!" She smiles.

We head back into the living room, where we talk for another hour or so. I tell her what I am looking for in a new home and the type of neighborhood I want.

"I can have your house listed tomorrow. I will swing by and put up the sign first thing in the morning, and I will make those calls I told you about for your Spokane home. I wish you luck, Michael, and only the best for you and Hunter. We'll talk soon!"

She leaves in Gwen's pants and it doesn't bother me at all. I offer to wash hers, but it turns out, dry cleaning only. I actually feel pretty good letting something of Gwen's go. I have to start moving on, and this is the very first thing I've done to start that domino party. I wave good-bye and then go back to my rocking chair. I sit there for the next two hours, watching the world go by, and I smile.

My day feels like it is going pretty well, until I remember what I found last night—the petal. *Who in the hell would plant a Toad lily petal in a light? The only person who knew about those flowers was...Mitch!*

Chapter 10

"HOW IN THE hell am I supposed to talk to Mitch when I disowned my father? This is just great!" I go inside and slam the door behind me. "That little shit! What did I ever do to him? Why is he doing this to me?" I run upstairs and open my e-mail account; maybe I have his address and can send him a private message. I scroll through my addresses; I never realized how many I have. The number shows 289. but I only know a handful of them. I don't even know how I got all these damn things on here. I find his name and send an e-mail to him, hoping it goes through and my dad doesn't see it. I try to make it sound as calm as possible, even though I want to wring his neck:

> Dear Mitch,
> Is there anything you need to tell me? I found something in my yard, and I have a feeling you had something to do with it. This isn't funny, either, because if you are working with the

Lavettis, then not only is my life at stake, but yours is, too. Tell me the truth.
    Michael

I am the worst when it comes to waiting. I have no patience. I used to, but I have no idea where it went. This will drive me crazy until I hear from him; that is, *if* I hear from him. I decide to go online to look at homes in Spokane; maybe that will keep my mind busy enough. I put in my requirements and up pop hundreds of homes. "Holy shit! This may take a while." I decide to look into homes with property. I've always lived in close neighborhoods where everyone knows everyone. I think I want the opposite now, and according to this site I have a few dozen to look at. I didn't realize how big Spokane is, and it's pretty close to Seattle. I have a feeling this will be a great move. I click back on my e-mail to see if I've received any mail...nope. Damn. I go back to the real estate site and click on a property around Fish Lake. "Now, that would be cool, living on a lake! Hmm." I begin to click on pictures, but my phone rings.

"Hello?"

"Hi, Michael, it's Kathy. I have some news about Spokane for you! Is this a good time?" she asks me.

"Yeah. That's ironic, though. I was just online looking at some properties over there. So what's up?"

"Well, according to my friend, who's a realtor in Spokane, there are houses that aren't even on the MLS yet, and she wants to know if she can contact you about them. She didn't want to contact you if there was another agent you were dealing with."

"No, I haven't talked to anyone but you. That would be great if she can send them to me. What's her name?" I ask.

"Her name is Missy Allison. I've known her since we were twelve years old. We grew up together, so I can speak honestly when I say I adore her. She's perfect for you!"

I can tell she is smiling a wicked grin. "Um…Kathy? You aren't trying to set me up, are you? Because it kinda sounds like you are."

"No, I am just making sure that the person I find for you is worth your time! Okay, yes, I am. I'm sorry, Michael, but I had this incredible feeling after I left your house. I haven't talked to my friend in a while, and she happened to call me the minute I got into my car! It was fate, it had to be, because she was just telling me how there are no great men left in Spokane and here you are—moving there!"

I can actually hear her clapping. "Are you jumping up and down and clapping, Kathy? Because it sounds like you are jumping up and down and clapping."

The sound stops. "No."

"Uh-huh. Kathy, please listen to me. I'm not looking for anyone, okay? All I want is to sell my home and find another one as soon as possible. That's it. Please don't set me up with anyone, not now," I explain to her.

"Okay, I understand. Did you still want her to send you those homes, though?"

"Yes, I would. Thanks, Kathy. Have a good night. Bye." I hang up the phone and start shaking my head. "Women." I go back to looking at the house on Fish Lake. "Three bedrooms, three baths, on ten acres right on the water. Sounds perfect to me!" I hear a *ding* telling me I have mail. "Oh, I hope it's Mitch!" I minimize the screen and pull up my e-mail. Unfortunately, it isn't Mitch, it's Missy.

Hello, Mr. Bali,

My name is Missy Allison and I am a realtor in Spokane, Washington. I heard from Kathy that you wanted to see some houses over here, so I am sending some pictures to you. These aren't on the MLS yet, so you have an advantage over most people right now. Let me know if anything suits you! I look forward to meeting you in person!

Missy Allison

P.S. I love your books!

"Wow, that was quick! Either she's hurting for business or hurting for a man." I can see a small picture of her in the top corner, so I click on it. "Wow...she's...hot. Maybe I should be more open to dating again." I read her bio, and it turns out she's a widow, no children, studied art at Washington State University, and plans to travel the world. She sounds interesting, and she has jet-black hair;

I've always loved black hair. Suddenly, I feel like someone is standing right behind me. I look up from my computer screen and just kinda sit there, waiting...for what, I have no idea. As quick as a flash, I turn around to see nothing there, but I do feel a slight breeze flow through the room. I look at the windows; they are shut, and I know the downstairs ones are shut as well. I sit there, the hairs on my arms starting to rise up, my skin starting to get goose pimples. I shiver, but go back to looking at my computer, until this overwhelming feeling of guilt comes rushing through me, like I am looking at porn or something. To the left of my computer is a picture of Gwen. When I look at it, I know exactly what I am feeling: guilt. Guilt that I'm even considering another woman, guilt that I am moving out of this house to start my life again, guilt that I am moving on. I turn the computer off for the night, and instead begin writing things down that I need to do before I move away. I know I miss a bunch, but my list starts to become quite lengthy, not to mention unattainable on my own. I will need Cheryl to help me with this, and I know she's not going to be very pleasant. I look at the clock and it's only eight. I pick out a movie and watch it in bed until I fall asleep.

The next morning brings me sunshine and a migraine. These suckers can last all day, and I haven't had one in a while, so I guess I am due. I take some medicine for it and go back to bed to sleep it off; I sleep for the next twenty-four hours. When I wake up, my throat feels like I have been screaming all night, it is so dry. My eyes have to adjust to the light and are quite puffy. I hobble into the bathroom and look at myself in the mirror—not good. My entire face is swollen and my eyes are red. It looks like I've been in a fight. Then I start to shit my pants. "Oh no! No, no! Please tell me nothing happened!" I look all over my body, but I don't see blood or scratches and my clothes are fine. I take in a deep breath, then exhale and drop my head back. I close my eyes and can feel my neck crack. When I open them, they are looking directly at writing scrawled on the ceiling:

I'm waiting...

"Oh my God!" I run downstairs to the front door. "How in the hell did he get in? I just changed the locks!" I check the door, but it is closed; so is the back door, and the side one as well. I run through the house, checking all the windows, but they haven't been tampered with at all. "Maybe I didn't see it, that one night when they wrote on my mirror? That has to be it! There's no way they could have broken in here, not again!" I run my hands through my hair and go back to my room. "I need to calm the hell down. I can't have my son seeing me like this!" I take a quick shower, then grab some food. I go into my office and turn on my computer, crossing my fingers that Mitch has returned my e-mail. I scroll through the thirty or so e-mails and there it is:

RE: Your question
Although our relationship came from the genetic form, I must tell you that my hatred for

you never really left and, in fact, has risen to a new high. I want to thank you for yanking my father out of my life by being the quintessential and returning son of the dead. I, too, have decided to become a writer, Michael. My destiny has started...just like yours did, although you didn't know it at the time. Say hi to the Lavettis for me! See you soooooooooooooooon.

M

"What the hell is he talking about? This is just great!" I slam my hands down on my desk, causing the picture of Gwen to fall over. I pick it up. "Son of a—!" It shocks me when I notice it—the eyes. My picture of Gwen has its eyes blackened out. I jump out of my chair, knocking it over. "Holy shit! What the fuck? I...what the fuck?" I fall to the ground, sobbing uncontrollably. "I can't do this, Lord! I need your help! Please help me." I cradle the picture in my arms and lie there for a while. Memories start running through my mind, taking me back to the first book and when I met my beloved. She was so beautiful and exquisitely feminine; her eyes alone could tell a story. I weep with complete and utter remorse. My phone starts to ring, breaking up my pity party of one.

"Hello?"

"Michael, it's Kathy. I came by yesterday to put the sign up, but you never came to the door. I guess you weren't home. I didn't hear from you so...how do you like the sign?" she asks.

"What sign?" I sniff quite loudly.

"The *for sale* sign, silly! It's in your yard, and I've already had a few calls! Anyway, I need to make sure you have the house sparkling clean when we begin walk-throughs. I've scheduled the first one for the day after tomorrow, okay?"

"Oh, wow, that was fast, Kathy! Um...my cleaning lady has been out of town, but I will call her and...we should be good." I express my appreciation after I blow my nose.

"You okay? You sound...funny."

"No, I have allergies and they just got to me, that's all." Man, I lie very well.

"I understand, I have them, too. So okay, then, we are set for day after tomorrow. Oh, did you get a chance to look at the houses Missy sent to you?" she asks me.

"Some. I ended up falling asleep, but I will today, now that I know people are interested. Thanks again, Kathy." I hang up the phone and run downstairs to see the sign. In big bold letters, there it is:

For Sale
Luxury Property

So it's begun—my fresh start. Not sure how I feel about it now that it's happening. I go inside to call Cheryl.

"Hello?"

"Hey, Cheryl, how's it going?" I think I sound way too chipper.

"It's going all right," she responds, and yes, she's not happy.

"Well, good news, I need you and Hunter to come home—like, today."

"Today? Are you sure?" She sounds hesitant.

"Yes, I am sure. The house is officially on the market, and people will start coming through day after tomorrow."

I don't hear anything for a few seconds, and then this is what I get.

"And you need the house cleaned, right? Sure, Michael, Hunter and I will be home soon. Bye." She hangs up.

I shrug my shoulders. "I can't help the way she feels." I hang up the phone. I feel like I'm going a million miles an hour, considering everything that's happened, from the e-mails to Mitch to the house. I don't know where to start. I guess the smart thing would be to get my *to-do* list and do it.

Chapter 11

THE DAY COMES and goes; the day is now night and I am freaking starving. I'm not in the mood to cook, so I run out for some Chinese food; orange chicken is sounding ever so good. I call ahead to make sure it is ready so I won't have to deal with... anyone. I pull into the parking spot marked Takeout Only and run inside. I tell them my name and then wait, impatiently. The restaurant seems way more crowded than usual, so the seating area is nil. I stand in the corner, trying to blend in with the wall; thank God I'm wearing a hat. Not two minutes after I get there, I feel fingers tap my shoulder. I look over and it's a little boy, standing on the bench so we are eye to eye.

"Hi," he tells me.

"Hi. Do you like Chinese food, too?" I ask him.

He shakes his head. "No, ick. I like hamburgers!" he tells me.

"Oh, well, I like hamburgers, too! What's your name?" I ask.

"Luke."

"Oh, Luke, that's a cool name! My name is Michael. Nice to meet you, Luke." I extend my hand to shake his.

He puts his hand in mine and begins to shake like my son would, full fist. I begin to laugh, until I see who his mom is.

"Hello, Michael." Her eyes look very scared as she begins to look around the restaurant.

"Lena, how are you?" I have no idea what the hell to say to her. "Looking for someone?" My sarcastic wit beguiles me.

"No, but you should be," she says under her breath as she stands up, waiting to be seated with her two boys.

"So...where's your husband? Killing someone?" I shouldn't have said that.

She looks back at me. "You know, this isn't easy for me, either. I didn't know what kind of monster I married until it was too late. I am trying to help you, Michael, and you are only making it difficult for me to want to do that anymore," she retorts.

"Did you know your sons are named after my brothers who were murdered by the Lavettis? Did you know that?"

Her face turns ashen. "What? What do you mean?" She looks at her boys.

I start to feel bad for her. "Look, the family you married into are pieces of shit, killing shit. I think you should be looking at a way to get out, for your boys' sake. I know firsthand how he fathered his children. I can't imagine what he wants those two to do for him when they are older."

I can tell I've gone too far telling her that; she looks sick to her stomach.

"Look, I am sorry for telling you all this, but I think you should know what you might be in for yourself. The Lavettis, from as far back as when I was a kid, were the worst people to ever know. They are pure evil, and I was praying it would all be done once the last bastard was dead, but now that he has two more children, I'm afraid their reign of terror will never end, unless you intervene." I look up as they call my name. "Look, I have to go, but please remember what I've told you. Take your boys and get the hell out of here, and don't look back. I'm afraid it's too late for me. I've been in this game, and I'll be here till the end of it. Take care, Lena."

I grab my food and go. I don't even look back at her, but I can tell she's watching me, wondering what the hell to do. I feel sick to my stomach after seeing her and those boys. It makes me miss Hunter so much, but thank God he's coming home in a few hours. When I arrive back home, I go straight up to my room. I scarf down my food and then lie down in bed. It doesn't take long before I fall asleep, with leftover orange chicken in hand. Something stirs me awake. I look at the clock: two forty-five. I sit up, wondering if I just dreamed something or if I heard something, but the slam of a door remedies that question. I jump up, thinking it's Lavetti, and now I'm awake to fight. No more sneaking-in bullshit tonight. I sneak out of my bed, orange chicken falling to the floor. I tiptoe across the room. My door is already cracked open, so I just move it some more so I can see down the hallway. There is a light on downstairs, but I don't hear anything. I slowly walk from my room to the top of the stairs, peering over the banister. Still nothing, and now the light has turned off. I can hear footsteps coming my way. I don't know what to do; I forgot to grab my bat! I can hear someone walking up the steps. I crouch down behind the big-ass plant. I feel like a ninja. My vision becomes impaired, since the leaves on the dumb cane are huge, but I manage to see the top of someone's head bopping up the steps. He/she is only a few steps away from me now. I get into my pouncing stance, ready for action. I slow my breathing so he/she can't hear me and begin to count in my head—one, two, three—and I jump.

"Not tonight, you fucker!" I yell. Now, this would have been a great opportunity to have worn a cup, but I didn't, and my balls become one with Cheryl's size ten. "Mother fuck!" I yell, to say the least. I drop to the floor.

"Ah!" she screams. "Michael! What the hell are you trying to do? Kill me?" She puts her hand to her heart and stoops over. I lie there in agony while Cheryl kneels down, clutching her chest. "Is this your way of greeting now? Because I could do without it," she tells me.

I moan; that's all I can do for about five minutes. When the blood finally comes back down, as well as my balls, I stand up. "Sorry, Cheryl, I didn't think you'd come home in the middle of the night! You scared the shit out of me!" I continue to hold my junk, wiping the sweat away from my face with the free hand.

She catches her breath. "I didn't think you would hear us. Your sleeping pills usually knock you out. I didn't even think about calling you. I'm sorry."

"It's okay, I'm just glad you're home. Is Hunter asleep?" I start to walk to his room.

"Well, he was! Who knows, now that you turned into the night stalker?" she loudly whispers.

"Oh, hardy-har-har! I don't hear him, so maybe he slept through it." I walk into his room where he is just sacked out. In fact, saliva has formed a nice puddle on his pillow and he has on one shoe. I walk back into the hallway. "Where's his other shoe?" I ask her.

"Oh, it's still in the car. He got so excited when he found out we were coming home that he started taking his shoes off and throwing them in the air. I'll look for it tomorrow. Go to bed, I'll see you in the morning. Good night." She starts to walk toward her room.

"Hey, Cheryl" I begin.

She turns around. "Yeah."

"Sleep tight, don't let the bedbugs bite." I smile and so does she.

That next morning, which is only a few light hours of sleep away, begins with Hunter's feet in my back. I turn around and there he is, sound asleep. I look at the clock and it's still early, but not too early to wake him up. I start to tickle his neck, and he begins to squirm until his eyes slowly open.

"Daddy!" He hugs me, tight.

"Hey, buddy, I am so glad you're home! I missed you so much!" I hug him even tighter, and my eyes begin to tear up. Hunter looks at me and asks why I'm crying. "I...I just missed you so much, buddy!"

He wipes away my fallen tears. "Don't cry, Daddy, I'm here now." That is all I need to hear; full-blown tears have left the building.

He jumps out of my arms, yells for pancakes, and then out he goes, in a flat-out run downstairs. I hear him in the kitchen before I can even crawl out of bed. I go in to brush my teeth and remember the writing on the ceiling; I didn't clean it up. I look up. "Oh shit." I grab a chair and a washcloth, then start to scrub. It looks like whatever it was written in is coming off pretty easy. Thank God, because in walks Cheryl.

"Michael, I don't think you need to be scrubbing the ceilings!" she says with a giggle.

"Oh, I know, but I thought it might help." I get off the chair and throw the washcloth in the hamper.

Cheryl walks over to it. "Hey, looks like someone knows how to do his own laundry! Nice!" She looks back at me.

"I'm not a complete idiot. I can take care of myself." I try to sound tough. I suck at it.

"Oh, I'm sure you can! In fact, I love what you've done to the backyard! Are those bullets?" she asks.

All I can think right now is, *Oh shit. Come on, Michael, think of a doozy.* "Oh, yeah...um...well, Easter is around the corner, and I thought Hunter could do a bullet hunt, just to get him some extra training for the big day, you know." God, that was so stupid.

Cheryl just looks at me. "Bullets? You thought that a three-year-old needed some training for an Easter egg hunt with bullets? Are you trying to kill him? There are hundreds of bullets out there! What were you thinking?" she snaps.

Yeah, maybe that wasn't such a great plan.

"Pancakes, anyone?" That was my defense.

I finish brushing my teeth and then head to the kitchen, where the aroma of those fluffy bastards is filling my nostrils with heaven and butter, lots of butter. I sit down next to Hunter, grab a forkful of bacon, and then a pile of cakes. He's already mastered the shovel technique; I am so proud. He starts to laugh when I try to imitate him, then he does his best with his interpretation of me. Together we are a laughing mess of bacon bits and flapjacks. This is the best morning ever!

I help Cheryl with the dishes, thinking that I can ease her into the notion of us moving without her with kindness. She figures it out before I can even finish drying. "I know what you are doing, Michael, and I appreciate it."

"What am I doing? You don't want me to dry?"

She smiles. "I'm going to miss you." She stops what she's doing and slaps me upside the head. I flick water in her face and tell her I will miss her more.

We don't say anything more, we just finish the dishes.

I look out the window and think to myself that this would be a great time for some father-son time, especially with all those bullets crying out to be picked up. I show Hunter all the shiny objects out there and say, "Look outside, buddy, at all those little shimmery things in the grass! Did you know that the Easter Bunny asked me if he could put all those on our lawn?"

"Why did he do that?" he asks me, his nose pressed against the window.

"Well, he picks out the smartest kid on the whole block, and then drops all these little things on his lawn so that kid can practice before any other kid on how to do an Easter egg hunt! It's obvious he wants you to win, because look at how many things he wants you to pick up! He picked you as the smartest kid, Hunter! We can't let him down, now, can we?" I sound convincing enough.

"Yeah! Let's go, Daddy!" He is very excited.

"Well, let's get dressed first, then we need to find something to put them in!" I tell him.

I can see his little brain thinking. "Oh, Daddy! I know what to get! I'll be back!" He runs off to his room.

I stand up and put my hands on my hips. Smart thinking, Dad, until in my peripheral vision I see Cheryl looking at me.

"Really, Michael? Why don't you tell me the truth now? What happened?" Her eyebrows are up.

I shrug my shoulders. "Just what I said. I don't have any control over the Easter Bunny, woman!" I stomp off in a huff.

Hunter comes running down the stairs with a large box in hand. "We can use this, Daddy!"

"Where did you get that?" I ask him.

"From Mommy's closet! It has a lid and everything!" He smiles from ear to ear.

When he gets closer to me, I realize he has the Blue Bonnet box, the one that housed the hat that killed Trudy. Shivers go up and down my spine. "Hey, that's a great idea! I'll tell you what, I will put this here and you go get dressed, okay?"

"Okay!" He runs back upstairs, and I just stare at the box. That same cold chill flows through my veins. I look around, expecting to see Cheryl, but again, no one is there. I pick up the box and take it into the kitchen.

"Look what Hunter found." I put the box on the table.

Cheryl turns. "Oh, wow. I haven't seen that since..." She stops.

"Yeah, me neither. He wants to use it to pick up the bullets. What do you think?"

"I think it's a great idea. I wanted to talk to you about going through Gwen's things and—"

I interrupt her. "I've been thinking about that, too, and it's time. I need to get rid of it, all of it," I tell her, then I walk away, back up to my room to get dressed.

Hunter runs out of his room, camo sweats on and all, ready for battle. "Come on, Daddy!" He grabs the box and heads outside. I'm right behind him. With each bullet he puts in the box, he counts: one, two, fwee, four, five, seven, two, four. According to his calculations we've picked up one trillion and two bullets. It only takes us a half hour to pick them all up, and Hunter is beaming with pride. "The Easter Bunny will be so proud of me, Daddy! I win!"

"Yes, you do, son. Yes, you do!"

He tries to pick up the box, but ends up grunting, "Uh, Daddy, I can't get it." I pick up the box and take it into the garage. Hunter follows me. "Daddy, why so many cars?"

I look at him, then at the cars. "You know, Mommy used to ask me that all the time!" I start to laugh.

"Why so many?" he asks me again as he starts rummaging through the bullets.

That gets me to thinking. I never thought I would say such a thing, but I do, and out loud. "You know what? I'm going to sell these cars and just keep one. What one should I keep?" I ask him.

Hunter looks up from his loot. "That one," he says, and points to the right.

"I had a feeling you would pick that one. It was Mommy's car, you know." I walk over to it and brush the door with my hand.

"I know. That's why I want that one. It's pretty, Daddy." He runs over and gets in the driver's seat. He pretends to drive, even making car sounds. Man, I love this kid.

As he plays in the car, I do a walk around and visit my other children: a 1964 canary yellow Mustang convertible, a 1969 Boss 429, and a 1970 Boss 302. It's going to be hard getting rid of these, but I know I have to. I guess I need to put that on my to-do list also.

"Come on, buddy, let's go inside. You did an excellent job today! The Easter Bunny will be so proud of you! I know I am!" I help him down from the car, and he runs inside the house.

I stay back, still admiring, still contemplating. I walk over to my '69 Boss 429 and sit inside. I feel the steering wheel in between my fingers, the leather seats cool against my jeans. I sit back and begin to recall the day I bought this beauty. It was exactly one year from the time the first book came out. I was on the prowl for a new investment after my '64 convertible got my attention. I pulled into the dealer and four guys came running out, each one trying to get to me first. They did their spiel, told me what was hot and what was not, asked if I was out to buy or trade in, and wanted me to be their best friend for the next hour. What I've learned is that I don't buy anything from anyone who comes out to greet me; I wait and look for the person I want to deal with. That's the day I found Justin. He ended up being the coolest gay man I've ever known. On the outside, he was very metrosexual, but when he spoke, holy moly, there was no hiding it. He was very gay, but man, did he know his cars. We sat and talked about Mustangs, Thunderbirds, Corvettes, and any other muscle car we could think of. He knew his shit and I trusted him. I don't care what you do in your personal life because it doesn't affect me. After the years of torment I went through just due to the way I looked, I have a soft spot for anyone who wants to live his life, the way he is, come hell or high water. I had a feeling those douchebags gave him hell, since they had been staring at us the whole time I was there. As Justin walked me over to the car I eventually would buy that day, I asked him how he got along with the other guys there.

"Well, we're guys and we are all competitive. You do that math." He smirked, looking back at the main building, and then back at me. "Then try being gay among these assholes."

"You know what, Justin? Today is your lucky day, my man." I put my hand on his shoulder. "I'll take two."

"Two what? Cars?" His voice sounded higher than usual.

"Yep, you heard me. I'll take this one, and that one over there." I pointed to this cherry-looking 1970 Boss 302.

"Um...are you kidding me?" He started to fidget. "Do you have any idea how much that one is?"

"No, and I don't care. I want it and I will buy it, today, so start the paperwork, my man!" I extended my hand to him and we shook, then walked back to the shop. He had the biggest shit-eating grin on his face after I signed the papers and handed him a check for the full amount. Before I opened the door to leave, I said, in my loudest indoor voice, "Thank you, Justin, for your expertise and honesty. We all know that those two traits aren't something easily found in a place like this. I plan on buying a few more of these bad boys, and you are the only one I will come to!" I winked, then waved to everyone else. I know Justin had a damn good commission that day, and I got the two coolest cars ever! It was a win-win, as I saw it. The cherry on top of this story was when I came back later and asked if Justin could drive one of the cars home for me while I took the other one. You should have seen the faces on those butt-hurt salesmen. It was a good day—no, a great day!

I get out of the car and take one final glance at her. I smile and then leave the garage, taking only my memories with me—and the Range Rover. Two days later I sell my cars; now, that is a hard day. I even sell them to one guy, a collector, and a damn lucky one. He asks why I am selling such beauties and my only response is the truth: it is time. With the garage now empty, I can start unloading other things that were hiding in here, such as the snowmobiles we never used and my riding lawn mower. Figuring I will sell this house long before I need to mow, it probably is a good idea. I am looking through boxes of crap that apparently I hoarded for a good part of the last five years or so. I come across the box I took from my mom's; the only surviving article of my past. I sit down in the middle of my empty garage and start to go through it. I must be getting old because I don't even remember what's in this thing. As soon as I open it, I remember all too well. The mass of drawings I made when I was a kid, all having to do with death, depicted the gruesome tale of the Lavetti boys—all but one. That's when it hits me. *Oh shit! How could I have known the way they would die?* I begin to look at each picture with a heavy heart. The first is John. I can feel that throw-up feeling in my throat; my drawing shows his arms torn off, and I remember that's what happened to him. The next one is a kid set on fire; that's how T. J. died in my mom's house. My hands are sweating and I feel faint when I see the third drawing. It shows two people on the ground with an *X* over each eye. Nick and John Junior were found dead in the woods, on the ground and covered in blood. The last picture shows a man begging for his life and another man holding a bat. I stand up quickly and cover my mouth. *Oh man! Oh no! What is going on? Did I kill everyone the way I drew it? This can't be happening!* I run out of the garage and into the house, beelining it for the bathroom as I hurl my guilt through my mouth.

"Are you okay, Michael? Are you sick?" Cheryl knocks on the door.

"No, I'm fine, I just...I'm fine." What the hell should I say to her? *Oh, Cheryl, by the way, I killed a couple people—well, four so far, and it looks as though number five is around the corner—and the worst part is I know how I do it!* I sit back against the wall, covering my face with my hands. "There's no way I could have done that, no way," I tell myself. I lean over the toilet and launch my troubles again, then again. I emerge from the bathroom white as a ghost.

Cheryl starts to freak out. "Oh, wait! You are not fine! What's wrong with you?" She goes to the fridge and takes out a Gatorade, then hands it to me. She sits down across the table, apparently waiting for me to spill it—my guts, not my drink. "Well?" Her eyes are wide open and staring right through to my soul, as black as it is.

"Cheryl, it's nothing. I think I inhaled fumes when I was in the garage and it made me sick, that's all." I gulp down the Gatorade. What the fuck do I do now?

Chapter 12

"YOU KNOW, MICHAEL, I've been noticing something about you," Cheryl starts in. "And I've noticed it for the past couple years or so."

I look up at her. "What?" I ask, after taking the last gulp of Gatorade.

"You used to have really bad anxiety attacks, and those seem to have subsided. In fact, I can't remember the last one you've had. That's real good!" She gets up from the table and pours herself a cup of coffee.

"I guess you're right, I really haven't had many. That's weird, huh?" I've never even thought about that until she brings it up.

"Another thing that's changed about you...you don't swear as much, either. When I first met you, it was eff this and eff that. Now, not so much. You are really calming down and that's a good thing! I thought for sure after Gwen's passing, you were going to be hell to live with, but you've surprised me. And I think—no, I know—it has everything to do with that little boy over there." She points to his room where he is playing.

"You're right, Cheryl. Hunter has changed my life for the better, and I thank God for him every day. It's going to be hard to say good-bye to you, you know?" I tell her.

She smiles slightly, then comments, "I know." She pats my hand, then gets up and finishes cooking.

I start to look around the house, knowing that possibly this could be the last month I live here. That reminds me to look on my computer for those houses Missy sent me.

"I'll be upstairs if you need me," I tell her as I dart off like a ten-year-old in an arcade.

I run into my office and turn on my computer, totally forgetting what I just went through in the garage. I open the e-mails from Missy; she has sent me thirty-six houses. I scroll through each one, handpicking the good from the bad. Since I don't know Spokane very well, I'm relying on her to guide me to the right area, where there's not a lot of traffic and I can have property—for what, I have no idea. I am able to minimize the list to four houses, all on the same side of town. I decide to call up Missy and talk about my finds.

"Hello, this is Missy," her soft voice tells me.

"Oh, hey, Missy, this is Michael Bali. You sent me some—" I get interrupted.

"Oh, Michael, so nice to hear from you! Kathy has told me a lot about you! So, did you like any of the houses I sent to you?" Way too uppity for me; it hurts a little.

"I did, and I picked out four of them. I would like to see them in person—soon. Is there a better time for you when I should fly in?"

"No, any time is good for me. I can even pick you up at the airport if you'd like!"

"Oh, no, that's okay. I need to get a rental car anyway, and learn the roads over there. I will call you after I know for sure when I will be in your neck of the woods."

"Sounds great. Oh, and would it be possible for you to sign my books? I just loved them so much!"

I cringe now when someone asks me that.

"Of course I will. Talk with you soon, Missy. Bye."

We hang up. That wasn't so bad. I go online to book a ticket for myself. I figure Hunter would be too confused if I put this on him already, considering he doesn't even know we're moving yet. I book my ticket for tomorrow, coming back three days later. I go downstairs and fill Cheryl in on my itinerary.

"Wow, that was fast! You sure you want to do this?" she asks me.

"Yep. I need to, Cheryl. I've made up my mind."

"And you think three days is enough? You might want to reconsider staying longer."

"You trying to get rid of me?"

"Yes, yes, that's exactly what I am trying to do. You idiot! I just think if you are planning on moving somewhere you've never even been to, you might want to take in some sights, you know, get to know the locals. You might end up hating it. Just saying." She shrugs her shoulders.

I hate it when she's right because that means—she's right. "Well, you might be right, but for now, I will plan on my three-dayer. If I need more time, I'll just extend it. Better, Miss Pissy Britches?"

I can feel her glare on me as I walk away. Funny how you get to know someone so well, and yet still have to say good-bye to her. I will miss her, immensely. I go upstairs and start to pack my bag, and Hunter comes in.

"Where are you going, Daddy?" He walks over and puts his Star Wars figure on my bed.

"I have to take a quick trip someplace, but I will be back in a couple days, okay?"

"Where? Can I go, too?" He climbs onto my bed and gets into my bag.

I smile. "Not this time, but next time, I promise! Hunter, how would you feel about moving away, out of this house?" Like a Band-Aid, just rip it off and wait for the pain later.

"We can move into my friend's house! He has a dog!"

"No, son, I mean far away, but to a fun place!"

"Do they have ice cream there?"

"Yes, they do."

"Okay, let me get my pillow."

"Oh, no, Hunter, we aren't leaving now. I just wanted to know how you would feel if we didn't live here anymore."

"Oh, okay. Bye, Daddy!"

Hmm...no separation anxiety here. I finish packing my bag, then head downstairs for dinner. As I enter the kitchen, I see Hunter looking at something.

"Whatcha got there?" I ask him.

"Bad pictures, Daddy!" He hands me one. It's my drawing from the garage! "I don't like these!" he tells me, then jumps down and runs off.

I look down at the one he was looking at. It's the one with the bat, and I am quickly brought back to the third book, my father's murder plot, and knowing the end of Marty is upon me. Cheryl asks me what I want to drink with dinner. Turns out I'm not even hungry—not anymore.

"I have an early flight, so I'm just going to go upstairs and read for a while." My melancholy voice doesn't fool her.

"What's wrong? It has something to do with that picture, doesn't it? Did you draw that?" she asks me.

"Yeah, I did, when I was a kid. See, I told you I was a screwed-up nut job!" I try to laugh it off, but my faux laugh sounds retarded. I crumple up the picture, but don't throw it away.

"Uh-huh, yeah, because this is a face of someone who believes you!" She raises one eyebrow and crosses her arms. "What's going on, really?"

"It's all happening, the move and all. I sold all my cars and it's just...sad." It's the truth, some of it.

"You know you don't have to go! We can take the sign down, and poof! Back to normal!" She smiles, even though she knows...

"I'll be upstairs," I tell her as I walk away, wearily, and somewhat defeated by my own past.

I sit on the corner of my bed, choking back tears as I smooth out the crumpled-up drawing. I am almost numb, to the point of wishing this whole thing was over right now, tonight! I fall back on my bed; I can feel a headache coming on. I turn to my left, opening my nightstand drawer and retrieving ibuprofen. "I hope this isn't a migraine," I tell myself. I look at the clock and it's only six. I turn the TV on and begin to scroll through the menu. "Aha! *The Golden Girls* is on!" I start to sing the theme song at the beginning while tapping my fingers to the beat. I watch two episodes with my headache still intact, which means it's a migraine. As I go into the bathroom for my migraine medicine, Hunter appears in his monster truck pajamas.

"Are you going to bed, Daddy?" he asks me.

"Not now, but soon. It looks like you are ready, though! Did you brush your teeth?"

"Not yet!"

"Well, you better go do that first! The Easter Bunny is proud of you. Now let's make sure the tooth fairy is, too!"

"Okay! Bye, Daddy!" He hugs me.

"I love you!" I tell him.

As he walks out of my room, he yells, "I love you more!"

I giggle as I find my medication. "That kid kills me." I take my pills and then head back to bed, not even bothering to change out of my clothes. I figure my hunger will be awakened soon, and I don't want Cheryl to see me in my Skivvies if I end up in the kitchen. I don't know when I do, but I fall asleep, hard.

The morning comes through my windows as if I asked it to show up, but I didn't. My flight leaves at eight, so I know my ass needs to get up and in the shower or I will fall back asleep. I rise out of bed and nearly yell out in pain. "Ow! What the hell is that?" A horrible pain shoots through my neck. I start to rub it and it feels wet. When I bring my hand down to see it, it's covered in blood. "Holy shit!" I get out of bed and realize my clothes are dirty and covered in blood—again. "No, no, no, no! This isn't happening!" I run into the bathroom and look at myself in the mirror. My face is bloodied and my knuckles once again are bruised. I take off all my clothes and throw them in a pile on the floor. I study my naked self in the mirror, looking at the cuts and bloody marks. I drop my head back. "Oh God, not again! Please, no!" I fall to my knees, burying my face in my hands. The dirt is getting into my eyes and they start to burn. I jump in the shower, scrubbing the night away and freaking the fuck out. I start to hyperventilate. "Oh shit, oh shit, oh shit! What's going on?" My whole body aches, but my back feels like it was hit with a bat or something. "Oh no! A bat! Marty!" I jump out of the shower and dry off as fast as I can without ripping open any new wounds. I take the pile of bloody clothes and shove them under my sink, way back in the corner. I look in the shower to see if any remnants of my body are left behind, then I get dressed in the first thing I find. I look at the clock; I still have thirty minutes before I have to be at the airport. I can hear Hunter in the kitchen. "Doesn't that boy ever sleep in?" I ask myself as I grab my bag. I look back to see if I forgot anything, and that's when I notice my sheets and the blood all over them. "Oh shit!" I throw my bag on the floor, then start to tear the sheets off my bed, including the blanket and comforter. "How am I going to get this by Cheryl?" I bundle up everything, not knowing where to stash it. My heart is pounding so fast, I start to feel lightheaded. "Oh, I can put this in my office, then lock it!" I start for the door, but can't see my feet; I end up tripping over something, and fall face-first into the mound of bloody sheets. After I unravel myself from the red-stained linens, my eyes fall upon what I tripped over—a bat. I drop everything from my arms and reach over to grab the bat. My eyes are bulging out of their sockets when I see the droplets of blood on the bat. "Oh my God!" I gasp. "What the fuck did I do last night? What the hell did I do?" I gather my wits, then grab the bat in one fell swoop. I pick up my sheets and comforter, and walk swiftly to my office. Sweat has now found its way down my back, soaking my shirt. My head feels like it's on fire after the sweat falls onto my wounds. I'm circling the room, trying to find the perfect place in case Cheryl does find a way in here. "Aha!" I have this old trunk in which I keep all my manuscripts that I wrote when I was younger, with the rejection letters attached. I open up the trunk and stuff what I can inside. The comforter won't fit, but everything else does, including the bat. I take the comforter and throw it in the closet. I grab my keys and lock the door behind me, making sure it's truly locked. I go back into my room and change my shirt, and do another once-over before I head out. I have to calm myself down before the family sees me. I take a few deep breaths and go downstairs.

Hunter is at the table, eating his cereal, and Cheryl is at the sink.

"Hey, did you want some coffee before you go?" she asks me.

"No, I am running late, so I'm leaving. Hunter, be a good boy, and I will see you in a couple days, okay?" I kiss the top of his head.

"Okay, Daddy. Bye." He waves his little hand at me.

Cheryl looks at me. "You okay? You kinda look like hell. Did you sleep?"

Well, by that question, at least she doesn't know I left the house. "I had a migraine, so I didn't sleep all that well. I'll see you later!" As I start to walk away, I hear Hunter rat me out.

"Daddy, you left!" he says.

"No, I haven't left yet, but I am now, buddy!"

"No, Daddy, you went bye-bye when it was dark outside!"

"When did he do this, Hunter?" Cheryl asks.

"Last night. I saw him go out the door with a baseball bat!" He continues to eat his cereal.

"A bat? What in the world is he talking about?" She looks at me.

"I have no idea, but I have to go! Bye, guys!"

I run out of the house as fast as I can. I jump in my car and take a deep breath. "Holy shit!" I push the button to open the garage door, then look behind me to pull out, and that's when I see him—Marty. He's lying there in my backseat, bloody and dead. I start to scream, but quickly cover my mouth. I just stare at him. "Oh my God, what the hell do I do now?" I say under my breath. I start to feel dizzy and sick to my stomach. I pull out onto the street, narrowly missing a passerby. My mind in gone, my mental capacity is somewhere near psychotic. I just drive;

I have no idea where I'm going. I completely forget about my trip until the news updates the weather conditions for outgoing flights. "Oh shit, my flight!" According to the clock, I have about fifteen minutes before check-in. I take the highway that will lead me straight to the airport and the lake. The great thing about the area I live in, there are a lot of lakes around—some big, some small—and right now I don't care which one I get to first, as long as this body goes away. As I get closer to the airport, I begin to look around for side roads or more densely treed areas. I eye an area just up to the right; it looks as though construction has started on something quite large, but since it's a Saturday, no one is there. I pull into the large, carved-out rocky road; my body is jiggling all around, but you should see the one in the backseat. I have to put my hand back there to stop him from falling closer to me—ick. I look around for anyone who might be there, but it looks clear. I drive up slowly to the edge of the bank, making sure I get close enough so people won't see the body. I get out, still keeping a sharp eye about me. I open the back door and grab Marty's feet; he only has one shoe on. "What the hell? Where is the other one?" I ask myself. I look around the car, but don't see it. Even though I have never done this before, I do know that bodies will only sink if something heavy is attached to them. I grab a bunch of rocks from the ground and start stuffing them down his pants and in his shirt. I tuck his pants legs into his socks so the rocks won't fall out. I give my surroundings the once-over before the body fully comes out of the car. I drag him about three feet and push him into the lake. I look around again, just to make sure no one is looking. I look back at the sinking body; my heart rate is off the charts. I wipe the sweat from my face, then get back into my car and take off. I only have four minutes to spare. I find a spot pretty close and run as fast as I can to the gate. Ever since 9/11 happened the paces the TSA puts you through are ridiculous, especially when you have the minimal amount of clothing on, but they still want to physically check you. It's a bunch of bullshit if you ask me, but what can I do about it? I stand there, hands straight out from my body, shoes off, waiting for the pat down.

Before he begins, the guy looks at my clothes and asks, "What's with the blood?"

"Huh? What blood?" I look down at my shirt. "I don't see any blood," I tell him.

"On your hands. It looks like you dipped them in a bowl full of blood. Now, what happened?" He stops his wand and waits for my answer.

"I just got off work, and had to make it here pretty fast or I would miss my plane, and I didn't have a chance to wash it off yet. I work construction and it gets pretty messy. Sorry about that." *Phew! Please believe me.*

He looks at me with a serious-like asshole face. "Well, wash them before you get on the plane, understand?" He waves me through.

"Yes, sir, I will. Gross, huh?" I grab my carry-on and run to the bathroom. I didn't even see all the blood I have on me. Thank God that guy believed me or I don't know what would have happened. The intercom comes on and announces the departure of my flight. I grab my bag and run out of the bathroom to my gate. I hand the lady my ticket.

"You just made it! It looks like you're running from the cops or something!" the attendant blurts out.

"Nope, just hid the body and needed to make a fast getaway! This is going to Mexico, right?" I smile at her, but she just hands me my boarding pass.

"Have a pleasant flight." You could tell that was hard for her to say.

I continue smiling at her as I walk away, a free but very tired man. Five hours later I'm in Spokane, Washington, and I couldn't be happier. The farther away I am from the body, the better. After I acquire my rental car and purchase a map, I phone Missy.

"Hello, Missy, it's Michael Bali. I'm in town and en route to house one. Are you available now? Because I can wait and just drive around my new hometown."

"No, actually, it's great timing! I just finished showing a house to a couple and now my afternoon is free. I will meet you at the Tudor-style house in twenty minutes."

"Twenty minutes? Is that how close I am from the airport?"

"Yep. You'll find that the area we will be looking at is pretty close to everything you need! See you soon!" She hangs up.

I turn on the GPS and start making all the correct turns until I am at house one, and there is Missy. She's very tall and dark-haired—raven-haired, if you will. She's wearing a black suit with bright pink heels.

"Michael, hello! Nice to finally meet you in person!" She extends her hand to me.

"Nice to meet you, too, Missy. So this is the house, huh? It looks pretty cool." I start to walk around and she follows me, closely; a little too close...maybe.

"Yes, it's quite unusual, and it's on ten acres with a barn. Let's go inside." She takes me through the whole house and I love it. It doesn't take me very long to decide if I like something or not. It's all about the feeling I get immediately after I pull up, and so far, so good. We walk around the grounds as she tells me about the history of the house and all the updates. My mind should be on listening to her, but all I can think about is the guy I just killed and buried.

"You okay, Mr. Bali? It looks like you're a million miles away. Does this house not fit your needs?" she asks.

"No, I just have so much going on right now. My mind is everywhere, but I do love this house. How close it the next one?"

"Oh, um...ten minutes or so. I'm sorry, Michael, but you don't look so well. How was your flight? I know I get a little squiggly after I fly." She makes a squished-up face at me.

I laugh, "No, Missy, my tummy doesn't feel squiggly, although I do know what one would feel like if, by chance, my tummy became a squiggly one." I continue to laugh.

"Oh gosh, that probably sounded so dumb! I was with my niece and nephew last weekend, and I guess I'm still in aunt mode. Squiggly, wow!" She puts her hand to her forehead, then brushes her bangs away.

"That's okay. After being around my son for a while, Pop-Tarts and Cheerios become part of my daily diet!" Then we both start laughing.

I follow her in my car to the next house, then the one after that. My stomach starts making noises so loud she can hear them.

"Oh, are you hungry? We can save the other houses for another day if you want to go eat," she tells me.

"That sounds great, where should we go?" I just assume...

"Oh, I didn't mean to sound like I was inviting myself!" Her face looks horrified.

"No, I want you to go! Please, it would be selfish of me not to invite you! Where shall we go? You pick, I buy."

"Well, there's a great restaurant around here called Chap's. Great food and the décor is simply to die for! Very eclectic! Shall we?"

"Sounds perfect! You lead the way and I shall follow!"

We both get into our vehicles and drive to the eatery. It turns out to be one of the best meals I've ever had, and she was right about the décor—amazing, to say the least. I know I am going to love Spokane.

After I settle into my hotel room, I start to think again about Marty. My hands still show the bruises from the night before, and my soul bears the same likeliness. I call home, but forget I'm three hours behind; no one answers. I leave a message telling them I made it and everything is looking great here. I try to fall asleep, but it doesn't work out so well. My back is still hurting pretty badly, especially when I bend over. I take some pain meds and turn on the TV, waiting for them to kick in. I turn the channel to *Platoon*. Awesome fucking movie; I can watch it over and over again, and it never gets old. When that movie is over, I start to watch *Forrest Gump*. To me, this is one of the best movies ever made. Now, every time I hear "Sweet Home Alabama," I think of Forrest learning how to dance with Jenny. But the part that really gets to me this time is during the war scene, where Forrest goes back into the kill zone to bring out his men who were shot but still alive. When he goes back to get Bubba, I freeze. That's when it hits me: Dave will be coming to find me when he realizes Marty is missing. Those Lavettis stand together, no matter what the evil circumstances are. I just pray he comes after me and not Hunter. Maybe it wasn't such a great idea to leave him there? I will call first thing in the morning and have Cheryl bring Hunter to me in Spokane.

I crack open my eyes around seven in the morning. The sky looks as if it took some personal time off from Baltimore and decided to come here instead; hello, rain. I pick up my cell phone and call the house, but no one answers, again. I leave another message, this time asking Cheryl to book a flight for her and Hunter to come to Spokane ASAP. I've lived with and trusted this woman long enough that I gave her my credit card a few years back and left it at that. She's never been one to go crazy with shopping; in fact, I am ten times worse. I came home one day after finding this awesome antique store that had just opened. I didn't see anything wrong with a two-headed dog statue with the words *Bad Ass* on the front. She just rolled her eyes and walked away. Come to think of it, I haven't seen that statue since I bought it. What the hell is that all about? As I hang up the phone I begin to panic. What if Dave is there now? What if he kidnapped them and is holding them for ransom? I start to pace the room and rub my hands together. My phone rings as I take my fourteenth lap around my room.

"Hello?"

"Michael, why do we need to come out there? Is something wrong?" Cheryl asks.

"Where have you been? I called yesterday and this morning!" I'm pissed but thankful at the same time.

"Well, considering you left me here to get the house ready for the walk-throughs your agent has set up, I've been rather busy!" Now she's pissed.

I put my hand on my forehead. "Ugh! I totally forgot about those things. I'm sorry for freaking out like that." I start to calm down. "How did they go? Wait…how many people came through?"

"Oh, jeez, I'd say around seventeen since you've left. Kathy only brought in, like, five; the rest were just drive-bys. One guy really loved the place. In fact, he kept saying how much of a fan he was of yours. He couldn't believe he was in Michael Bali's house! Come to think of it, he was kind of a weirdo. He said he had started over now that his older boys were gone. He has two little ones. I tried to get him to answer my questions, like is he married and what does he do for a living, but he was rather standoffish. When he left, his truck was blowing so much exhaust I about gagged."

"Wait, what color of truck?" I ask her.

"Green. Why? Do you know him?"

Oh my God, he was in my house!

Chapter 13

"**M**ICHAEL? ARE YOU there?" Cheryl continues asking me. "Hello?"

"Cheryl, I need you to get on a plane with Hunter and come to Spokane today, do you understand?" My voice is stern.

"I can't, I still have people coming by! I can't just leave!" she retorts.

There's a knock at my door. "Cheryl, hold on, someone's at my door." To my surprise, it's Missy, with coffee in hand.

"Hey, good morning! Thought I would bring you coffee!" She smiles and hands me the cup.

"Hey, this is great, room service. I could get used to this. Wait, how did you know where I was? I didn't tell you what hotel I was in." I take a sip of the delicious java; oh Lord, heaven!

She smiles, "Well, I do have a few feelers out there and I just asked around. You're not upset, are you?"

"No, it's just surprising, that's all." Then I remember I am on the phone. "Oh shit! Cheryl!" I run back to the phone. "Are you still there? Sorry about that."

"Who's there? Is that a woman in your room? Michael, you dog!" She starts to laugh.

"No, it's not a woman, it's Missy."

I realize what I just said and I look over at her; she looks embarrassed, to say the least. She mouths to me that she's leaving, but I tell her to stop and I hold my hand up, as if I have the power to control this strange woman with my appendage. It works.

"Cheryl, just please get on a plane today. Call me later and tell me your flight info, okay? Bye." I hang up the phone, then walk over to Missy.

"I'm sorry about that. That was my nanny/sitter/ housekeeper/life-keeper. I really want Hunter to see this place, so she would have to bring him." Why am I explaining this to her?

"Oh, Michael, you don't have to explain anything." Now she tells me! "I should have called first. My mistake."

"Well, now that you are here, are you hungry?"

"Yes, I am, and I know the perfect place, but we'd better hurry! It gets pretty busy on Sundays!"

We decide to take her car since she knows where she's going. About ten minutes later, we pull up to Chap's again.

"Um, Missy? This place again?"

"I know it's weird to go back to the same place hours later, but you have no idea what you're in for! They have this oatmeal tha   t doesn't even taste like oatmeal! It's more like a dessert, and I've never been able to finish the bowl! Trust me, okay?"

She is right about it being busy; holy shit, the line is long! It takes about twenty minutes to get a seat, but the staff is quite incredible. I order the oatmeal, like an obedient man, even though I am seeing these plates of huge pancakes and French toast and slabs of ham. I am in hog heaven looking at this meat, but I sit here calmly, waiting for my oatmeal. All I can say is, this better be the best freaking oatmeal I have ever had, if I am letting this beautiful meat pass me by.

It takes only minutes for our waitress to bring us our meal, and I have to say, the blueberries on top? Nice choice! I pour the cream on and swirl the berries into the oatmeal. I look at Missy and she is wide-eyed, just waiting for me to take my first bite.

Then it happens. I have found food euphoria in oatmeal. In oatmeal! I throw my hands up in the air and actually yell out, "Halleluiah! What is in this culinary delight you call oatmeal, my lady?"

The waitress starts to laugh, and all she says is, "I know, right?" I high-five her and she walks away. I look over at Missy, who is also enjoying her oatmeal.

"Okay, okay, you are right, again. This is the best oatmeal I have ever had in my life!" I tell her as I cram another spoonful of bliss into my mouth. She doesn't even have to say anything; her smile says it all. Unlike Missy, I finish my bowl, but cannot eat another bite of anything, including that ham steak that just walked past me. I sit back in my wooden chair and just take it all in;

the awesome décor, the compassionate staff, and one of the best food establishments I've ever eaten it. As we leave the restaurant, I notice the other businesses right across the way.

"Hey, what's over there?" I ask her.

She looks to where I am pointing. "Oh, there's a vet clinic, a tanning and hair salon, another restaurant, and a little shop where you can buy trinkets and things. This is a really cool area."

"Oh, yeah? Let's go over there. I can use a good haircut, and I can find something pretty cool for Hunter in that shop, too. Oh, wait, I'm just taking up all your time. Do you have time to do this? Because I can come back."

"No, it's fine, my entire day is yours. Let's go! In fact, Elite Salon is where I get my hair done."

The salon gets me right in and my stylist does exquisite work. After my perfect haircut, I head next door to Foxy Horse and Hound. What a cool store this is, and I am able to find some fun things for Hunter and Cheryl. This area is freaking awesome, and now I can't wait to move here. As we walk back to the car, I mention to Missy that I would like to try Latah Bistro next for dinner. She says she is free tonight and to plan on it. Wait...is this turning into something more than just an agent-buyer relationship? It's been so long since I've had a female tagging alongside me, other than Cheryl. It's kinda nice.

She drives us to the next house, and when we pull up I know this was the one. It has everything I want; a huge yard already landscaped, it sits back from the street, and there are no neighbors who can see into my living room. The ten acres puts it at the top of my list of final picks. She takes me to the last houses, but none of them measure up to the one I saw earlier.

"I want to put in a bid on the blue one," I tell her.

"Great, but didn't you want to wait for your son and Cheryl to see it first?" she asks as we drive away from the final house.

"That's right! I haven't heard from her yet, have I? I need to call her." The phone rings once, twice, three times…no answer. "Not again," I say under my breath.

"What was that?" Missy asks.

"Oh, nothing, just talking to myself." Come on, pick up, Cheryl! It goes to voice mail, again. "Cheryl, it's me. I haven't heard from you about your flight, so call me back right away!" I hang up the phone and then drop my dome back on the headrest.

"Everything all right?" she asks me as we wind down Cedar Road.

"It will be, once I have my son with me."

I look over at her and smile slightly. She can tell my mind is elsewhere, so she offers to take me back to my hotel to lie down. I agree.

"I will get those papers drawn up for you still, if you'd like, and I will call you a little later?"

"That sounds good. Thanks for your help, Missy." I wave as she drives away.

I walk into the hotel, unaware that the front desk attendant is motioning me over there. I walk straight to the elevator.

A woman approaches me, nearly out of breath. "Mr. Bali, I have a delivery for you! Would you like us to take it to your room for you?" she politely asks me.

"A delivery? From who?"

"I don't know, Mr. Bali, but they are beautiful!" She smiles.

"They what? What are beautiful?"

"Your flowers! We have a huge bouquet of flowers waiting for you at the desk. I will have someone bring them to your room. Oh, and by the way, I'm a huge fan! I love your books, and I can't believe you're in Spokane!" She nearly skips away.

I get into the elevator. "Who in the hell would send me flowers?" I push the button for the Tower Suite while I ponder the thought of a man receiving flowers. The elevator doors open and I just shake my head as I walk to my suite. "Flowers?" I open the door to find the coffee Missy brought me earlier sitting on the desk. The light is flashing on my phone, as if it's screaming at me that I have a message. "Yes, I hope it's Cheryl!" I listen to the message and it's not from Cheryl; instead, my heart sinks as the voice from the other end is that of Dave Lavetti.

"Found ya," is all he says.

"Fuck!" I throw the receiver down and it breaks. I run my hands through my hair as my eyes begin to tear up. He knows I'm here and my son is not. I am just about to call Cheryl, when there's a knock at my door. I look over, wondering who the hell it could be. When I get to the door, I look through the peephole, but all I see are flowers. I open the door and the lady just bursts right in.

"Aren't these the most beautiful flowers you've ever seen? They are so unusual. I don't even know what they are!" She sets them on the table and begins to arrange them so they are more perfectly sound. "Oh, whoever sent you these must be someone special, Mr. Bali. Do you know what kind of flowers these are?"

I pause and then look down at the ground. "They're Toad lilies."

Chapter 14

"**T**OAD LILIES? I'VE never heard of those! They are just lovely. Anything else I can do for you, Mr. Bali?" She folds her hands together and smiles at me.

"No, thank you. Oh, wait; do you know where they came from? I mean, was it a local florist?"

"Oh, I don't know, but I can surely check for you! I just have to tell you how proud we feel that you have chosen to stay here, at the Davenport Hotel. It's not often that we get two brothers who became authors here in the same week!"

"Wait, what? Brothers? Ma'am, I think you're mistaken."

Her face looks confused. "But isn't Mitch Bali your brother?" she asks me.

"Yeah, but I don't understand." I get interrupted by her beeper.

"Oh, excuse me, Mr. Bali, I am needed downstairs. I will check on the florist for you, though!"

"That would be great, thank you." I walk her out. "Mitch is a writer? When did this happen, and why would he be in Spokane, of all places?" I turn around to look at the evil display of foliage sitting on my table. "Now, let's just see which psycho fucktard sent these to me," I say to myself as I reach for the card. This is what it says:

Amor et melle et felle est fecund issimus…
M. Bali

I start to freak out once again. "Latin? I don't know Latin shit!" I grab my phone again and Google in the phrase. My mind immediately goes to the worst: my kid has been kidnapped, my house has blown up, my kidneys will disappear from my body overnight. What the hell does it mean? My phone matches up the phrase and delivers the translation: *Love is rich with both honey and venom.*

I fall down onto my bed; my mind is racing a thousand miles per hour. "What the hell does Mitch want with me now? I haven't done a damn thing to him, and now he's a freaking writer?" I grab my phone and Google his name. Seconds later I see his name alongside his book titled *Adsum*. I immediately Google that word, and what comes back is: *I am here.* "How in the hell did he write one so fast and get it published?" I just at stare at his name on my phone, until an eerie feeling comes over me that makes me shiver. "Wouldn't that be something if he had manuscripts show up on his computer like I did, ha-ha-ha." My laughter turns into nausea. "Oh God, what if it happened to him? What if this isn't finished, and it's starting all over again, but now he's at the wheel? Oh shit!" I think about it for a while, then realize how stupid that sounds. "What am I saying? This couldn't happen to him...not in a million years." I laugh it off for a few minutes, until my phone rings.

"Hello?"

"Michael, it's Cheryl. The house has been flooded with people in and out! There is no way we can come to Spokane now," she tells me.

"I don't care how many people, I need you and Hunter here with me now. Why is this so hard for you to understand? Get on a plane!" I am so irritated there is no way of sugarcoating it.

"Okay, you need to tell me what the hell is going on, because you jetted out of this house just a couple days ago without even wanting or asking us to come with you. You told me how important it was that this house is in perfect for-sale shape, and I was needed here to do that! You even told me of walk-throughs that would be happening in the next couple days, and now...you want us there? It doesn't add up, and you are sounding totally crazy!" she yells at me. She actually is yelling at me.

I take a few deep breaths, then say, "The man you told me about that sounded crazy when he found out he was in my house...well...that was Dave Lavetti, and I am terrified that he will hurt you or Hunter."

"Are you kidding me, Michael? This isn't funny!" she exclaims.

"It's not a joke, Cheryl. In fact, it's quite real. Now, I need your ass on a plane, okay?"

"Damn it! I wish you would have told me this earlier! Now I am freaking out! Okay, okay, I will call the airlines right now and call you back. Bye." She hangs up.

About ten minutes later, she calls me back. "Okay, we are on the next flight, but it doesn't leave until tomorrow morning. We should arrive in Spokane around noon. Don't worry about us, Michael. If anyone touches one hair on Hunter's head, I will kill them myself. I have a concealed weapons permit, and I'm always packin'."

"Damn, it's Annie Oakley in the house! Actually, that makes me feel better, but I don't know why. Keep an eye out and I will see you tomorrow." I hang up, a little relieved and somewhat petrified.

After Cheryl writes down the ticket confirmation next to the hotel information, she begins to panic. She now realizes a Lavetti was in this house and that he had spoken to her and Hunter.

"Oh shit! Hunter!" She runs outside to where he is playing. "Hunter!" she yells as she looks for him in the backyard. "Hunter! Come on, buddy, we need to go inside and start packing!" When she turns the corner, she stops in her tracks.

"Packing for what? Going somewhere?" His voice sounds just as evil as he looks.

"Dave," Cheryl states, "let him go."

"Now, how do you know my name?" he asks as holds a gun to Hunter's back. Hunter looks up at Cheryl, unaware of what's happening.

"Are we going to see Daddy?" he asks as he continues to play in the sandbox. Cheryl doesn't say a word.

"Yeah, Cheryl, are you guys going to see Daddy?" Dave mocks the little boy. "I hear Spokane is a lovely place to live!" He smiles at her with his yellow-stained teeth and tobacco-filled cheek. He spits out his chew, and some of it gets on Hunter's arm.

"Ew, gross! Cheryl, get it off my arm!" Hunter looks up at her; she's frozen in place. He lifts up his arm. "Look, it's icky! Wipe it off!" He beckons for her cleaning talents, but she doesn't move.

"That's a good girl, Cheryl. We don't need any sudden movements, do we?" Dave's evil voice sends shivers down her spine, causing her to snap out of it.

"Don't you touch him!" Her voice is firm but shaky.

"Now, would that be something I would do? I think you have me confused with Michael, because I'm not the one who killed my own sons!" His voice rises up and starts to scare Hunter, but Dave gives him another piece of candy and he is back to playing in the sand.

Cheryl's face is petrified as she tries to think what she can do, and then she remembers the gun she has in the waistband of her pants. She doesn't take her eyes off Dave and his gun as she moves closer to them.

"Wait right there, lady. I don't think Hunter here would approve of you coming any closer, considering the shiny object I have in my hand." He conveys his anger through a soft voice that only a deranged mother could love.

Cheryl stops in her tracks, still keeping an eye on the gun, and replaying in her head what she told Michael just minutes ago about killing anyone that hurts Hunter.

"Hunter, remember that game I showed you, when I say goose? Do you remember what you do after that?" she asks him.

He looks up at her with a big grin. "Uh-huh!"

"Okay...goose!" she yells.

Hunter then shouts, "Duck!" while he drops to the ground. As quick as lightning, she grabs the gun from her waistband and swings it around to Dave's face, firing off one shot, hitting his left shoulder, but not before Dave is able to get a shot in as well, hitting Cheryl in the chest. Hunter jumps up, putting his hands over his ears and screaming. Dave shrieks, then grabs his bloody arm; he jumps up and runs off, leaving a trail of blood behind him. Cheryl lies there, blood spilling from her chest. Hunter is screaming and crying so loudly that the neighbors, Jerry and Nancy, hear him and run to the backyard.

"Oh my God! Jerry, call nine-one-one!" Nancy yells to her husband. She tries to comfort Hunter, but he is freaking out so much that he is able to pry himself out of her grip, and he runs to Cheryl's side. He grabs her arm, desperate for her to look at him. He calls out her name, but she doesn't respond. Blood has now made its way to his clothing, soaking it in crimson red. His tears have taken over his face as Nancy pulls him away from Cheryl.

"No! No! No!" he yells, while he tries with all his might to free himself from her grip, but it doesn't work. His strength gives way to his pain, and he just drops to the ground, sobbing uncontrollably and yelling for his daddy. The paramedics show up within minutes of the call and immediately go to work on Cheryl. Blood is everywhere and it doesn't look good. They start CPR and feel for her pulse, but can't get one. Cheryl dies from a bullet wound to her chest that day, protecting Hunter like she promised she would.

Chapter 15

"DADDY! I WANT my daddy!" Hunter screams, while they take Cheryl's body away in an ambulance. Nancy is having a hard time keeping him calm. She takes him into the house, followed by a couple officers. It's a good hour before Hunter is able to speak.

"Do you know this family?" the officer asks Nancy.

"Yes, I do. They moved here a couple years after we did. I can't believe this happened. That poor woman." She wipes away tears as she continues to cradle Hunter.

"Do you know where the father is?" the officer asks.

"No, I don't. That woman who was shot was the housekeeper. She's been with this family since they lived here. His wife died about three years ago. I think that's why they were moving, too many memories for him," she explains.

The officer writes everything down verbatim. "Hunter? Do you know where your daddy is?"

Hunter shakes his head no. He sits in Nancy's lap, sucking his thumb, tears still falling heavily.

"Is it okay if I take him upstairs to clean him up?" Nancy asks the officer, and he obliges. As she starts to walk away, she notices the note by the phone. "Um, this might be a clue. It's information about a flight and a hotel in Spokane." She hands him the note, then takes Hunter's hand and walks him upstairs.

The officer looks at the note and asks Nancy, before she gets too far away, "What is the dad's name?"

"Michael Bali, the writer," she answers. Hunter starts to cry again when he hears his dad's name.

"The writer? Hmm…don't know him," the officer says to himself, then picks up the phone and calls the hotel.

"Thank you for calling the Davenport Hotel. How may I assist you?" the kind voice on the other end asks.

"Hello, my name is Officer Tate. I need to speak with Michael Bali, and it's an emergency."

"Yes, sir, let me ring his room for you. Thank you for calling the Davenport Hotel."

"Hello?"

"Mr. Bali?"

"Yes, who's this?"

"Mr. Bali, my name is Officer Tate, and I'm afraid there's been an accident at your residence today."

"What? My son! Did something happen to my son?" I holler.

"No, Mr. Bali, your son is fine. I'm afraid the accident involved your housekeeper. Now, we don't know for sure what happened, but there was gunfire and it hit her in the chest."

"Oh my God! Oh my God! How is she?"

"I'm sorry, Mr. Bali, but she didn't make it."

I don't think I hear him correctly. My heart is beating so loudly, I can't hear anything he's saying. "Um, I'm sorry, what did you say?"

"She died, Mr. Bali, and we need you to return to Baltimore as soon as you can."

I fall to my knees; tears are streaming down my face. "No! I don't believe this! Where is my son?" I try to ask between sobs.

"He's here at the house, but I'm afraid that until you return home, he will be put in the state's care."

"I am on the next plane home. Please tell my son I'm on my way." I hang up the phone. I try to dial the airlines, but my tears are larger than my eyes can hold. I put my hands over my face and sob uncontrollably.

"That fucking Lavetti! I know he did it, I know that bastard did it!" As distraught as I am, booking my ticket home is easier than I think. They must have heard it in my voice that I need to get home; I am able to get on the flight that is leaving in two hours. I throw all my belongings in my bag and book it to the front desk. I jump in my rental car, and twenty minutes later I'm at the airport. I leave the keys inside because I don't have time to check it in. I yell at the rental place agent that the car is in the parking lot outside and to just charge my card.

I couldn't care less at this moment what they charge me. I run to my gate just in time. My phone rings as soon as I'm on the plane and seated.

"Hello?" My voice doesn't hide my pain.

"Michael? Are you there? I can barely hear you. It's Missy."

"Oh, Missy, I totally forgot about you. Um…I'm on my way back home. I will call you in a few days. There's been an accident and I have to go home."

"You sound horrible. You okay?"

"No, I'm not okay, Missy. I'm as far from okay as someone could get."

"Well, I have the papers on that house ready for you to sign. What do you want me to do?"

"I don't know, Missy. This isn't a good time. I will call you in a few days, okay? Bye." I hang up the phone just in time for the flight attendant to ask me if I want a hot towel. I love first class.

Five hours later I'm in Baltimore, flagging down a cab. I tell him the faster he gets me home, the bigger the tip. I live about forty-five minutes from the airport and we get there in thirty. I give him an extra twenty and make a dash for my house. Cops are still there, taking pictures and making sure no one goes in.

"Um, yeah, I live here. Where's my son? A cop said he's a ward of the state, but where do I go get him now? Please tell me, now, Now! Where?" I am so frantic; I hope they don't think I'm high on something.

"Excuse me, sir, who are you?"

"I'm Michael Bali. I live here."

"Oh, yes, sir, I am sorry for your loss. Let me call in and see which family has taken in your son, okay? Please wait here."

"What? I can't go into my house?"

"No, sir, it's a crime scene now. After the warrant has been issued and a thorough sweep has been done, you will be allowed to go back in, but right now, you cannot," he tells me as he makes his phone call.

Nancy and Jerry see me come home; they run out to meet me.

"Michael, I am so sorry about Cheryl!" Nancy hugs me.

"I can't believe this happened in our neighborhood—and to Cheryl, for Christ's sake." Jerry extends his hand to me.

"Thank you both for caring for Hunter. I just need to be with him right now. I don't know what else to do. I can't go into my house yet. Did you see any of this take place?" I ask them.

They both shake their heads no. "All we heard was the gunshots, then Hunter screaming. We ran out to find him with Cheryl. She was shot in the chest and on the ground. We didn't see anyone else. I was able to take Hunter upstairs to clean him up and change his clothes. They had blood all over them. I didn't get a chance to even throw them in the laundry. The cops wanted me in and out," Nancy explains.

"Where did this happen?" I ask them.

"In your backyard. I am so sorry again, Michael. Let us know if we can help you in any way possible." Nancy hugs me again, then they go back to their home.

I just stare at the big white house in front of me with yellow-and-black tape all around it. I sit down on the grass, feeling like my world just ended again. I can't believe this has happened to Cheryl. She had decided to change her life and do things for herself for once, so she had lost 120 pounds this last year and a half. She started exercising, had her hair done. She was really doing something to make herself feel and look better, and now this...

Oh my God, I wonder if anyone has called her sister yet. I hope someone did. I get up and approach one of the officers there. "Um...how do I find out if her family was notified about this or not?" I ask him.

"I will check for you, Mr. Bali, give me a minute." The officer speaks into his radio on his shoulder and then turns back to me. "We didn't have a number to call, so we were waiting for you to come home," he tells me.

I look down at the ground. "Oh, man...okay...um...I will call her sister. I have her number on me. Thanks," I tell him as the taste of throw-up enters my mouth. "How in the hell can I do this?" I ask myself. I dial her number, praying that God gives me the strength to finish this call without having to start over again.

"Hello?" her soft voice answers.

"Hello, Shelly? It's Michael."

"Oh, hi, Michael. It was so nice having your little boy here! I hope they can come again soon. How have you been?" she asks me.

I close my eyes and begin to tell her the tragic news.

"I am afraid that I have some bad news, Shelly. I don't know how to tell you this, but...um...something's happened to Cheryl and it's not good. I was out of town while she and Hunter stayed here to help sell the house, with walk-throughs and such. Well...I am so sorry, Shelly, but Cheryl passed away today." I begin to cry.

"What? What did you say? I don't belie—what did you say again, Michael? I don't think I heard you right. Will you repeat that last thing, please?" I can tell by her voice, she heard me.

"Cheryl passed away today. I am so sorry, Shelly."

A bloodcurdling scream comes from the other end of the phone. She is hysterical and yelling things that I cannot understand. I try to interrupt with, "I'm sorry," but she can't hear me. She's totally gone, and I can't blame her one bit. I stay on the phone for another five minutes before she calms down enough to hear me.

"Shelly, I don't know all the details yet, but I do know she was protecting Hunter. She was shot in the chest, but no one knows who did it." I choke back some tears myself. I stay on the phone with her another fifteen minutes before she hangs up. Shelly is Cheryl's only living relative. They were as close as two people can be; this pain will last a lifetime for her.

The officer returns with the address where my son is, but he says I can't get him without a judge signing off on it.

"What? I want to see my son now! Please! Tell me how and what I need to do so I can have my son in my arms tonight!" I convey my anger and complete anguish to him.

"Trust me, Mr. Bali, I am on your side. I have an officer en route to the judge as we speak. You will have your son soon."

It takes about forty-five more minutes before I get the okay and the address of where my son is. I pull up to the house and knock on the door. Considering it's late, I hope he's asleep. It's probably the best thing for him right now. I follow the lady into her house and to the bedroom where he is.

"He was having a very hard time up until a half hour ago or so. That's when he just conked out. He will be so happy you're here. That's all he's been talking about," the nice lady tells me.

I walk over to the bed and put my hand on his back, feeling him inhale and exhale. I start to tear up, knowing my little boy is safe, but also knowing what he's been subjected to at such a young age. He begins to move around, so I whisper, "Hunter. Hey, buddy, wake up, I'm home." I continue to rub his back. He turns over and sees me. His eyes get as big as saucers and he jumps up into my arms.

"Daddy! Oh, Daddy! Don't ever go away again, Daddy!" He starts to cry hysterically. I pick him up and take him to my car. Having to let him go just to put him in his car seat is hard, but I eventually secure him in it and drive away.

"Don't worry, Hunter, I will never leave you again," I explain to him. I search for a hotel and pull into a Marriot.

We're both drained. Thank God Nancy was able to clean him up. That wouldn't be the most ideal thing—having to explain the bloodstains on a three-year-old. I carry Hunter all the way to the room. As I lay him down on the bed, he's still sniffling.

"Cheryl, Daddy, Cheryl—" He starts to talk but I don't let him.

"Shhh, buddy, we don't need to talk about that now. Let's just lie down and think of good things, okay?"

I lie down next to him, still cradling him like he is an infant. He sniffs and wipes away his tears, then asks me to tell him a story. My mind is nowhere close to story time, but I know he needs to hear something, anything, to keep his mind off Cheryl. We both fall asleep.

The next morning, I wake up with Hunter wrapped around me like ivy. I feel so drained and so incredibly sad that I don't even want to get up. I know the longer Hunter sleeps, the better. I hope his mind doesn't allow him to remember any of it, but I know that's a wish that probably won't come true. He starts to stir about, then opens his eyes. He frantically sits up to make sure I am still there, and then sees me and smiles.

"Hey, buddy, sleep well?" I ask him as I move his hair out of his face. He just nods his head and doesn't say anything. He continues to lie next to me, arms around my waist, holding on to me as if I would float away without his help. I reach for the remote and turn the TV on. I channel surf until I find cartoons, his favorite. We just lie there and watch TV for a while until hunger sets in.

"Daddy, I'm hungry."

"You are? Well, what would you like to eat?"

He ponders his answer while flicking the buttons on my shirt with his little fingers. I hear him sigh right before he tells me he wants pancakes. I know what he was thinking, and I don't want to bring it up.

"Pancakes sound great! I will call room service and have them brought to us, okay?"

He nods his head yes and then goes back to watching TV. I get on the phone and order everything on the menu. I want this to be a good experience for him, and food has always been our comfort thing. I also ask the front desk if they could send up a couple toothbrushes and some toothpaste. They oblige, and within ten minutes, all the glorious menu items plus my hygiene requests are at my door. Hunter gets a huge smile on his face when he sees the array of nummies parade in. He jumps off the bed and climbs onto the chair. It looks like he has forgotten all about yesterday, at least for the moment. I don't realize how hungry I am until that first bite. We devour that entire table of food, leaving only the strawberries and eggs—yuck. I sit back in my chair, sipping my coffee and watching my little boy enjoy this moment. When he sits back in his chair, he lets out the biggest belch I've ever heard.

"Hunter, oh my God! What do you say, little boy?" I ask him as my eyes widen to the size of plates.

He starts to giggle. "Sorry, Daddy, 'cuse me!" He puts his hand over his mouth and brings his knees up to his chest.

I start to laugh with him; it is a good ending to a great meal. I hand him his toothbrush and ask if we can brush our teeth together. He agrees, and we go into the bathroom and scrub our sadness and pancakes away. Then I run him a bath, making sure to put enough bubbles in it to make him want to get in. It works, and he starts playing like a three-year-old should play, carefree and happy. He doesn't want to get out of his bath until he's all pruny. My cell phone rings a few minutes later.

"Hello?"

"Mr. Bali, this is Officer Tate again. Sorry to bother you, but we have a search warrant for your house, and I wanted you to be aware of it. You have two choices: either you give us the code to your front door, or we kick it in."

"Why would you need to search my house?"

"Since the incident happened at your residence and the victim lived at your residence, then it's SOP."

"SOP? What does that mean, exactly?" I ask.

"Standard operating procedure, Mr. Bali. Now, what's it going to be?"

I give him the code and he tells me I'm not allowed in my residence until it's been cleared. Soon after we hang up, my phone rings again.

"Oh, Missy, hi. Thanks for calling me again. Things have been quite chaotic since yesterday. How are you?"

"Well, I'm fine, but I am worried about you. You left so quickly that I didn't get a chance to talk to you about the house. Is now a good time?"

I look over at Hunter, still playing in the bath.

"Um, well, not really. I'm with my son right now. So how about we speak tonight—say, around seven?"

"Okay, Michael, take care."

"Hey, buddy, are you wrinkly enough now to get out?" I ask him.

He looks at his hands, then announces he is. I grab the big hotel towel and lift him out of the tub. I dry him off and he starts to laugh. Apparently I find his tickle spot.

"No, Daddy, that tickles!" He falls to the ground laughing. I don't want to put his dirty clothes back on, but I don't have a choice. He doesn't mind at all.

I don't know how long it will be until I'm allowed back into my house, so I take Hunter to the mall for some clothes—and toys, of course. When we get to the mall, Hunter hightails it to the toy store. Why is it they always know where one is, even though they've never been to that particular mall? I start to run after him, until something catches my eye. The large department store next to the toy store is having a linens sale, and that's when it hits me, like a fucking brick.

"Oh my God! My comforter, and those sheets, and the bat! I hid them in my office and I know those cops are going to find them! Oh shit! What the hell do I do?" I ask myself.

"Daddy, over here, come on!" Hunter hollers at me.

"Okay, buddy, I'm coming!" Oh my God, oh my God! I don't know what to do!

While Hunter roams the store, I follow close behind, but my mind is not on toys.

"Hey, Daddy, can I get this one?" he asks.

"Sure, buddy, whatever you want." I don't even look at what he picks out. The next thing I see is a cart full of crap. "Wait, what are you doing?" I ask him as I look over the loot.

"You said!" He points at me. Damn it, he's right.

"Okay, well, that's enough. Plus, we still need to find some clothes."

"I want to go home, Daddy. Can we go home now?" he asks me.

"Soon, buddy, real soon." We walk around the mall for another hour or so, then my phone rings.

"Hello?"

"Michael, it's Missy, I have the papers ready for you to sign! They accepted your offer on the house! Is there a fax machine I can send them to?" She sounds damn giddy.

"Oh, um…I'm at the mall right now, but you can still send them to the house, even though I'm not there," I tell her.

"Oh, great, I will do that. Congratulations, Michael! Do me a favor, though, get them back to me as soon as you can, okay?" she tells me.

I don't want to tell her about Cheryl yet, not with Hunter standing right here. "Okay, sounds good. Bye, Missy." I look down at Hunter as he starts looking through the bags of fun that he got. His smile lights up my whole world, but I know deep inside, he's struggling with the memories of seeing a murder.

Chapter 16

TWO DAYS LATER, the police call and tell me to meet them at my house, as they are done conducting their investigation. I tell Hunter we are going home, and he can't stop jumping up and down. He is so excited that he ends up peeing his pants. Thank God for shopping malls. Missy has called me a few times, but I don't pick up the phone. I can't tell her what's happened until I am alone, and I haven't been alone since it happened. Hunter has been at my side twenty-four/seven. We arrive at the house and there's a police car in the driveway—always a good sign when trying to sell a house.

"Mr. Bali?"

"Yes, that's me. I thought this was all done?" I ask him, hoping I don't hear anything about the comforter. I watch him as he walks closer to me, making sure he's not going for his cuffs.

"Oh, it is. I just wanted to tell you that in person, and to let you know what we found."

Oh shit, here it comes. "What did you find?" I can feel my hands starting to stiffen up.

"Why don't we go inside? Please, after you." He motions for me to go first.

I type in my code, then walk inside. Hunter walks in slowly, looking around like he's trying not to be scared.

"It's okay, buddy, no one's here. You can go to your room if you want, and take your toys, too," I tell him as I hand over the bag from the toy store. He looks at me, and I'm not sure if he's okay with being alone yet, until it hits him that the rest of his toys are now waiting for him to play with.

"Okay!" He grabs the bag and runs upstairs.

"So, what did you find, officer?" I ask him as I walk into the kitchen. "Do you want some coffee?"

"No thanks, Mr. Bali, I won't be here long. I wanted to tell you that there is still some blood residue on the patio in the back, and some of the sand became soaked in blood, too. I wanted you to know before your son saw it first. Also, we will need to talk to your son about what he saw. I know this is something that will take a long time for him to recover from, but at some point we will need to talk to him. It's probably a good idea to set up some kind of therapy for him, too. I'm afraid he will need it, Mr. Bali."

I nod my head in agreement, then I think to myself, *That's it?* Maybe they didn't even look deep enough in my office to find it, or they would have my ass down at the station, for sure. My hands start to loosen up again.

"Well, thanks, officer, I appreciate you thinking of my son. Is there anything else?"

"I noticed a bat in your office."

"Oh shit, there's a bat in there? Vampire or fruit?" I start to laugh at myself. *Please don't arrest me, please don't arrest me!*

"No, a baseball bat."

"Oh? I didn't know I had a bat in my office. News to me."

"You didn't know you had an autographed bat from the 1961 World Series? You didn't know you had a bat autographed by Yogi Berra? This isn't your bat?"

"Oh, that one. Sorry, I sort of forgot about it. Yes, it's mine. Is there something wrong?"

"No, I just wanted to know where you got it. My son and I are huge fans, and I thought this would be an awesome gift to get him on his eighteenth birthday." He smiles.

"Oh, that would be a good gift! I got it at an auction a couple years ago. I paid a pretty penny for it, too." My mouth doesn't stop talking when it should have. "Did you see the blood on it?" *Oh shit, you idiot!*

"Blood? Why would there be blood on it?" he asks me in his cop tone.

Think, Michael, think quickly. "Um...I slammed my finger when I was trying to be a wannabe baseball player, and my finger fell off. See?" I show him my missing index finger, even though I lost that during my fight with the Lavettis one Halloween night.

"Oh, man! That sucks, man! No, I didn't see any blood on it. I just wanted to know where I could find one. Thanks for your cooperation, Mr. Bali."

I see him out, and after I shut the door I run up to my office. I burst through the door and head for the closet. When I open it, there's no comforter.

"What in the hell? Where did it go?" I turn around and open the trunk, but the sheets and the bat are both missing, too. "What's going on? I know I put them in here!"

I start rummaging through my drawers, trying to find those bloody items. When I turn around, I notice my bat lying on my desk. I pick it up, looking for all the blood, but it's been cleaned off. There is not one drop anywhere. I am dumbfounded, and suddenly I think I'm losing my mind. Did it really happen? Did I even kill Marty? I start questioning what really happened that night, running through each moment in my head. I look at my knuckles that still bear the wounds, although those have almost disappeared. I scratch my head.

"Maybe I put them in my closet?" I run into my room and start digging through the closet, but I find nothing in there, either. "This is crazy. I know I had those things. I know I hid them. Where the fuck are they?" I say out loud.

Hunter walks into my closet. "Daddy?" His eyes are huge and staring right at me.

"Oh, yeah, buddy? What's wrong?" God, I hope he didn't hear me.

"What's fuck?" he asks me.

I stare at him blankly, wondering what the hell to say. I start to laugh, but I turn my head so he doesn't see me.

"Um…Hunter, that isn't a good word. Daddy made a mistake and shouldn't have said that. So I don't want you to say that, okay?" I explain to him.

He nods his head like he understands. "Can I have a Popsicle?"

"A Popsicle? Why, yes, you can! That sounds great, Hunter. Let's go get one!"

We head downstairs and into the kitchen. I walk over to the freezer and Hunter walks to the back door. I turn around to hand him his Popsicle, but he's staring outside.

"Hey, buddy, here ya go!"

I walk over to him, but he doesn't even glance my way. Then I remember what the officer said about the blood. I look outside to see if I can see anything, but the sandbox is to the left of where we can see. Hunter is pale as he looks down.

"Daddy, I miss Cheryl Daddy." He turns to me and hugs my legs. I pat his back with my one free hand.

"I know, buddy, and it's okay to feel that way. I miss her, too. Here…do you want this?" I hand him his Popsicle and he takes it. He walks over to the table and sits down, still looking quite melancholy. I sit down next to him. "I need to ask you about that day, okay?"

He doesn't say anything; he just continues to eat his Popsicle.

"Do you remember that day? I mean…do you know who was there, or what he looked like?"

He still doesn't answer me.

"Okay, buddy, we don't have to talk about it now."

I sit back and watch him finish his snack. It doesn't take him long to scarf it down, then he runs back upstairs. I continue to sit there, glancing out the window. I get up and open the back door, then walk outside. I start to feel sick to my stomach, knowing what happened here just a few days ago. I walk around to the sandbox and stop in my tracks. I look down at the patio and see the bloodstains. My eyes start to fill with tears as I walk closer to where it all took place. The cop was right about the blood in the sandbox, too. I take my shoe and quickly cover up what I can. I get a horrible chill throughout my body that nearly knocks me to the ground. I turn around and go back inside; I lock the door behind me. I walk backward a few steps, not taking my eyes off the door. The phone rings, bringing me out of my coma.

"Hello?"

"Michael, it's Shelly. How are you doing, dear?" she asks me.

"You're amazing, Shelly. I mean, with all that's happened and you are worried about me. I'm okay, Shelly, but how are you doing?"

"Okay. It's still hard to wake up every day, but I'm doing well. I just called to tell you that I've made funeral arrangements for Cheryl. She has a plot here, so I called the funeral home to make sure her remains were brought back here. The funeral is tomorrow."

"Tomorrow, um, okay. Where and when?"

"Heritage Funeral Home on Kindler Street at three. I have some friends that offered to take care of Hunter, so he doesn't have to be there if you don't want him to be. I will leave it up to you. I'll see you in the morning, Michael."

She hangs up, and now I feel sick. I don't want Hunter to see me upset, so I walk into the laundry room and shut the door. I have a little cry fest for myself, wondering how I can get through this and help Hunter at the same time. I lean my back against the door and begin to bang my head on it. I take a deep breath and then regain my composure. Just as I am about to open the door, I notice something on the washing machine. I walk over to the pile of clean sheets and comforter. On top is a note from Cheryl:

Do I even want to know?

"Oh my God, here they are! I wasn't losing my mind! I wonder how she got in my office." I look up to the sky and say, "Thank you." I can only hope she is looking down at that same time. She probably saved my life and doesn't even know it. I take the items and bring them back to my room, shaking my head about what just happened. I put the sheets down on the bench and then put the comforter back on my bed. I feel heavy hearted, knowing in just a few hours I will be truly saying good-bye to a dear friend. Hunter walks into my room and asks what's wrong.

"Oh, um…that was Aunt Shelly that called earlier, and she has arranged Cheryl's funeral. It's tomorrow. How would you feel about that, Hunter? Do you know what a funeral is?"

"Yes, it's when someone dies and you put them in the ground."

"How did you know that?"

He starts to explain to me how Cheryl taught him about life and death, and how important everybody is to the world. Even during the car ride the next morning, he continues to talk about Cheryl and all the things she educated him on, including forgiveness and hate. I think for sure he will sleep the whole way, considering we have to leave around six in the morning. He falls asleep ten minutes before we get there. He does so great during and after the funeral; he is a champ. Afterward, Shelly comes up to me and hands me a letter.

"It's from your dad. I called to tell him about Cheryl. He came to pay his respects yesterday and left before you showed up. He didn't want to cause you any more grief, but he did leave you this."

I stare at the envelope, not even wanting to know what it says, but curiosity gets the best of me. I sit down outside, finding the rickety rocking chair to be an old friend, and open the letter:

Michael,

First, let me say how sorry I am to hear of Cheryl's passing. It came as quite a shock to us that such a wonderful woman would be gunned down like that. Now, I know I said I wouldn't contact you again, but I feel like this is an exception. I also feel like this is a good time to tell you some things you don't know about me. I never thought I would have to tell you about them, but now I have to, for your sake and your son's. A long time ago, I was bullied, much like you. I was on the verge of suicide, when a book showed up on my computer, telling me if I hit Send all the bullying would go away. That's right, Michael, it happened to me, too. Didn't you ever wonder why I didn't freak out when you told me the truth? By the time I was twenty-five, I had three published books, but you'd never find them. I changed my name afterward because I was so mortified by my actions, I didn't want anyone to know who I was. Now, I know anything I tell you in this letter will be our secret for life, considering...

My birth name is Walter O'Malley. Yep, that's right, we are Irish, full-blown Irish. Ever wonder why you swear so much? It's a genetic thing, don't think anything of it. Have a temper, too? Yep, it's a package deal. You are welcome! I know humor probably isn't what you want to hear right now, but it's gotten me through a lot of shit, Michael. Trust me, after reading the rest of this letter, you will be finding ways to make yourself laugh, too. It's not a pretty picture. Here goes.

The first book I "wrote" detailed things in my past, much like your first book. I did find out a few things I never knew about my father and grandfather, though. When I asked my dad about it, he said it was an old wives' tale, but the further I looked into my past, I found out that gypsy curses were quite real. The second book I "wrote" detailed things that I eventually did. I had bullies, too, Michael, and as you know about the football player I killed, well, he wasn't the first one, nor was he the last. Over that next year and a half, I killed four people, including my own father. It was ruled an accident but, as you know, it wasn't. I strangled my father as he slept after a weekend of binge drinking and beating the shit out of me and my mom. I hid his murder by throwing him down the stairs and breaking his neck. His alcohol level was three times the legal limit, so they ruled it an accidental death. The only good thing that came out of it was his life insurance money. The third book I "wrote" detailed the last of the men I would kill, but it also included one woman. Now, I'm not going to get into who they were and what they did. Just know it happened, and the guilt I felt caused me to start drinking, heavily. The third book also came after I met your mom. She didn't know anything about what I'd done; she just got to witness my guilt through alcohol. The last thing the third book said was that I would have a son, born with the same genetics, born with the same curse.

I had to change my life, including my name. I chose Bali because it was the one place I've always wanted to visit; that's the name's only significance. I felt so guilty and horrible about the things I did, I turned to God. I figured if I gave my life to the Lord, I would be forgiven for the sins I'd committed, and somehow the curse would be broken. Now, here you are, in the same mess as I was. Please understand, I did not know this curse would be transferred to you until I looked into our family's past after you admitted to me about your books. My father, your grandfather, didn't change his name as I did. His name was William Edward O'Malley, and he was a famous writer in his time, but with works not his own. Just the other day I found out about Mitch and his first "book." It will never end, Michael; no matter what you do, your life and your son's life have been written in verse. I am so sorry.

Dad

"This is total bullshit! There is no way I would ever believe in a gypsy curse! How stupid do you think I am, Dad?" I say to myself, and I crumple up the letter and throw it on the ground.

Shelly comes out with a glass of pink lemonade for me. "Here you go." She looks up at the sky. "Mighty fine day God gave us, isn't it?" She smiles and sits down next to me. She starts rocking away, looking like she hasn't a care in the world.

"Shelly, you are an amazing person. I mean, you and Cheryl were all that's left of your family, yet here you sit, smiling and thanking God. I don't know if I could do that," I tell her.

She looks down at the letter I threw away. "I believe family is who you love, and who loves you just as much, no matter what. I have been blessed with friends throughout my life that are as close as my dear sister and I were. They are surrounding me today, Michael, just as you are—my family. That letter down there is from your family, Michael, the same family that will be there when you pass on." She smiles and pats my hand. "Hunter is looking for you, my dear. He is holding up quite well, considering what he's seen, but I know he wants to get home. Thanks for coming, Michael. I know Cheryl is looking down and smiling at us right now." She gets up and I do, too. We hug good-bye and I tell her I love her.

Hunter comes running out, followed by a few other kids. They have been playing tag and Hunter is the safe zone.

"Daddy, save me!" He wraps himself around me, nearly knocking me over. The other kids come over and beg me to stay longer. I have to let them down easy, because I appreciate them for wanting to play with him, instead of making fun of him.

"Hunter, we have to go home now. Say good-bye to Aunt Shelly, okay?"

He runs off with his followers, laughing all the way. I look down and pick up the letter. I smooth it out and put it in my pocket. Shelly is watching me from the doorway.

"You're a good man for doing that. I'll see you soon, baby." She walks inside, closing the door behind her.

I don't know it is going to be the last time I see her. She dies just few days later from what I believe to be a broken heart. It turns out I am partly correct; it is her heart, all right, but those clogged arteries make it impossible for the doctors to save her. Now she and her sister will be laughing it up in heaven and looking down on me, with Cheryl probably giving me the finger. I love both of them, and she is right, they are my family.

I don't go back for Shelly's funeral, though. I think it might be too much for Hunter to handle, but I do send flowers—a lot of flowers—to the funeral home. That same week, I sign the papers to the house in Spokane and tell Hunter we are moving. He seems excited at first, and then asks if bad people live there. How do you tell a child that there are bad people everywhere? I do my best at comforting him with a very broad answer. "Nope."

I decide to look into what my dad said in his letter about some gypsy curse with our family. I log onto my computer and start to Google anything I can find: my dad's name, my grandfather's name. I don't know what I would have done before computers were around. I guess I would have to go to an actual library, and that would be so weird. So while Hunter sleeps, I am elbow deep into my family history. I even sign up to learn about my ancestry on one of those websites. I type in my dad's name and my grandfather's name, and bam! My entire family history is right in front of me, just dangling on all those branches. It goes all the way back to the 1800s. I click on every name that is there, including the really old ones. Turns out, every man since the tree began was a writer. They all started out wanting to do something else, but ended up writers. One name in particular looks quite odd to me, as it isn't an Irish one. The name is Simza Petulengro. She was a woman from a small town in England. According to this, she met and married my great-great-great-grandfather, Davis O'Malley, a struggling writer, when she was just fifteen years old. My grandfather and Simza eloped, which angered the Petulengro family so much they banished her and her future children from ever bearing the family name. The curse was placed by the elder of the family, and stated that any one man from this bloodline shall have the following three possessions placed upon them:

1) Their fortune generated only by the deaths of others,
2) Bear the shame on their face, and
3) Shall live by verse alone for three moons.

I laugh when I read it, thinking, *This is such baloney.* Then I start to kind of believe it. "Shall live by verse alone for three moons? That has to mean books, three books. Bear the shame on their face explains why we look like we do. Generate their fortunes only by deaths of others—

fuck, this is real! Oh, man, I've read about this stuff, but it never seemed logical. Could this really be happening to me?" I get up from my desk and start to pace the room, running my hands through my hair. "This means Hunter will have to go through this, too? I can't let that happen! But how do I...stop it?" I stand by the window, looking outside, knowing these surroundings will be someone else's soon. I drop my head back and pray to God that my son will be forever protected from any curse that may already be there. I turn off my computer and decide to forget about what I read, at least for now. I need to start packing for our new life, our new home, and a new beginning in a town called Spokane.

Chapter 17

THREE YEARS HAVE passed since we moved from Baltimore, and so far our move to Spokane has been seamless. My house was sold that very next week after the funeral, to a fan of mine who thought it was even more awesome that a crime had been committed there. I thought for sure my house would never sell because of that same reason. Funny how life works. Missy has been showing us around town, and Hunter has grown quite fond of her, and I have to admit, so have I. Hunter's six and a half now, and making friends quite easily in school. Spokane is very laid-back and we fit it pretty well here. I even bought Hunter and myself matching four-wheelers to drive on the property. No crashes so far; fingers crossed that our driving record maintains the status quo. Even though the love I still have for Gwen is just as strong, I've been able to see past it and start feeling deeply for Missy. It isn't easy the first time we have sex, but I soon get over that fear. I find myself wanting her as much as I did Gwen, and I finally don't have the guilt anymore. It's like Gwen gave me the okay to go ahead with my life. I will always be grateful for what she gave me and allowed me to feel, and I still miss her every day. My relationship with Missy is ever evolving. I never ask where she goes or what she's doing, I tell her every day that I love her, and I am actually thinking of asking her to marry me. We have a mutual respect for one another, and besides, it's kinda nice to get up every day thankful for what I have and not feeling bad for what I don't anymore. Of course, I'm still wary about my whole "past," as my father put it in the letter he wrote me. I still haven't seen hide nor hair of Mitch or Dave Lavetti since I've been here, and I feel like I'm constantly looking over my shoulder, waiting...

Hunter came home from school today and told me he met a couple kids that just moved here.

"Hey, that's great, buddy! What are their names?"

"Andy and Luke," he tells me as he gets a juice box from the fridge.

"What did you say?" My heart has just stopped.

He stops sipping. "Amos and Lucy. They're twins. I'm going outside." He opens the door and leaves me in the kitchen, mouth wide open and virtually numb.

"I could have sworn he said Andy and Luke. What the hell is wrong with me?" I try to shake off hearing those names. I'm still on edge every day, expecting the worst to come, expecting the cops to show up at my door and arrest me for Marty's death. It's been over three years now and I haven't heard even a snippet of news about the Lavettis. I don't know it that's a good thing or not. As I start to read the newspaper, Hunter comes barreling in.

"Hey, Dad, can we play?" he asks me.

"Of course, buddy, what would you like to do? A puzzle, or Play-Doh, perhaps?"

"No, I want to ride the four-wheelers!" he yells.

"Hey, that sounds awesome! Let's go get our helmets on and ride like the wind!" I get up, and we both run out the back door and into the garage. We ride for a good hour until it starts to get dark, and then we come inside for some grub. "Tacos sound good?"

"Yeah, I love tacos! Where's Missy?" he asks me.

I look at the clock and realize she hasn't called at all today. "Hmm, I don't know. I will call her in a bit."

We finish our meal and Hunter helps me clean up. I marvel at this kid, knowing how well his therapy has gone, even though he doesn't remember a lot of it now. We've tried to get him to tell us who did it or what he looked like, but he's blocked it out so far. There's hope he will remember one day, but we don't push it, as that might send him further into denial. He's a good kid and handling everything with grace. He's had to grow up way too fast for his age. I try to do as many kid things as possible so he knows he's still a kid.

"Can we get ice cream later? It looks like ice cream weather, doesn't it?" he asks me.

"Ice cream weather? What does that look like, exactly?" I snicker at his obvious trickery.

He looks outside and then back at me. "Any day I'm alive is ice cream weather, Daddy!" He laughs, then jumps down from his stool. "Can we go?" he asks again.

"We'll see. I'm kinda nervous about Missy, though. She hasn't called at all," I tell him as I put the last dish in the dishwasher.

"Hope she's okay, Daddy. I don't want anything to happen to her...like Cheryl." He looks at me with a sad face.

I stop what I'm doing and kneel down to him. I put my hands on his arms and tell him how proud I am of how his therapy is going. I ask if he needs anything from me and if he still likes it here. He tells me he loves Spokane and has a lot of friends at school. I think it helps that he was so young when Cheryl died. His moving on has been a blessing, even though there have been no leads or arrests in Cheryl's slaying.

"Do you want to talk about it? I know you've been talking to Ms. White about it when you go to her office, but I'm just wondering if you want to talk to me now." I cock my head to the side.

He breathes out like he's angry. "Daddy, I am so mad!" he yells.

"Okay, it's okay if you're mad. You can be mad with what happened. Someone took our friend from us, and I'm mad about that, too!" I respond.

"I'm scared he will come back for me, Daddy. He knew my name and everything!"

He starts to cry, so I grab him and hold him so tight. "No one will ever hurt you, son, ever! I will always be here to protect you, no matter what, okay?" I try to console him.

"Daddy, you weren't there to protect Cheryl!" He pushes me away, runs to his room and slams the door.

"Breakthrough, perhaps?" I ask myself, then Missy comes through the door. "Where have you been? You didn't call today and I was worried!" I walk over and hug her.

"You were worried about me? That's not like you. What's wrong?" she asks as she takes off her coat.

"Well, I've grown quite fond of you, and so has Hunter." I kiss her cheek.

"Aw, how sweet. Where is Hunter, anyway?" She looks around the room.

"He's upset with me, but I think it might be a breakthrough with his memory about Cheryl," I tell her as I walk her into the kitchen.

"Ooh, that would be somethin', huh? What happened?" she asks as she sits down at the table.

"Well, I was asking if he wanted to talk to me about it, and that it was okay to be mad. That's when he got upset and yelled that I wasn't there to protect Cheryl. He ran into his room, and that's when you came home. I'm hoping it's triggering his memory so we can find the asshole that did it, even though I know who did it—Dave Lavetti."

"Lavetti, Lavetti, why does that name sound so familiar? Oh, wait! Now I remember! There was a big story on the news a few days ago from your hometown about a Lavetti. He was dredged up from the lake by the airport. Do you think he's a relative of the Dave guy?"

She gets up and pours herself a cup of coffee. I just sit there, staring straight ahead.

"Oh, I don't know, Missy. Do you know his first name?" I ask her, even though I know the answer.

"No, I don't remember, but that name isn't a common one, right? It has to be his son or his brother."

"The last thing I want to think about right now is the Lavettis. Tell me how your day was. Why didn't you call?" I ask her.

"Oh, man, I was so busy today! Home sales are definitely up, and it seems like people are moving from the East Coast in droves. I'm lovin' every minute of it!" She smiles.

"That's great, babe, it's nice to see you love your job. I think that's the most important thing, finding your niche."

"What about you and your writing? You haven't written anything in a while. Have the written word lost its luster for you?" she asks me as she fixes a taco salad for herself.

How do I tell her about this? The answer is, I don't. She will never know about the books—ever. I sit with her while she eats, then Hunter emerges from his room. He peeks out from behind the door at us, but only enough for us to know he's there.

Missy starts first. "Man, I wish Hunter was here so I could tell him about my day! I know of a new ice cream shop that just opened, and I was hoping he'd want to go with me someday!" She continues eating her salad.

"Oh, you know what's funny about that? He was just asking if we could go get some ice cream later today, but I think he's too upset to go. Maybe we should postpone it for another day." I wait for him to make his entrance and he does, right on cue.

"No, I want to go!"

"Oh, hi, Hunter, I didn't see you there!" Missy tells him, and he runs over and hugs her. They play and giggle like a real mom and son would; I smile just watching them.

"Okay, well, let me finish my salad and then we'll go, okay?" she tells him. He kisses her, then runs off to his room.

"Okay, Mommy!"

We both look at each other. "Wow, did you just hear that?" she asks me.

"Uh, yeah, it's pretty cool that he thinks of you that way. He never knew his mom, and Cheryl was the closest thing to a female parent that he had. I never thought I would hear those words from him. How do you feel about that?" I ask her.

She sits there, tears welling up in her eyes. "I thought it was the most beautiful sound I've ever heard, Michael. I've always wanted children, and he's the closest thing I've had to a son. I love it." She wipes away her tears, then gets up and puts her salad in the fridge. "There's no way I could eat that now!"

She starts to cry some more. I get up and hold her in my arms, loving how this feels. I think that just sealed the deal.

Hunter comes running out with his coat on. "I'm ready!"

"Hey, Hunter, do you mind if I come, too?" I ask him.

"Of course you can, Daddy. Why wouldn't you come, too?" he tells me.

"Well, you didn't seem too happy with me before. I wish I had been there, Hunter, I really do. I'm so sorry I wasn't. Do you forgive me now?" I ask him as I walk over and put my hand on his shoulder.

He looks up at me and smiles. "Yeah." That's all he says.

We all head out to get some ice cream, although it's frozen yogurt, but he doesn't have to know that! On our way to get the ice cream, Hunter asks Missy if it is okay if he calls her mom. She looks at me with a kind of "help me" face.

"Well, Hunter that is a good question. Can I ask you why you want to?" Missy asks him.

He ponders the question for a minute or so, then announces, "I'm the only kid who doesn't have a mom and I don't like that feeling. I don't want to get made fun of anymore."

"Wait, kids are making fun of you for that?" I ask. My blood starts to boil immediately, since that is a form of bullying. "What have they been saying to you?"

He looks out the window. "They said I was too ugly for my mom to want me."

"What?" Now I am full-on pissed off. I pull the car over so I can talk to him face-to-face. "Hunter, look at me."

He looks over his shoulder. "Daddy, it's true, isn't it? Mommy died because I am so ugly, huh?" he asks.

My heart is literally breaking in two, and Missy is even having a hard time hearing this.

"Buddy, you are not ugly. In fact, you are the most beautiful little boy ever created! Mommy was so excited when she knew you were coming, but her body just gave out. You are a loved little boy, and anyone who says something different is just jealous of you. That's right, they are jealous, because you are the coolest kid around and they wish they were as cool as you." My explanation lacks the subtle yet feverish anger I am feeling right now.

Missy chimes in with, "Hunter, I would be proud if you called me your mommy. There's no one else on this earth who I would want more to call me that than you, little one!" She smiles at him. "Now, let's go get that ice cream, okay?"

He smiles and nods his head yes. She looks back at me, and I have the dumbest grin on my face.

"What's that face for?" she asks me.

"You really surprise me, that's all. I love you, and I just wanted you to know that," I tell her as I lean over and kiss her cheek. I look at Hunter in my rearview mirror and he's smiling. Life is good...no, life is great.

The next couple of days I really start thinking about asking her to marry me. I am completely nervous, but at the same time, completely confident she'll say yes. I go into a couple ring shops and just look around. I am about to leave the last store when it catches my eye: it is the one. The one I am looking for, the exact color and size. The big sign above it says it is on sale and will "make all your friends jealous when they see it." I know she will love it as much as I will love buying it—hello, fifty-inch plasma TV! When I arrive home with the giant box, she is actually thrilled.

"Oh my gosh! How cool is this, Hunter? Your dad just got a really big TV!"

"Yeah, Daddy! Now we can watch Spider-Man on it!"

"Yes, we can, buddy. Do you want to help me set it up?"

"Yeah, cool!" He sits down next to me.

Missy decides to start dinner. "Hey, any requests from my guys?"

At the same time, we both yell, "Pizza!"

"Okay...saves me from cooking! I'll be back shortly. Don't blow anything up, Michael, okay? We just painted." She smiles, grabs her purse and leaves.

I make sure she has left before I tell Hunter my plan. "Hey, buddy, I have something to show you!" I take out a ring from my pocket.

"Ooh, Daddy that's pretty, but I like the TV better," he tells me, as he continues to go through the plastic shielding in the box.

"Well, it's not for you, it's for Missy. How would you feel about her becoming your real mommy?" I ask him.

"Oh, yeah, I really would, Daddy!" He jumps up and hugs me.

"I was hoping you would feel like that, buddy, because tonight I'm going to ask her to marry me. So don't tell her when she comes back, okay? It's a surprise!"

We get the TV all done, and now we are just waiting for Missy to come home with the pizza. I look at the clock and realize it's been over an hour. I start to get nervous, so I call her cell. I can hear it ringing in the other room, so I follow the sound and it leads me into the kitchen. I keep the phone to my ear as I track the ringing, and when I take my first step onto the tiled floor, I find Missy standing there—with Dave Lavetti, his gun to her head.

"Michael!" She stops.

"Shhhhhhh," Dave says to her as he strokes her cheek with the gun. Tears are streaming down her face as his hot breath whispers something into her ear.

"Dave, don't do this, please. Let her go!" My voice is demanding but quiet, as I don't want Hunter to hear me.

"Daddy, when is the pizza coming?" Hunter yells from the living room.

"Oh, um…it's on its way, Hunter, so why don't you go play with your friend next door for a little while until it gets here, okay?" I choke back tears as I stare at Missy. Her eyes are screaming at me to help her, but I don't know what to do—yet.

"Okay," he yells, then I hear the front door slam shut.

"It's so good to see you, Michael. Tell me, how's Cheryl?" He starts to laugh and then holds Missy even tighter.

"Dave, please stop. I won't tell anyone you're here. Just let her go. You have my word!" I tell him as I take one step closer.

"Stop right there, Mikey. You expect me to believe you, after you killed my son and dumped him in the river?"

"I didn't do anything—" I begin, but he interrupts me.

"Shut up! Do you think I am so fucking stupid that I would actually believe you right now? I know you killed my boy, and now your little whore is going to pay for it!"

"No, please don't!" Missy screams, and starts bawling.

"Shut up! I don't want to hear your pathetic crying! That's all you women do is cry and whine about everything! Trust me, little girl, you won't win with your tears this time!"

Click.

Chapter 18

"**N**o!" I scream, and lunge at them. The gun misfires, leaving me only seconds to react. I knock them both down as we fight for the gun. Missy escapes unharmed, but Dave and I grapple on the ground, leaving me only one choice: I have to kill him. The gun becomes so slippery with our sweat that it's nearly impossible to grab. I begin to punch him in the face; blood starts to flow from his nose. I can hear Missy in the background screaming for help. She dials 911 and tells them Dave Lavetti is in her house and trying to kill us.

"You won't live through this, Mikey. You will die today, and so will your son!" He punches me in the gut, knocking the wind out of me. For a moment I think I'm done, until Dave reaches for the gun, and that's when I get my kidney shot in—POW! He falls down on top of me, moaning in pain. I get out from under him and start to pound his face some more. I grab his head and slam it against the tile floor.

"Fuck you, Lavetti! Tonight you're the one who's going to die!" I yell, and I slam his head to the ground again and again. Missy is yelling at me to stop, but I don't—I can't. My anger has now taken over my body, and physically I can't stop, but mentally I am having the time of my life. Dave takes hit after hit after hit, but just when I think he's had enough, I hit him again. I stand up, covered in blood. My face doesn't look the same, as hatred has given me a new gaze. I look over at Missy, who is now on the floor and covering her face. She is petrified and crying uncontrollably. I reach down to touch her, but she flinches.

"Get away from me!" she yells. "Look what you've done, Michael, look!"

She points to the bloodied-up body of one Dave Lavetti. I look over at him…I just smile. I walk over to him and kick his leg to see if he'll move. He doesn't. I lean down to grab the gun, but he grabs my arm before I do and pushes the gun away from me. He's able to drop me to the ground again, and now he's on top of me. He smiles. Blood has filled his mouth, his eyes are deep red, and his nose is broken. He takes out a knife and thrusts it into my stomach.

"Ah fuck!" I scream.

Missy has now fallen to her knees, begging for Dave to let me go.

"Shut up! I told you this was your day to die! My revenge is now complete!" He stands above me, ready to thrust the knife straight into my heart. "Say hi to your wife for me!" He laughs.

Then I hear a gunshot. Dave drops to his knees, then looks down at me. He falls to the ground, dead. I look up, and there stands Mitch with a gun.

"Oh my God!" Missy runs over to me and puts her hands on my chest, keeping a steady hold on it.

Mitch comes over and kneels down beside me. "Hey, you. Now, how did I know what was going to happen?" He smiles, then tells me I will be all right.

The cops burst through the door, clearing the way for the paramedics.

"Thank you, Mitch, brother. Thank you."

He grabs my hand and tells me it's not over yet. The paramedics carry me away on the gurney. Missy stays with me, but my only thought is about Hunter. I turn to Mitch.

"Mitch, I need your help. I need you and Missy to go next door and get Hunter. I need you to take him away from here, but don't tell him what's happened. Missy, I need you to go with him so he knows it's safe. Please don't let Hunter see me like this."

"Of course we will. Anything for you, brother," Mitch tells me, then kisses my hand as they put me in the ambulance.

As luck would have it, while this whole thing happens, Hunter has gone to the park with his friend from next door and the friend's mom. I have completely forgotten that every Friday she takes them to the park to watch the skateboarders. Thank God for miracles.

I am only in the hospital overnight. The knife wound hit nothing vital; I just have to take it easy for a few weeks. Missy asks the next-door neighbor if Hunter can stay the night, which she doesn't mind at all, and neither does Hunter. Missy is able to clean up the mess before Hunter comes home the next day. Mitch talks Hunter into staying a few days with him and his girlfriend by bribing him with Silverwood tickets. I've heard about this amusement park from many people; I guess they have Boulder Beach on one side and rides on the other. Hunter is quick to say yes, as long as he can wear his Spider-Man cape.

"Dude, I wish I had a cape like that! Man, you are the coolest kid in town!" Mitch tells Hunter, and that makes his day.

Another murder, another investigation, but this time, it doesn't take as long. The sheriff's department here is top-notch. They have their investigators in and out; the witnesses and the testimonies are done within a matter of days, and life goes back to normal before Hunter comes home. But the best news of all? Dave Lavetti is fucking dead! Dare I say it's all over? Can this whole nightmare be finally done? I lie on the couch watching TV while I wait for Missy to come home. Ever since the whole Dave thing, she's been acting very strange and standoffish to me. When she comes through the door, I ask her to sit down next to me.

"What's wrong?" I ask her. "You've been acting kind of strange ever since—"

"Michael, you scared me that day. I never thought I would see that ever in my life. You turned into a monster!" She purses her lips together and looks up at the ceiling.

"Look, I'm sorry, but he was going to kill you and threatened to kill my son! I had to do what I had to do. I would do anything to protect my son, and when I saw him with a gun to your head, I lost it. Please don't be scared of me, Gwen."

"Missy."

"What?"

"My name is Missy, not Gwen." She gets up, goes into the bedroom, and slams the door behind her.

"Oh shit, I really fucked this up."

A few weeks later, after dozens of flowers and "I'm sorry" cards, Missy starts to come around. I guess what brings her around is the dancing bear in a tutu I send to her workplace, along with a poem of how much I love her. When she comes through the front door that night, she runs into my arms and tells me she forgives me. Good thing my wound has healed nicely. Our lives go back to normal. Missy's back to selling houses, I start redoing the kitchen floor, and Hunter is none the wiser. I decide to hold off on asking her to marry me. Too much has happened, so I don't think it would be a great idea; plus, I lose the ring. It falls out of my pocket when I am in the hospital. I ask Mitch to go with me to pick out another one. It's a good time to ask him about his "books."

"So, how's the wound?" he asks me as we sit down at Latah Bistro for lunch.

"All better, thanks to you! I can't believe you showed up and...shot him," I say quietly, so the waiter doesn't hear me.

"Well, it was written in the stars!" We start to laugh, but the laughter quickly turns to silence, as we both know it's a serious matter.

"So how did you find out about them?" I ask him.

"Dad. He came to Jesus shortly after he got back together with my mom. I didn't believe him, so I Googled his real name and up popped his 'books.' I started reading the first one, but then stopped. I realized I didn't want to know who this man was; I like who he has become. Anyway, I also started to look up the ancestry, since the story he was telling me sounded so crazy. I know about the curse, Michael, but I'm not sure if I believe it. Honestly, it sounds too hokey. I grew up in a household that believed in God, not in gypsies."

"I understand, Mitch, it was hard for me to believe, too. I looked up our ancestry line, though, and I did find out about the curse. It's real, Mitch, and it dates all the way back to the 1800s. The curse tells of three things that will happen to each man born in this bloodline, our bloodline. The first one says our fortunes will be made through the deaths of others. Think about that one, Mitch. How have we made our money so far, huh? Our book sales go through the roof each time we hit Send. How many people have died in your books so far?"

He doesn't answer me.

"The second curse tells of us bearing the shame on our faces. Look at us, man! We bear the curse, just like our father did and his father did, and so on and so on. And if you have sons, they too will bear it, just like mine does. The third curse says we shall live our lives through verse alone for three moons! That means books, Mitch! Three books will show up on your computer, and you will live your life exactly how those books say you will, until every last word has been accounted for. How many books have you written so far?" I ask him.

"Two. And so far, everything has happened the way they've said. Shit! I can't believe this, Michael! What can we do?" He puts his elbows on the table and covers his mouth with his hands. "What the fuck is going to happen to us?"

"Oh, and the swearing is because we are Irish. Did you know that?"

"I'm fucking Irish now?" He starts to laugh. "Man, that explains a whole lot of shit."

We both start laughing. We decide to finish our lunch without mentioning any more of the curse, and as it turns out, he's one funny motherfucker. After we finish lunch, we head to the mall downtown. He helps me pick out a new ring for Missy, and this time, I don't even look at the TVs.

"So, how are you going to do it? Soft and romantic at a nice restaurant, perhaps, or just down and dirty and throw it at her?" He takes a sip of his water.

"I haven't even thought about it. To tell you the truth, I used to be confident that she would say yes, now...not so much. I guess I'm flying by the seat of my pants now, considering I don't have any more books to live by, unlike you. Do you think about it? Do you think about what would happen if you didn't hit Send?"

"Nope, because I didn't hit Send on this last book. It did it for me. There's no getting out of it. I have one more book to live through; then I can actually live my life the way I want. Come on, let's get a pretzel."

Later that night I start to think about how I should propose. Should it be over the top, or not so much? Would she care if I had flowers and Perrier or pizza and Dr. Pepper? Considering we both don't drink makes it way easier on me; there's no way she can "blame it on the booze," either. I remember my mom telling me how my father proposed to her: "Will you marry me? And I'm not drunk, either." Smooth...he was a real smooth talker, that one. I can't have this proposal anything less than spectacular! She deserves flowers, but...flowers in Spain, as we coast along the Mediterranean on a beautiful sailboat while sipping our Perrier in tall fluted lead crystal glasses. I know this will be the perfect setting, so I go ahead and book the entire vacation, with us leaving next week. I call up Mitch to see if he can take Hunter for the time we are gone, and of course, he says yes. I even offer for him and his girlfriend to stay at the house. I guess it is a blessing in disguise that the college he goes to is fifteen minutes away. He decided to be an Eastern Eagle, thank God! When Missy walks through the door, I take her into my arms and swing her around like you'd see in a Bogart movie or something.

"Hey, what's going on with you?" she asks, giggling during our last twirl.

I stop and look deeply into her eyes. "I love you, Ms. Allison, and I want to spend forever dancing with you. Would that be all right?"

She stops laughing and straightens up after she catches her breath. "Um…what?" She looks like she's going to be sick.

I just stare at her, thinking, *Did I just say that out loud?* I let go of her after she gains her footing again. "What's the matter? You look a little sick," I tell her as I wipe my sweaty hands on my jeans.

"I…um…well…it's the…oh." She just stops and looks at me.

"I get the feeling you're trying to say something to me." I smile at her.

She nods her head yes, then starts to tear up. "I…um… when you…oh, I should…um…kitchen." She walks away.

I follow her, smiling, because I know I just freaked her out. "Babe, what's going on?" I ask her as I sit at the table and watch her fidget with the coffee.

"Uh, nothing. How are you?" She spills the coffee grounds all over the floor. "Oh…poo!" She grabs a towel and starts to clean up.

"Oh, poo? Who are you, Mary Poopins?" I start to laugh myself silly.

She stops cleaning and stands upright, putting her hand on her hip. "Um, Michael? I feel that maybe we swear too much and that's not good for Hunter to hear, so…I am trying to change that, okay?" She bends back down and finishes cleaning up the spilled coffee grounds.

I think about what she said, then I nod my head in agreement. "That's a great idea; I shall start with poo, too!" I walk over to her and kneel down beside her. "Hey."

She continues to clean, but says, "Hey," back to me.

I grab her hands and make her stand up with me. "I didn't propose to you, if that's what you're freaking out about. All I said was I wanted to dance with you forever." I grab her face with my hand, lean in and softly kiss her.

She looks at me with her doe eyes. "Oh, you didn't?" Her voice sounds surprised.

I shake my head no. "I'm sorry if I disappointed you, but I don't think we are ready for something like that, at least not now. Don't you agree?" I'm dying inside, knowing that when I do propose, she's going to shit her pants, but those pants will be soiled in Spain, baby!

"Oh, yeah, you're right. It's not like we haven't had a lot of things happen to us this last year. It's a good idea to, you know...wait." She takes the towel and washes it off in the sink. If anyone were to walk in the room right now, you could cut the tension with a butter knife, and I'm lovin' every minute of it.

"Maybe we should go on vacation instead, you know, somewhere we both have never been before. Somewhere that we could just let loose and no one knows who we are. Someplace where the water is so blue you can see right to the bottom, and the sands of the beaches are white as snow. The colors of the buildings remind you of a rainbow, and the sweet smell of the local cuisine makes your mouth water." I paint a great picture, don't I?

"That sounds amazing, and it sounds like you've already picked out a spot, so why don't you just tell me, instead of this whole *Casablanca* story you got goin' on." Her hand twirls in a circle around my face.

"Spain!" I tell her.

"Spain? I've always wanted to go there! Oh my God, that's awesome!" She starts to clap her hands and jump up and down like she's five years old. "Yeah, we are going to Spain!" She continues to laugh and jump around, then stops all of a sudden. "Wait! I can't go to Spain! I have a job, with a bunch of clients that are coming into town soon! Oh, man!" She starts to pout.

Oh shit, how do I remedy this? I already bought the damn tickets!

"This is a chance of a lifetime, babe! Can't you find someone else to help them? You aren't the only one that works in that office, right?" Now I sound totally paranoid, but that's only because I am totally paranoid.

"It's not that easy, Michael! These people contacted me because I helped someone they knew! I can't just toss them to the side like that! Oh, I am so sorry, but my job is way too important for me to do that to anyone. Plus, the other agents in my office would just love to get their hands on my clients. It really is a cutthroat business, Michael, and those girls would use a dull knife if they could. Please understand that I can't go, not now."

"Okay, I understand, but I must tell you that I already purchased the tickets, planned out the entire vacation, and paid for everything, including the hotel, car rental, scuba diving, private boat rides, and a couple massage after a day at the spa. But I understand. I'll just call and cancel it. I'm sure it'll be fine." I start to walk away, knowing what I am about to hear. I know women better than they think!

"Wait! I'll call them right now!" She breaks the sound barrier as she whizzes by me and grabs the phone. I just lean against the wall and smile—I win!

That next week flies by, and the next thing we know, we are landing in Madrid and it's freaking glorious. The weather is hot and the sky is a shade of blue that looks like Renoir would have created it himself. Every day is better than the first, but when it comes to the boat ride, my stomach is in knots—and so are my lower intestines. I shit myself running to the bathroom after lunch that day. I have no idea what I ate, but whatever it was could not wait to see what the fabric of my Hanes briefs looks like.

"Honey, are you okay?" She knocks on the bathroom door.

Now, usually I would answer her in a normal and kind tone, but this isn't one of those times. "Holy Mother of God! What the hell is that? I didn't eat that!"

Missy just walks away and heads downstairs to the gift shop, and stays there for a while. An hour later I find her sitting at the bar, sipping on a lemonade spritzer. I slowly sit down next to her, easing my ass on to the chair. I realize I am sitting up on one cheek when Missy decides to imitate me.

"Ha-ha, very funny! How is it you feel fine, but my asshole feels like it needed a vacation from my butt! I think I just backed myself into a new wardrobe." I wave the waiter over and order hot tea with lemon.

"Ew, you are so gross! We haven't been together long enough for you to say those things to me!" She holds her nose and pretends I stink.

"Oh, trust me, we have, and it'll only get worse—I mean better!" The waiter brings my drink. "Thanks, my man. Tell me something." I start to dunk my tea bag into my water. "How's the surf and turf here?" I lift up one eyebrow.

"It's delicious, sir, and may I compliment you on your choice of entree. Were you ready to order?" he asks us.

"Sure, um...I will have the gazpacho to start, then the paella and gambas ajillo." She just rattles it off like it's nothin'.

I have a more difficult time ordering. "And I will start with some pulpoaee fiero, then I'll try that, um, coochi fritos." I hand him the menu and smile at Missy. I know I just sounded hot! He takes the menu and smiles at me, then rolls his eyes and walks away. "Did you see that? He just rolled his eyes at me!"

"Well, it's probably because you just trashed his native language! Do you even know what you ordered?" she asks me.

"No, but I'm sure it will be great—plus, we are on vacation! We need to be more spontaneous!" I tell her as I sip my tea. It takes only minutes before we get our first course, and Missy's looks good.

"Ooh, this looks so nummy! What did you get?" She looks over at my plate.

I look down at it, then up at her. "I don't know, but it looks like I already created this upstairs in a big white bowl!"

"Oh...my...God! Did you just say that out loud?"

Now she rolls her eyes at me. What's with all this eye action I've been getting? I take my fork and begin to pick through it, trying to look for something familiar, then I notice a tentacle.

"Oh shit! This is octopus!" I say out loud, probably a little too loud, since the waiter sees me and walks over.

"Is everything okay, sir? Is there something wrong with the pulpo á feira?" he asks.

Missy just smiles at him while I have to come up with a doozy. "No, it's...great! I love a good pulpafeeroa!" I smile at him and pretend to take a bite of the octopus.

"That was smooth, Michael, really smooth!" she says, and takes a sip of her delicious-looking soup. Why didn't I order soup? She looks at me. "Aren't you going to even try it?"

I am immediately taken back in time to the time when Gwen fixed this dish, or at least tried to fix it. My heart sinks a bit when I remember it. "Um...I think I should tell you that the first and last time I've ever been served octopus was with Gwen. She tried to make it and nearly burnt the house down, so it kinda brings back those bittersweet moments for me. I'm sorry, but I want to be completely honest with you when it comes to things like that."

"That's okay, Michael. I have memories of my ex-boyfriend whenever I eat popcorn, but time usually takes care of that kind of stuff. Plus, I hated him, so that helped a bit. I'm glad you feel like you can share these things with me. Makes me feel like I mean a lot to you." She takes another sip of her soup. *Stomach, stop growling...*

The entrées show up and Missy's once again looks awesome; mine, not so much.

"This looks so good! I love shrimp!" She picks one up and puts it in her mouth, then moans afterward, "So good!"

I look down at my plate, cringing at the scene. "What did I order?" I ask her.

She takes another bite of shrimp. "Fried goat, genius," she tells me.

"What the fuck? What is wrong with me?" I take a piece of the goat and put it in my mouth, then spit it back out on my plate. "Oh, no, no, no. I...no...this can't happen." I look over at her plate of shrimp that is half gone now. My mouth is watering and my stomach is pissed off at me. At least we have breadsticks on the table.

The waiter once again comes over and asks how everything is. Noticing my plate is still full, he says, "Sir? Is this not to your liking?"

I look at him, then down at my plate. "Oh, you know what? I didn't know this was goat, and I'm allergic to... um...goats."

"I understand, sir. Can I bring you anything else? Dessert, maybe? We have a wonderful crème brûlée."

Now, I do know what that shit is. "Yes, I will have two of those. Missy, would you like one, too?"

"Yes, please, and can I get a box for the rest of this?" She pushes her plates to the waiter and he takes them away.

"So, all you're going to have for dinner tonight is dessert?" she asks me.

"I don't think I have a choice!"

Chapter 19

GOOD THING I am able to change our boat ride to the next evening. "Are you excited?" I ask her as she slides into her slinky yellow dress.

"Yes, I am, although I've never been on a sailboat before. We aren't going to tip over, are we?" She looks at me, doe-eyed and a little paranoid.

"No, babe, it's not *that* kind of boat. We will be on calm waters and not too far out. Don't worry; it's my job to protect you." I kiss her lips and tell her to get her butt in gear so we won't be late, then I slap her ass.

"Ow!" She rubs her tush. "I thought we had another hour before we had to leave?"

"Well, I want to get there early. Plus, there are a couple things I need to pick up at the gift shop downstairs."

"Like?"

"Like gum, some Pepto just in case, and…Dramamine."

"Dramamine? Are you telling me you get seasick?"

"Maybe…actually, I don't know. I've never been on a boat before."

"Oh my God, then why did you book it?"

"Because it will be romantic, and we should always try new things. I mean, how will I ever know if I get sick on the water if I never go on the water?"

"Good point."

"Shall we?" I lead her to the door and start the ultra-gentleman-like stuff. "After you, my lady." As she walks past me, I begin to panic. "Oh shit, where's the ring?" I ask myself. I pat down my jacket until I feel the bulk of the box. "Whew."

Missy turns around. "Anything wrong?"

"Nope. Let's roll, sweet cheeks." I slap her ass again.

After I buy my assumed tummy and butt necessities, we head down to the pier where *The Lady Awaits*. Missy thinks that is the perfect name for the boat. I, for one, think *Kumbar Megashnog* would have been a lot better—catchier, if you will. The captain salutes us as we board the vessel—or should I say the soon-to-be *Yes, Michael, I will marry you, so take me now* boat. We set sail shortly after we board, and the night can't be more perfect. The moon is absolutely huge and it glistens on the water like diamonds. The breeze is warm and smells of spices, roses, and Spanish bluebells. We both stand by the railing and watch the shore fade in the distance. The waiter comes out with a bottle of Perrier and a plate full of Spain's best fruits and chocolates to start with. I am smart enough to ask what everything is before I order the entrees; I really didn't want another night of goat and octopus hanging over my head. We dine to our hearts' content, and then sit and cuddle each other on the sofa, watching the stars dance like they can hear music. I know this is going to be it, the moment. I sit her up from my lap, then kneel down beside her. I take the ring from my pocket and look up at her.

"Missy, it's not easy to reduce my feelings for you to mere words alone, because it seems words can't adequately express how I perceive you as a woman. You are what every man should look for: beautiful, a lady, honest, self-respecting, very loving and kind. There's nothing about you that other women shouldn't be jealous of, and they should want nothing more than to be like you. I was and always will be very attracted to you for all these reasons. You are everything I could have wished for. I feel so proud to have you on my arm, and I appreciate you for standing behind me during all those difficult times I have had to face. You have had to go through many troubling times because of issues that have come up in my life, but your support and love for me has never wavered. You have always been there for me, emotionally and physically, when I have needed you the most. You have opened my eyes on numerous occasions my putting a different perspective on an issue that was troubling me, and in many cases, you saved me from making a decision that would have made a situation worse. You are the guardian angel for my son. In the Bible, angels are sent by God to perform many difficult tasks. You do this daily. Although my son can take this for granted, I do not. I appreciate all you do for him, and often I am amazed at your persistence and patience. You have been nothing short of gracious and wonderful to my son, and I owe you a sincere debt of gratitude. This again is another testament for who you are as a person—or, like I said before, an angel. Will you marry me?"

Tears stream down her cheeks as I slip the ring on her finger. I look up at her, waiting for an answer. She pauses, trying to gather herself before her reply leaves her soft, mango-infused lips. "Yes," she replies. "Yes, yes, yes!" I quickly stand up to greet her loving arms. I twirl her around and around while the song "At Last" plays in the background. I stop, gently placing her feet on the ground. I take her face into my hands and I kiss her, for as long as my breath lasts. We start to dance, slowly and methodically, to what is now our song.

Two hours later, the boat docks and we return to our room. I don't think our feet touch the ground the entire way back. If someone had taken pictures of us, the caption would be: "Look, Ma, I swallowed a hanger!" That night turns out to be so perfect it is scary. I haven't had something *not* happen in quite a while; my defenses are up, but I don't want them to be.

The next morning proves to be just as exquisite, blue sky and a naked fiancée right next to me. I wake her up by kissing her spine all the way down to the bend in her back. She turns to face me, her eyes still swollen from the night's tears.

"Morning, babe," I say to her. Her lips make a kissing motion with an "I love you" whisper attached. "So how does it feel?"

She looks at her hand, admiring the two-karat yellow canary diamond, and replies, "Damn good! How do you feel?"

I look at my hand. "Hmm...empty."

"Aw, does Michael want to find a ring today for himself?" She starts to tickle me.

"Yes, I do, in fact. I think I want an unusual one, too; nothing too gaudy, like yours." I smile at her and then smack her bare butt.

"Hey, you know that's going to leave a mark one of these times. Then what are you going to do?"

"Smack the other cheek, what else?" I tackle her.

As we start to pack our bags, there's a knock at the door. "These were delivered for you today," the nicely uniformed young lad says.

"Thanks." I take the bushel of flowers and set them on the table. I unwrap the covering to unveil the present, and that's when my heart sinks.

"Oh, nice, who sent those?" Missy asks as she comes over and grabs the card attached.

See you soon!

"Hmm, do you know who these came from? There's no name." She hands me the card.

I don't even want to look at it, considering my table is now housing Toad lilies. I call down to the desk and say, "Someone delivered flowers to us. Would you by chance know where they came from?"

"All of our flowers come from the florist down the street called Belle's Flowers, sir."

I hang up the phone and tell Missy I'm going to go to that flower shop to find out who sent them.

"Honey, what's the big deal? Who sent them? Obviously it's someone from back home, like your brother." She looks like I'm crazy, and I know I probably do look that way, but I need to find out.

"You're right, but I'm a little OCD. I need to find things out. I'll only be gone for a few minutes." I kiss her good-bye and head straight for the flower shop.

In the shop, I hand the lady the card from the flowers. "Hey, I had flowers delivered to me today, and this is the card that came with them. Do you know who sent them?"

"Oh, yeah, I remember this! These are very hard to get, and it's the first time someone has ordered them before. Let me pull up the order form. Just give me a moment, please."

She walks in the back and I start to look around her shop. It's pretty nice. I've never seen so many carnations before. You usually only see them during funerals. I'm leaning down to smell the flowers as the lady comes back.

"Okay, I found the slip. The order came from Spokane, Washington, from L. Lavetti. Does that help?"

"Lena!" I say out loud.

"Excuse me?" she asks.

"Oh, nothing. Thanks for your help, Miss..."

"Belle Rose. Come in again soon, Mr. Bali!" She shakes my hand and walks in the back again. I walk out of her shop sick to my stomach.

"I totally forgot about her! I guess I had hoped that once Dave was dead, the whole family would cease to exist, and I fucking forgot about her and her sons! Oh my God, I have to tell Missy!" I book it back to the room, checking my watch to see how much time we still have before the plane leaves. I walk into the room and Missy is there, packing up the last of her stuff.

"So, did you find out who sent them, Sherlock?"

Now I think to myself this isn't a good time to tell her, because we just got engaged and I don't want her to freak out on me. I'll tell her in a couple days—hopefully, I'll still be alive then.

"Um, no, they couldn't tell me, but you're probably right about Mitch. Are you ready to go?"

"Yep. This was a great vacation, Michael. Thank you so much for everything! I love you!"

She kisses me, then we pick up our bags and go, but not before I slap her ass one more time. I smile at her, but inside I am totally freaking out about Lena. I thought for sure this shit would be done, but it looks like it's not over. On the plane ride back home, I start to relive my conversation with Mitch that fateful day. He said it's not over, and maybe this is what he meant by it.

"Daddy!" Hunter comes running over to me. "I missed you so much, Daddy!"

"Oh, I missed you, buddy! Did you and Uncle Mitch have fun?"

"Uh-huh, and I got some new toys, too!" He runs into his bedroom to retrieve them.

"Thanks again, Mitch, for taking care of him, very cool of you. But, I would like to introduce you to my future wife!" I point to Missy and she's dancing around.

"Missy, that's awesome, congratulations!" He hugs her and then we fist pound it. It's how we roll. "So, let's see the blinger!" He grabs her hand and lifts up one eyebrow, then whistles. "Looks like he spent some dough on you. I think he likes you!"

"Hey, where's Isabella? Did she finally see you naked and now that's scared her off?" I punch him in the arm.

"No, man-whore, she's at work. But she's off early today, so I thought we'd all have dinner together and you can tell us about your trip."

"Sounds good to me. There is something I'd like to talk to you about, Mitch," I tell him quietly, but not softly enough because Missy hears me.

"Yeah, I love the flowers you sent to us! They were gorgeous, but we couldn't take them on the plane, so we had to leave them there!" she tells him.

"What flowers?" he asks.

She looks at him. "You didn't send us flowers? Hmm, I wonder who did, then." She grabs her bags and takes them into the bedroom.

"What flowers, Michael?" he asks me.

"Well, that's what I wanted to talk to you about, but I didn't want to in front of Missy. We received flowers yesterday and they were Toad lilies, and the card said 'See you soon.' Toad lilies, Mitch! Now, you tell me if you know something about this from your book, because Lena sent them!"

Mitch shakes his head. "No, man, I don't know anything about Lena. I've never even met her before."

"I can't help remembering what you said that day Dave died. You said it's not over. Now, what did you mean by that?"

Mitch sits down on the sofa, rubbing his hands together. I sit down next to him, ready to hear my fate, when Hunter comes bursting in.

"See what Uncle Mitch got me, Daddy!" He shows me his Spider-Man figurines and his new bike helmet.

"Wow, buddy, those are so cool! Why don't you go show them to Missy, okay? She's in the bedroom," I tell him as I kiss his head. After Hunter leaves the room, I look back at Mitch. "Tell me what you know."

"She is out to get you, but I wasn't sure of that until you told me about the flowers. Watch your back, bro, that's all I can say."

"That's all you can say? Why didn't you tell me this before?"

"Michael, my books don't go into detail like yours did. I know blanketed statements and very vague descriptions of people. It's like I have to guess myself what's going to happen. I'm telling you to watch your back because I don't know anything else. That was the end of the second book, flowers being sent to you by someone...it didn't even say by whom. At least you know they were from Lena."

I sit back on the sofa, hands on my head and pissed off. "What the fuck am I going to do? Missy knows nothing of these books, and neither did Gwen, and look what happened to her, Mitch! Maybe I should end it with Missy before she gets hurt." I stand up and walk into the bedroom. I find her and Hunter sitting on the bed together. He's admiring her ring.

"Daddy, it's so pretty! Now I have a mommy!" He gets on the bed and starts to jump up and down until I stop him.

"Hey, buddy, I need to talk to Missy, so will you excuse us?"

"Okay." He jumps off the bed and runs out of the room.

"What's wrong?" she asks me as she continues to unpack her bags.

"Oh, I've just been thinking about us and—"

She interrupts me. "Oh, crap, hold that thought, Michael. I have to make a quick call first!" She grabs her phone and starts dialing. "Sorry, babe, I had a message on my phone to call ASAP when I got back, so give me a minute, okay?" When her friend answers, she says, "Hey, Marla, it's Missy, what can I do for you?" While she talks, I leave the room and sit back down on the sofa with Mitch.

"Well, what happened?" he asks me.

"Nothing. I was about to tell her when she had to make a call. I don't know if I can do this, man," I tell him, and cradle my face with my hands.

"Then don't. You don't know if something is going to happen to her. You are just being paranoid. Don't end it because of that!" he tells me.

"I just don't want to hurt her, that's all." I stop talking as Missy comes into the room, dressed up.

"Babe, I'm sorry, but I have to go meet a new client." She leans down and kisses me.

"What, now? Why the urgency?" I ask her.

"I know it's bizarre, but I'll explain when I get home. My phone is dead so it's on the dresser charging, so you won't be able to get ahold of me. Love you!" And like that, she's out the door.

I look back at Mitch. "Good thing she loves her job, huh? Now, when's Isabella off work today?" I ask him as I get up and walk into the kitchen. He follows me.

"Oh, in about two hours. Talk about loving your job, she is in love with the coffee stand where she works. Not only does she drink free coffee all day, but I get them as well! She makes great tips, too, and it does help that she's a hottie. I think I did pretty well for myself."

"So things are going well for you two, huh? Are you going to pop the question?" I ask him as I grab a Gatorade from the fridge. He takes one, too.

"Um, not for a long time, I'm only twenty-one. We've talked about it before, and about having kids. It's on the plate, but right now, we are just enjoying the appetizers." He laughs as he opens his Gatorade. "What about you and Missy? Think you guys will have kids?"

"I haven't even thought about it, to tell you the truth. I'm surprised we've lasted through these past couple of years, with everything that's happened. She's a strong woman, and I am a very lucky guy to find someone. I still miss the hell out of Gwen, though, every day I do."

"I know what you mean, she was a cool woman. I can't believe how long it's been since her passing, though."

"It feels just like yesterday to me," I tell him, and gulp down my Gatorade.

"So, since Missy left, what do you want to do about dinner?" he asks me.

"I don't know. She can be gone for hours on things like this if someone wants to put in a bid today. Maybe we should plan it some other time."

"Well then, I will see you later." We fist pound again, but this time I grab him and give him a hug.

Hunter comes in. "Where you going, Uncle Mitch?" he asks.

"Home, buddy, now that your dad is back." He picks Hunter up and gives him a hug. "Thanks for being such a cool nephew!"

"You're welcome!" After Mitch puts him down, Hunter asks where Missy went.

"Oh, she had to go to work for a while, but she'll be back shortly."

An hour or so has passed, and Mitch and I continue to talk, not even looking at the clock.

"Oh shit, I have to go! I was supposed to meet Isabella at home twenty minutes ago, dude!" He gathers up his stuff and then opens the front door. "Hey, let me know when the best time is for you guys to meet up for dinner. Hey, Hunter, I'll see you soon!" He waves and shuts the door.

"See you soon?" I say to myself. "See you soon? Missy!" I call her cell phone and it starts to ring in the bedroom. "Fuck, I forgot she left it here!" I run into the bedroom and look through her contacts. I find Marla's number and call her.

"Hello?"

"Marla, this is Michael, Missy's boyfriend—I mean husband—I mean fiancé. Do you know where she went? I mean, she ran out of here a while ago to meet someone like it was an emergency, and I haven't heard from her. She left her phone here, so, do you know where she went?" I sound paranoid because I am paranoid.

"Oh, hello, Michael! I am a big fan of yours. So nice to speak to you finally!"

I interrupt her. "Marla, this—thank you, but I need to know where she is!"

"Oh, okay, let me look it up for you...it'll just be a moment...ah, here it is. This woman was very adamant about seeing Missy, and she needs a house today, that's what she said. It was a pretty sad story, though. Her husband was killed and now she has her twin boys to take care of all by herself. It was kind of heartbreaking—"

I interrupt her again. "Marla, I need the address of the house or houses they went to look at. Missy is in danger and I'm scared this woman will kill her. I'm not kidding, so please give me the fucking addresses, now!"

I write them down and yell at Hunter that we are leaving. We get into the car and speed off, leaving a cloud of smoke behind us.

"Wow, Daddy, that's cool!" Hunter says as he looks behind us.

"Okay, buddy, now listen to me. I will be driving pretty fast, and I need you to hold on and not talk, okay?"

He doesn't say anything. I look in the rearview mirror after I hear some clinking sounds.

"Hunter, what are you playing with?"

"Bullets, just like the ones the Easter Bunny wanted me to pick up, Daddy! Look!"

I look down to my left, where I can see his hand reaching to me; it's full of bullets.

"Where did you get those from?" I ask him as I swerve to the right.

"They were in this red heart box on the seat."

Oh shit! She is already here!

Chapter 20

"BUDDY, I NEED you to stay in the car, okay? I will be back in a few minutes, so just stay here, understood?"

"Why can't I go see Missy?"

"You will soon, but right now, please do as I say." I get out and lock the door behind me. I look around the neighborhood as I walk up to the house; Missy's car is in the driveway, but no other car is there. I walk up to the front door and ring the doorbell. I stand there for a minute or so, then ring it again—still no answer. I knock on the door and yell Missy's name—nothing. My heart is beating so fast, and I feel my hands stiffening up on me. "Oh Lord, please don't do this to me again."

I walk inside and I don't hear anything. "Missy, you in here, babe? It's Michael!" I call out, but no one answers me back. I look through the living room, still calling out her name. I look out the front window, where I can see my car and Hunter. I look back and continue through the house, opening the bathroom doors, then the bedroom ones—nothing. I walk down the hallway, still calling out,

"Missy, babe, are you here?" I look behind me again at my car; Hunter still safe inside. I turn around and I'm feet away from her body, lying on the ground in a pool of blood from a gunshot wound to the head.

"No! Missy!" I scream as I fall to the ground, feeling for her pulse. It's weak, but there is one. I grab my phone and call 911. Within minutes the ambulance is there. "Please clear the way, sir, we need to get her on the stretcher!" They have to pull me away, just as all my strength gives way to my heartbreak. I watch as they administer CPR and cover her mouth with an oxygen mask. All I can do is stand there and cry, until I remember Hunter. I run outside, praying he's in the car; he is, but starts crying when he sees the blood on my clothes.

"Daddy! Daddy! What's going on, Daddy? Blood!" He screams as I pick him up.

"It's okay, buddy, everything will be okay. Calm down." I stroke his hair as he lays his head on my shoulder. I don't realize he is facing the house until I hear him scream when he sees Missy on the stretcher.

"Mommy! What's happening to Mommy?" His cries would melt anyone's heart. I turn him away from seeing any of it only after it is too late. I tell Hunter that Missy was in an accident, and they are going to take her to the hospital and make her all better.

I call Mitch and tell him to meet me at the hospital. I jump in my car and follow the ambulance to Deaconess Medical Center. Mitch is only minutes behind me, and so are the cops. I grab Hunter out of the car and run inside to the ER. I watch as they lift her from the stretcher onto a bed. It seems like dozens of nurses are around her, all frantic and calling for a code red. They won't let me pass through; I have to sit and give my information to the lady at the desk. Sit and do this, are they kidding? The cops then come over and I give them my statement. As I pace the room, Hunter is freaking out. I pick him up and tell him everything will be all right.

Mitch comes rushing through the doors. "What the hell happened?" he asks me, but his question soon turns to an exclamation when he sees the blood on my shirt.

"Missy's been shot, Mitch, and they won't let me see her." I start to lose it, but I try to hold it together for the sake of my son. Mitch takes notice of this and asks Hunter if he wants to get some ice cream in the cafeteria. As soon as they leave my sight, I lose it. I fall to my knees and cover my face.

A nurse comes running over. "Sir, everything will be all right. Let's sit down over here and I'll get you some water." She brings me back a little paper cup and I can't even swallow it. My hands are now stiff as a board and my breathing is shallow. She calls another nurse over to help her put me in a wheelchair. They wheel me into a bay right next to Missy. I can see them working on her feverishly while blood drips from the table. I start to hyperventilate when I see the blood, so they try to sedate me. I am fighting off every person that comes near me. I have to see Missy, so I yell, "Missy! Missy, answer me! Missy, I love you, please answer me! No, you don't understand! We are supposed to get married! She's my life! Missy!" I scream at the top of my lungs. Four nurses, all men, have now surrounded me and belted me to the table. I feel the sharp pain go into my arm. "No, please, I have to see her! Don't let her die, please! Missy!" I scream, until the medicine makes its way through my veins, causing me to fall asleep.

I wake up dazed and confused, not even knowing what happened. As I look around the room, trying to figure out where the hell I am. Mitch comes in.

"Hey, you're up!"

"What happened, and where am I?" I lift my arm up to scratch my head, but soon realize I am in the hospital; the IVs give it away. "Mitch...Missy! Where is she? I need to see her!" I try to get out of bed, but my body won't let me.

"Hey, hey, you need to calm down, she's fine. You need to heal yourself before you can even see her, Michael."

"She's fine, really? Where is she? Take me to her, Mitch!" I try again to get up, but my body seems to hate me right now.

"I can't take you to see her, Michael, not yet."

"What aren't you telling me? I know something's wrong, so just tell me, damn it!" I yell quite loudly.

A nurse walks in the room. "Mr. Bali, I'm happy that you're awake, but you need to keep your voice down!" She patronizes me.

"Where's Missy? Where is she? Tell me now!"

"Missy who?"

"Are you fucking kidding me, woman? Missy who? Missy Allison, you dumb twit. Now, where is she?" I yell again.

"Michael! Knock it the fuck off! You don't yell at a woman like that! She wouldn't know where Missy is because she isn't here!" he tells me.

The nurse checks my IVs, says, "I'll be back in an hour or so," and leaves the room.

I look at him. "What do you mean, she's not here? I know she is, Mitch! I am the one who found her, shot, and called nine-one-one! What the fuck do you mean, she's not here?"

"Michael, nothing happened to her! You fell and hit your head after you got home from your trip. You've been in here for a couple days, bro! Nothing happened to anyone but you, you idiot!" He laughs.

"Wait, what are you talking about? I saw her bleeding from her head, and I had her blood all over my shirt. See?" I take the covers off me, but I am not wearing my shirt, only a gown. "Wait, where are my clothes?" I start to look around the room, but don't see them.

"I will ask the nurse what happened to them, but for now, calm the fuck down!"

I lie back down in my bed; my head starts to ache badly. I soon fall asleep to the sound of my own heartbeat. A few hours later, I am awakened by the nurse taking my temperature.

"It looks like you can go home today, Michael. I will let the doctor know and we'll get your discharge papers ready."

"Okay, thanks." I sit up with ease this time, no pain anywhere. I look outside and the sky is blue. The weather looks amazing, and now that I know I dreamed it all, I am one happy fool.

The doctor comes in with my discharge papers. "Good morning, Mr. Bali. You look a lot better, considering the last couple days," he tells me as he signs off on my papers.

"So there's no sign of damage or anything? I mean, I didn't have to have stitches, did I?" I ask him, feeling my scalp.

"Um...I'm not sure what you mean. You didn't hit your head, Mr. Bali. You were having an anxiety attack after you brought your fiancée to the ER. I am very sorry for your loss." He hands me the papers and starts to walk out.

"Wait a second! What do you mean, my loss?"

"Your fiancée, Ms. Allison, she passed away, Mr. Bali. I thought you knew that." He walks out of the room, leaving me there alone.

I immediately start crying. "What the fuck is going on? She died? She's not...oh my God!" I start pushing every button I can find on my bed; I even tear out my IVs. I fall to the ground, utterly devastated and wanting to die myself. "He told me I dreamt it! He told me she was fine! She's...gone." I sit on the floor, knees curled up to my chest, and I cry for what seems like hours.

Mitch comes in shortly after my meltdown. "How are you doing, Michael?" I don't answer him; I can't even look at him. "Hey, Michael...why don't you answer me? Look, I'm sorry I told you she was fine, but I know if I told you the truth you would've..." He stops talking.

I look at him. "You lied to me. You looked right at my face and lied to me! Why did you do that? Answer me, you coward!"

He looks right into my face and says, "Because if I told you that she had passed away, you would have killed yourself, that's why! You already lost Gwen, and now the only other woman you've ever loved is gone! What was I supposed to do? You are my brother and I love you! I am so sorry about Missy, but I did it for your own good! You have a son to raise, and I was scared you wouldn't have even thought about him if I told you the truth!" He starts to cry. "Please, Michael, I am so sorry for lying to you. Let's go home." He helps me get dressed and then we leave the hospital.

"I can't believe she's gone. I...how am I going to tell Hunter?" By now, we are both crying.

"I already did, Michael. He knew; he was there. He's been with me and Isabella since this all happened. He's become so attached to her that it may be hard for him to want to come back home." He opens the car door for me to get in.

"Wait, where's my car?" I ask him before I get in.

"It's at my house. Come on, get in."

I sit down and lean my head back on the headrest. "Did they catch her yet?" I ask him.

"Catch who?"

"Lena. She did this, you know," I tell him.

"No one knows for sure, Michael."

"Oh, bullshit, Mitch! I know she did it, and I will find her and kill her myself!"

"Take it easy, Michael! You just got out of the hospital. Do you want to go back in again?"

I just look out the window as we drive home; I begin to cry, and don't stop until we pull in the driveway.

"Hunter is still at my house. Did you want me to go get him?" he asks me.

"Only if he wants to come home. I won't make him until he's ready, but like you said, he may not want to come home."

I go inside alone; the house feels different and quiet. I walk into our room; her clothes are still on the bed, waiting to be put away from our trip. I sit down on the bed and just sob and sob. I pick up her sweater; her perfume wafts over me. I put the sweater up to my face and breathe it in.

"How did this happen, God? Why does this keep happening to me? Please, no more death." I look around the room at the things she had brought from her house. I remember how hard it was for me to get rid of Gwen's stuff; I ended up leaving it right where it was for three years. I'm not going to do that again. I start taking all of Missy's personal belongings and put them in boxes. I go through the entire house and pack up her things, leaving nothing behind. When I walk into Hunter's room, I'm not sure if taking the stuff she gave him is a good idea, but I know leaving it all wouldn't be, either. Instead, I leave just one item that she gave him, a stuffed koala bear named Floyd. I take the boxes and put them in the garage. Just as I was walking back inside, Mitch and Hunter come driving up. Hunter runs from the car and into my arms.

"Oh, Daddy!" He starts to cry, which makes me cry again. Mitch just waves and drives away. I carry Hunter inside and sit him down on the kitchen table.

"Do you want some juice, buddy?" I ask him as I wipe his tears away. He nods his head yes.

"Why do people keep dying, Daddy? I don't like it."

I turn around and give him his juice. "You know, that is a really good question, but something I can't even answer. I don't know why, buddy, I really don't. I love you so much! We just need to stick together, you and me!" I give him a hug, then lift him off the table and gently set him on his feet. As he runs off to his room, the phone rings.

"Hello?"

"See what happens? You took someone from me, now I've taken someone from you."

"Lena, is that you?" She hangs up.

I look at the phone number, but it was blocked. Now I know it was her for sure. That eerie voice will be forever embedded in my mind as the demon's wife. I told the cops who I thought it was, so I hope they follow up on it.

After I put Hunter to bed, I start to think about the curse. As I watch him sleep, I beg God for forgiveness and pray for his help in our healing. I decide to look further into this curse than I had originally. I turn on the computer, and for the next ten hours I am reading everything I can find about my family. I don't notice what time it is until the sun illuminates my room. I look at the clock and it's already time for Hunter to get up for school. I wake him up and help him get ready, then drive him to school. I go back home, tired but determined to fight this curse for all I'm worth. If I can find a way to end it, then Hunter won't have to go through this, and perhaps his life will be worth living. I read and read and read about gypsy curses, but nothing's coming up on how to end this specific one. I quit for a while and take a shower, allowing the water the wash my sadness and pain away. I get some food and then take a little nap, which turns into a four-hour one, but I need it. Mitch calls to see how I am coping, so I tell him my plan about finding a way to end the curse. He doesn't say much.

"I don't think you can end it, Michael. I mean, think about it—if there was a way, wouldn't someone in the family have figured it out a long time ago?" he asks me.

"I don't know, Mitch, maybe no one even checked. Maybe they thought this was it, or maybe they didn't even know about it. Hell, we would have never known if Dad hadn't come to Jesus that day!" We hang up and I go back to my research. Damn, I'm tired.

Chapter 21

I HAVE TO GIVE props to Missy's sisters. The funeral is absolutely beautiful and brimming with flowers galore. It is a hard day, but saying good-bye is the healthiest thing I can do for myself. Everyone is very nice, with words of support for me and Hunter. Of course, I am asked numerous times if her killer has been found, and I want to shout *Lena Lavetti* from the rooftops, but I can't, so "Nope" is all they get.

After the wake, Missy's sister, Monique, comes over and hands me something. It is Missy's engagement ring. "I think you should have this back. It won't do any good buried in the ground, and it surely can't make my sister any prettier than she already is, even in death. Please take it, Michael. She loved you so much."

I look down at the ring and start crying once again, but this time I am in good company—no, great company. I walk away from the wake a different man. I don't know how, but I have changed. Maybe it is the grieving family members, or the fact that I have to say good-bye to the only other woman I loved. But whatever it is, I feel a debt to my son, and vow to keep him safe for the rest of his life.

When I arrive home, I have a message on the machine from Mitch, telling me his third book has been published and to call him immediately because the news is not good.

"Hey, what's going on?" I ask him.

"Michael, I don't know how to tell you this, but it's not good at all. In fact, it's disturbing, to say the least."

"Okay, well, tell me. Nothing happens to Hunter, does it?" My heart is in my throat.

"No...not him...you."

I don't say anything; I just sit down on a chair, almost missing it. "What, Mitch? What happens to me?"

"You die, Michael. You kill yourself."

You could hear a pin drop between both phones.

"What do you mean, Mitch? There's no way I could—"

He cuts me off. "It's written in the book, Michael, it does happen." I hear his words being smothered by tears.

"When?"

"It doesn't say, Michael. Brother, I don't want this to happen! I don't want this life anymore! We need to stop it. We can do that, right? I mean, you've been reading about it and shit! Tell me you've found the answer. Tell me this isn't going to happen to you!" He starts crying.

The only thing I can tell him is the truth. "Mitch, I haven't found anything to stop it from happening. What I need to do is to update my will, making you Hunter's legal guardian if something—when something happens to me. Will you do that for me, Mitch?" I sound unbelievably calm right now, and oddly enough, I am.

"What are you saying? You're just going to give in to this? That's not the brother I know!"

"Maybe it's time for me to be a new brother, and give in to fate and stop trying to fight it. I love you, brother. I will call you soon." I hang up the phone before he can argue with me. My heart was once filled with anger and resentment toward my father; that has now lifted. I decide to call him and apologize.

"Hey, Dad, it's Michael."

"Michael...good to hear from you." His voice is quiet.

"I need to say something to you before it's too late, Dad. I'm sorry for everything I've said, and for kicking you out of my life. It was wrong of me, and I am asking for your forgiveness."

"I am sorry, Michael, for saying the horrible things I told you. I should have never told you about the books. That letter was wrong of me, and by telling you the truth, although it still being the truth, it led to...this, and I wish I could take it all back."

"Dad, I need to know if you ever read anything about our family, and possibly found something that curtails the curse in any way. I really need your help with this one, Dad."

"What's the matter, son? You aren't telling me something."

"Dad, I just need to know."

"No, son, I haven't found anything about it. Your grandfather wouldn't tell me anything, either. Please tell me what's going on. I want to help if I can." His voice starts to break.

"Dad, trust me, it's all on me this time. But I love you and I will call you soon, okay?"

That next day I meet with an attorney to change my will, making my brother not only Hunter's guardian but the executor of my will. I ask him to meet me at Chap's to sign the papers.

"Michael, this says I get everything, and when Hunter turns twenty-one, he inherits a lot of money. Why are you doing this?"

"You know why, I have to. I have to protect my son, and I trust you more than myself right now. Does the book say how I do it?"

Mitch just looks at me. "Are you kidding me with this? No, Michael, it doesn't. Now, please, let's try and think of a way out of this. We can stop it, I know we can!"

I just smile at him, knowing we can't. "Let's just enjoy our oatmeal, okay?"

Since there is no way of knowing when this will happen, I decide to live my life in the fast lane. I take skydiving lessons, I zip-line 150 feet in the air, and I even get a few tattoos. Strangely enough, a few years pass without anything happening. Hunter is approaching sixteen and still there is no sign of Lena anywhere. Maybe she kicked the bucket? One can hope. I start to believe the curse isn't going to happen, considering how much time has passed. My father has been here visiting a few times and we've become close once again. He and Hunter have taken a few camping trips, including one to Australia. "What better way to get to know the outback than to actually be there!" That's what he says, at least. I have been on a couple dates, but I refuse to get involved with anyone else. My life is great, even without the accompaniment of a woman. I have a lot of friends and that's all a man needs—well, that and porn.

One day I am looking on the computer when a pop-up shows up. This one asks if I want to rid myself of a curse. "Hmm...how convenient would that be?" I laugh it off and click out of it, but it shows up again, this time announcing with a guarantee and my name:

Michael...if you wish to end this curse with your family, click here and I can tell you how!

"What the fuck is this?" I ask myself, but I still click out of it. "Yep, that's all I need is a virus to wipe out everything! What dipshits!" I continue on my search for Nile River cruises, but it pops up again. This time it freaks me out:

This is your last chance to stop it from continuing on to your son! Click here, Michael; it can end if you just click here.

"Fuck it." I click it, and up pops this ugly old woman in a purple scarf and gold jewelry. Below her is the text that stops my heart from beating:

Congratulations, Michael, for being the first one to get this far. This curse placed on your family is generations long, and you have the opportunity to end it once and for all! Here's the secret that you've been searching for, Michael.

The love you have for your son will be what stops this curse. End your life before the eve of his sixteenth birthday and the curse will not continue on, but if you don't, the curse will start for your son with his first "book." It's your choice, Michael…will you live or die for your son? Heed the warning of a new life before your time's done, for the curse shall continue through the eyes of a newborn son.

I sit there, staring at the screen, staring at the words in front of me. "This is what Mitch was telling me. I do kill myself for my son."

I push myself away from my desk, not really knowing what to think. I start to feel that puke coming up, so I run to the bathroom and throw up everything I have eaten for what seems like this last year. I lie down on the cold floor and start to cry. Memories of Hunter flood my mind, and I think of what I won't see when he's a grown man. I pick myself up off the floor and walk into the kitchen. I decide not to tell anyone about this. It would be like watching paint dry, waiting and wondering if today's the day. I know I will tell Mitch later; I will leave a note for him, explaining why I did it. I know he will understand, and I can only hope Hunter will forgive me. Just then, I hear the front door open.

"Hey, Pop! What's shaking?" Hunter comes in and hugs me. He's still a hugger.

"Oh, just…you know…not much. Why are you so happy?" I ask him as I grab a Gatorade from the fridge.

"Well, Dad, I've decided what I want for my birthday! It's coming up, you know—the big one-six!" He also takes a Gatorade from the fridge.

I start to feel dizzy, then nearly collapse, but he drops his drink in time to catch me. "Hey, Dad, you okay?" He helps me to the table.

I sit there, trying to get myself to see straight. My stomach is churning and I'm on the verge of a complete meltdown.

"Dad, you okay? Should I call the doctor?" He sits down next to me. I look up at his beautiful face, his curly brown hair and bright green eyes.

"No, son, I'm okay. I haven't eaten yet today, that's all." I take a sip of my Gatorade as I watch him move about the room. God, I'm going to miss him.

"Okay, so, what I was thinking for my birthday is a private party at the Airsoft place, you know, the one we went to a couple months ago? I think it would be so cool to have, like, twenty guys come for an airsoft fight. What do you think, Dad?"

My mind and my heart are in the same place, so I don't even hear him. "What, son? I'm sorry, I wasn't listening."

"Dad, are you sure you're okay? You don't look well. We can talk about this another time, but not too far off, since my birthday is next month! Can I make you something to eat?" He rubs my back.

"No...no, buddy, I'm fine. I think I'll just go lie down for a while, okay? Make sure you do your homework!" I tell him the same thing every night.

"Dad, it's Saturday," he tells me. "Are you going to bed already? It's only six, Dad, and you're still young. You're not dead!"

"Oh…okay. Well, make sure you get it done, then." I go into my room and shut the door behind me. I lean against it, slide down to the ground, and cry uncontrollably but quietly; I don't want Hunter to hear me. Truth is, I'm already dead. I look at the calendar and realize I have only a few weeks left with him. I crawl into bed. I can't stop crying.

Chapter 22

HE NEXT MORNING brings me pain…nothing but an intolerable pain that has stricken my heart. I lie in bed looking up at the ceiling. My eyes are still swollen from the night's weeping, and I don't feel anything but agony.

Hunter knocks on my door. "Dad, you up?" he asks.

"Yeah, son, come on in." I start to wipe my eyes quickly. He walks in the door dressed in his soccer gear.

"I have a game this morning, and I was hoping you could come to this one." He sits down next to me on the bed.

"I wouldn't miss it for the world, buddy! Can I drive you there?" I get up quickly and run into my bathroom.

"Oh, no…the coach likes everyone to ride on the bus together, but you can take me home afterward." He gets up and stands in the doorway to the bathroom. "Pop? You've been crying all night, haven't you? Don't lie to me because I can tell. Trust me, I've done enough of that myself these last few years."

I look back at him and his face is so sad. I go to him and wrap my arms around him; I never want to let him go, but soon I will have to.

"I've just been thinking about our time together, and it makes me sad that you're turning into a young man. You're not my little buddy anymore, and it's starting to kill me a little bit." I let go and he looks at me.

"Dad, no matter what, I will always be your little buddy." He smiles at me and then sticks his tongue out. "I love you, Dad, forever." He hugs me again, then yells as he leaves the house, "The game starts in an hour! Mitch and Isabella will be there, too! See ya!"

I hold my hand up, waving good-bye, even though he's already gone...already a man. I look back at the mirror; my reflection is not what it used to be. Age has shown up, and it's decided to walk across my face using a pitchfork as its feet. I'm glad I took Hunter in for his first surgery when he was twelve. His eye no longer droops, and they really smoothed out his skin. His second surgery was just last year; his face looks practically normal now. Either way, he's the most beautiful person in the world to me. Now that I know my time with him is limited, I need to be there for him every second I can.

I drive to his game and sit next to Mitch and his wife, Isabella. They married about six years ago, but so far, no children. The doctors say it doesn't look good for natural conception, and for them to look into adoption or surrogacy. I now have to thank God for little things like this because, according to the curse, if she gets pregnant naturally before my life ends, then the curse lives on and

I will have killed myself for nothing. How many people can say that in a lifetime?

"Hey, Michael, it's so good to see you!" Isabella leans over and kisses my cheek.

Mitch just slugs me in the arm. "So, have you thought of the big *par-tay* for Hunter yet?" Mitch asks me.

"Oh, he...um...said something about guns or something. I have to check with him again. Honestly, I'm not looking forward to that day at all."

"Oh, I bet, Michael! It's probably the hardest thing for any parent to watch his kids grow up and become these wonderful adults. He is a great kid, you did well. I know his mom would have been proud of both of you!" Isabella pats my leg and smiles.

If only they knew what I meant.

After the game, Hunter and I drive home together. Actually, I let him drive me home.

"So how do you like driving this?" I ask him.

"Oh, it's great, but I feel like an old person, though. Don't get me wrong, Dad, it's a cool car—but, you know, it's a grocery getter." He laughs.

"A grocery getter? Well, I was going to give it to you for your birthday, but I wouldn't want you to feel old or anything."

"Are you kidding me, Dad? That's awesome!" He starts to yell and throw his hands in the air, hootin' and hollerin'.

"Hands on the wheel, Mario! I said I was going to give it to you, but I'm not going to anymore. Turn left here."

"Where are we going, and why can't I have this car?"

"Because you already said you felt old driving it—make another left at the light—and I know how image is everything to teenagers nowadays! Make a right."

"Dad, when have I ever been like that?"

"Turn in here," I tell him.

His eyes light up when he sees where we are. "Um…Dad…what are we doing here? You really are giving me this and you're going to get a new car, huh? Yes! Woo-hoo!" He jumps out of the car and starts to look around the lot. "Hey, Dad, how about that one over there? You like red, right?" He points to a Mustang.

Oh, Mustangs…how I remember you…fucking Marty asshole dickwad!

"No, son, I'm not getting a new car, you are."

He looks at me with the biggest eyes you could ever see. "What, Dad? I am getting a car?"

My heart is so heavy right now that tears have made their way to my eyes once again. "Yep…I mean it, buddy."

He starts jumping up and down and screaming so loud, I started to get embarrassed, but only for a nanosecond. Right now I am enjoying the last days of being a dad. I watch him look at every car on the lot; he actually starts to skip, but then soon realizes he is skipping, so he quickly makes the transition to a short sprint. I watched his precious face light up when he asks the salesman questions about a car. I stand there, with my arms crossed, leaning on the side of my car and watching my little boy…grow into someone I will never get to know as a man. I am so proud to know the man he is right now, right at this moment. I have to choke back the tears when he looks over at me and smiles; my son, my little buddy.

"I will always love you, Hunter," I whisper out loud.

Hunter comes running over. "Dad, I found the car I want, but it's in the back so you have to come with me." I follow him behind the building, where they house the older-model cars. I look around at the heaps of metal crap that have price tags on them and I start to laugh. I am immediately taken back to my own 1979 Ford Fiesta and how proud I was of that car. Hunter is about ten yards ahead of me. "Dad, it's right here!" I catch up with him and he is pointing to a dark green Ford truck. I just stare at it like I'm looking at the demon himself. It's the Lavettis' truck.

"This one, Hunter? Are you kidding me? You can't have this one," I tell him.

His smile leaves his face and he asks me why.

"I can't tell you why, but not this one, okay! Let's look around some more." As I start to walk away, the sales guy stops me.

"This truck may look old, but we checked it out. It's a beauty on the inside, too, so if you are worried about safety, don't be."

"We aren't getting that truck"—I look at his nametag— "Todd, so how about showing us something else? Perhaps a newer truck, if that's what he wants," I tell him, and start to walk away again.

Hunter comes running up to me this time. "Hey, Pop, what's wrong with this truck?" He stops me with his hand on my arm.

"Hunter, will you just trust me on this one, please? If you want a truck, then we can look at some others, okay?"

His face starts to take on the look of a sad, sad dog. "Okay, Dad, whatever you say. I'll get what you want me to get, it's no problem. Thanks for getting me a car, Dad." He hugs me, then starts to walk away.

"Wait." My heartstrings are being tugged on right now. "If you want that truck, then let's get it. If you really want that one instead of a new one, like that yellow one over there, then we'll get it. I love you and it's your birthday, so...I love you."

His face once again lights up, and he runs over to me and picks me up in a giant bear hug. "Dad, you are the greatest dad that ever walked this planet! I love this guy!" he yells at the top of his lungs. Then he runs back to the green truck. I can't believe this is happening.

"So, where did this truck come from, Todd?" I start to grill him.

"Well, we just got it in last week from a lady who needed a smaller car instead, so I don't know the history on it." He takes out the papers from the glove compartment. "Looks like the last owner was from Maryland. Long way from home."

"Hey, that's where we are from!" Hunter says. My heart sinks even deeper knowing she's still alive.

I ask Mitch to come down and drive the truck home, since Hunter can't drive alone yet. I let the boys go ahead of me while I stay behind to talk to Todd.

"Can you tell me anything about the woman who brought this truck in?"

"Like, what are you looking for?" he asks me.

"Well…um…did she have anyone with her, or was she alone? Did she look sick, or possibly on her deathbed?"

Todd looks at me as if I am screwing with him. "Ha! That's very funny, man, and you got me!" He continues his faux laugh.

"I'm not kidding, actually. I think I know this woman, and I just want to be sure it's her,"

"I wasn't here when she brought it in. Sorry, man." He walks off.

I stand there, looking around the place for someone else who could have been here at that time. I can hear some guys in the garage, so I go in there. I know they did some work on it, maybe they saw her.

"Excuse me? Hey, man…I was hoping you could help me with something."

This old guy walks up to me, dirty as all get-out, and says, "Yeah."

"Um, I just bought the dark green Ford truck you had back here, and I was wondering…were you here when it came in?"

"No, but I know the guy who was, lemme get him for ya." He goes into the break room. A minute later he returns, followed by a young man.

"Can I help you?"

"Yeah, were you here when that dark green Ford truck came in? I just bought it, and I wanted to know a few things about the owner." Now, what he tells me next about kills me.

"Yeah, you're looking at him. My name is Andy. My mom and I brought it in last week. What did you want to know?"

I am looking directly at the bloodline of a killer. I freeze.

"Sir? You wanted to know stuff?" he asks me.

"Uh...I'm..." I don't even know what to say. He doesn't recognize me, but the last thing I want to do is say my name, just in case. "Um...I wanted to know if...you had... any...cats?"

He looks at me strangely. "No, sir, no cats. Was that all you wanted to know?"

"Yep. Thanks, Andy, for your help."

I turn and walk away quickly. I can't get out of there fast enough. I jump into my car and take off. I don't look back. "Fuck me! She's still here! Fuck!" I yell at the top of my lungs. I pull into a parking lot and try to calm myself down. My hands are starting to freeze up, and it's getting harder to breathe. I look in my glove compartment and grab my pills. Thank God for spit or I'd be screwed. I lean back and wait for the pills to take effect. "I can't believe I bought Hunter that truck! Oh God, it's still happening." I stay in that lot for another hour before heading home.

"Dad, I love that truck so much, thank you!" He runs and hugs me, just like he did when he was six years old.

"You are welcome, but you can't drive it until you get your license, so don't even try. Got it?"

"I know. Thanks again, Dad. You are the best! Now I'm going to call everyone I know!" He runs into his room and

I don't see him for another hour or so. He emerges with the biggest smile on his face. "Well, Dad, it's happened."

The first thought in my head is, *Oh shit...the Lavettis? Did you kill someone? Did you get a strange book sent to you?*

"What?" I ask him very nonchalantly.

"I'm in love...and it's great." He falls down on the sofa.

I smile at him, remembering what that feels like. "What's her name?" I ask him.

"Dad, you won't believe this, but her name is Gwendolyn and she goes by Gwen. How strange is that?" He looks at me with the "I'm so happy I could bust" look.

I want to throw up. "That is weird, but kinda cool, you know? I know your mom would have wanted you to find someone just like her. She was perfect, you know... completely." A sadness overwhelms me and I start to tear up, but quickly wipe them away before he notices. This is getting harder and harder each day for me, one day closer to... "So, do you guys go to school together?" I have to get a grip.

"No, she goes to a private school. I met her during one of my practices at the school. She was hanging out with her friends, and Dad, it was love at first sight! She's so pretty. I can't stop thinking about her."

"Well, it's Saturday night, you guys going out?"

"Yeah, if that's all right with you. She'll pick me up around seven."

"She'll pick you up? How old is she?"

"Oh, Dad, she's only seventeen. Yep...found me an ole woman just like you wanted me to, Pa!" He starts in with his southern accent.

"Well, jeehoeseefat! That's mighty good of ya, son! Make sure she's got thems breedin' hips and her own teeth!" I stand up and do a jig, which makes Hunter bust a gut.

"Dad, you're crazy, and I love that about you! I can't wait for us to grow old and look back at things like this. Too funny. Well, I have to jump in the shower. Gotta smell purty fer the ole gal!" He hops up and runs to his room.

"My little buddy." Pretty soon, choking back my tears won't matter anymore. God, protect him.

Chapter 23

Brother,

Well…what can I say to you…I love you, and I couldn't have asked for a better brother than you. Remember when you asked me if there was something we could do to stop the curse from happening? Well, I found it, and it turns out your book was right; my life had to end before another one started in our bloodline. I stopped it from happening, Mitch. I stopped it from continuing on. Now you and Isabella can have children, God willing, and not have to worry about this being inflicted upon them, or Hunter; he shall have a glorious life, too. I didn't kill myself because the world wanted me to; I did it because I love you and Hunter more than myself. That's what it took, a completely selfless act of love so the bloodline could continue without any further complications or death.

Take care of my son, take care of yourself, and take care of your future children.
Michael

Mitch walks into the room where Hunter sits, alone. He sits down next to him and asks, "You okay?"

Hunter shakes his head no. "I had to bury my dad today, Mitch. I'm not okay."

"I know, stupid question. Your dad left you this." He hands Hunter the envelope containing the letter.

Hunter looks at him. "Where did you get this?"

"They were mailed to me, Hunter. They are dated the day before your birthday. I got one, too." He gets up and leaves Hunter to read his letter by himself.

Hunter takes the letter and just stares at it; he doesn't want to open it. The sweat from his hands moistens the envelope, causing it to open. His tear-stained face looks down. He inhales a deep breath and takes out the letter:

My little buddy,
With a heavy heart I am writing this letter to you, hoping you will understand and one day forgive me for what I am about to tell you. Please believe what you are about to read, it is quite true. I love you, Hunter, more than my own life.
It all happened many years ago, when your great-great-great-grandfather fell in love with a young girl who was of gypsy origin. They

eloped, causing a great heartache for her family and, in turn, a great hatred for our family. A curse was placed on our bloodline and has been there ever since, until now. Every man born with Davis O'Malley's blood in him had a curse placed upon him from birth; this included me, your uncle, and you. Three abominations were placed on all of us:

1) Their fortune generated only by the deaths of others,
2) Bear the shame on their face, and
3) Shall live by verse alone for three moons.

I know this must sound crazy to you, but it's true. I wish it wasn't. I've done a lot of things in my past that I'm not proud of, and if I could take it all back, I would in a heartbeat. I've killed people and made money from it. I wasn't a paid killer by any means, but I did take people's lives, and reaped the rewards that came from it in the form of book sales—three, to be exact. We were born with faces like ours for a reason: to show the shame and guilt our family has bestowed upon us. So never believe, as I did, that God hated you. The gypsies hated us for a very long time. This curse had been on us since 1802, and I was finally given the blessed opportunity to stop it from continuing on to you and to Mitch's children. This is why I am not

with you any longer. It took a selfless act to stop the curse. I had to love something more than myself...and that was evident the day you were born. You are the one thing I did right, and I thank you for being my son. Mitch will be taking care of you now, Hunter, and I know he will do a great job. I am sorry to leave you the way I did, but...I loved you too much not to. I love you to the moon and back, my little buddy.
    Daddy

"Oh, Daddy! Oh my God!" Hunter falls to the ground, clutching his letter and sobbing uncontrollably, still loving his father just as much. There's a knock at his door, but he doesn't respond. The sound of it opening makes him sit up and see who's standing there.

"Hi, Hunter, is it okay if I come in?" Walter asks.

"Hi, Grandpa," he responds.

Walter walks over and sits on the bed. Hunter gets up and sits next to him, leans on his grandpa's shoulder, and continues to cry. Walter wraps his arms around Hunter and holds him until the tears dry up, somewhat.

"I can't imagine what you are feeling right now, but you need to know how much your dad loved you, Hunter. I am so sorry." He then sees the letter in Hunter's hands. "What's that?"

Hunter looks up to see what he's talking about. "Oh... um, it's from my dad. He wrote letters to me and Mitch about why he did what he did."

"Is it okay if I read it?" Walter asks him.

Hunter hands him the letter. Walter stands up and begins to read it.

A few minutes later he responds, "What is this? I don't understand what he's saying." He looks over at Hunter.

Hunter shrugs his shoulders. "The curse, Grandpa. I know you know about it."

"Of course I do, but…I'm…how did he figure out how to stop it?"

He shakes his head. "I don't know. I didn't even know about the curse until this letter. Why didn't you tell me? If you knew about this, and you knew it would be passed on to me, why didn't you tell me? My dad died because of you!" he yells, and storms out of the room.

Walter follows. "Hunter, it's not like that! Please don't walk away from me!"

Hunter stops and turns back to him. He just stares, tears flowing down his cheeks. Walter walks closer to him, but Hunter puts his hand up.

"Just stop right there! Let me ask you this, Grandpa. Do you know what it feels like to see your father hanging from the closet? Have you even the slightest notion of how unprepared a person could be to see that, especially if it's someone you idolize? I loved my dad so much and he's dead! I found him hanging there with a belt around his neck, Grandpa! I cut him down. I tried CPR, but he was dead. I will never forget that—ever. Do you realize I am an orphan now?" He wipes away the tears from his face and then looks out the window. "I had the greatest dad in the world, who loved me so much that all he cared about was making sure I would have a good life." He looks back at Walter. "Now, how can that happen if he's not in it anymore?"

Walter walks closer to him, slowly, making sure Hunter doesn't run away like a scared deer. He puts his hand on Hunter's shoulder and takes a deep breath.

"Hunter…there are no words that I can say to you right now that would take any of the pain away, and if there were, I would be the first one to say them. When you get to be my age, you tend to start looking back on your life and wishing you could make some things disappear by changing the way you live your life today. Trust me when I say to you that never in my wildest dreams would I have given this curse to someone that I loved on purpose. I really thought it wouldn't continue on to your dad if I wasn't around him. I know that sounds stupid, but that was my thinking back then. I was so ashamed of the things I had done that I figured God would forgive me, and somehow take the curse off if I left your dad to grow up without me—a piece-of-shit father myself. His mom, your grandmother, was a really nice person. She was kind and very forgiving; something I thought would rescue him from my fate."

"Rescue him? Do you really think I believe you, Grandpa?" Hunter huffs back.

"Yes, I do."

"Why? Why should I believe a drunk like you? That's all you ever cared about—booze! My dad told me all about you, and how you used to beat the shit out of Grandma. Now the words coming out of your mouth are of forgiveness and love? Tell me something, Grandpa, did you ever once look for a way out of the curse? Did you ever look into the past and try to figure out something you could have done to save your son from it? You know what? You don't even need to answer that because I already know the answer!"

"Wait just a minute!" Walter begins, but Hunter interrupts.

"NO! You wait for once, old man! There was a way out of it, and my father figured it out because he loved me enough to do that! So the answer to the question is a flat-out no! You never looked into it because you said it yourself; you just hoped it would go away with your abandonment of my father and grandmother! I hope when I have children I will love them as much as my dad loved me and not as little as you loved him. I buried my father today, and it sickens me to death knowing his killer stood right next to me and now stands in my home. Get ready to know what abandonment really feels like—Walter."

He storms out of the house, slamming the door behind him. Walter just stands there, alone.

Chapter 24

"**D**O YOU THINK we should start counseling with Hunter soon? I mean, he seems to be doing well, but, you know, losing his dad...I don't know if he's really okay." Isabella sounds concerned.

"I've been thinking that exact same thing lately. He hasn't really wanted to say much after his blowup with my dad, but...I don't want to push him, either. Sometimes kids need time to adjust, more than what we think they need," Mitch explains.

"Hey, what was the blowup about, anyway? You never did tell me why he's so mad at your dad."

"Oh, who knows—he was mad at the world that day, and my dad was the lucky recipient. Just think, Isabella one day we will become the lucky ones to get yelled at, too!" He smiles.

"You are right. It's just hard being a parent for the first time—to a teenager."

"Don't think of yourself as his parent but as his sister. That might make it easier on you. Plus, I don't think he even wants you as a mom."

"Oh, jeez, thanks for your kind words, ass munch!"

"No, I meant—hey, wait! Ass munch? Is that what you called me?"

"Yep. Need me to spell it for you, too?"

"You know, it's a good thing my dad is on his way over here to protect you from an ass whoopin'!"

Isabella rolls her eyes as Mitch playfully mimes his ass whoopin' to her.

A few minutes later, Walter arrives at the house.

"Hey, Dad," Mitch says as he hugs him.

"Hey, Mitch, how's it going?" Walter hugs him back, then he looks up and sees Isabella. "Hey, beautiful girl! How are you?" He goes over and hugs her.

"Oh, I'm doing just great, Walter. Where's Winnie?" She looks behind him.

"Oh, she's not feeling well so she's at home—a cold, I guess." Walter looks around the house. "You sure you want me here?"

"Dad, it's fine. Hunter is at school, so don't worry about it. He will come around, just give him time," Mitch explains.

"Coffee?" Isabella asks.

"Sounds great. With cream, please." Walter excuses himself to use the bathroom.

"I wish I didn't have to go to work. Your dad just got here." Isabella pours the coffee into two mugs.

"I know, but he'll come by again. Plus, this will give him and me a chance to talk about stuff," he explains. Little does she know he will be asking a shit load of questions about this curse.

When his dad emerges from the bathroom, Bella hands him his coffee, then says her good-byes. After she leaves, they both sit down in the living room. His dad looks very uneasy right about now.

"I can only imagine what you want to talk about, Mitch."

"I have some questions for you, Dad...about the curse."

Walter starts to shift his body on the couch, since he wears his emotions on his sleeve lately. "Mitch, I don't know much, but I will answer what I know."

"Good enough, then...tell me what you know." He takes a drink of his coffee while he stares at his dad.

"Well, first of all, no one in my family has ever admitted to this curse happening to them. This was all my imagination—at least that's what I was told, after your brother told me about the books showing up on his computer. I had asked my great-aunt and my cousins if they knew anything at all, and they all said no, and that I was just as crazy as my old man. What I looked up and found was dated all the way back to 1802. Your great-great-great-grandfather, Davis O'Malley, married a gypsy gal named Simza. Her family placed the curse on our family, and it's been there ever since. I looked deeper into it, but I couldn't find much else. Then again, I'm on dial-up. I think it would be wise of you to find out as much as you can about this and share it with Hunter. I know he doesn't want to see me, so I won't make him. After I read Michael's letter to Hunter, I was shocked that he had found out how to stop it. I couldn't find anything when I went looking, and now my son is in the ground. Mitch, if I had known how to stop it, I would've done the same thing. You believe me, right?"

Mitch looks at his dad. "Yes, I believe you, but that's because I grew up with you. Michael didn't, so of course Hunter won't believe you. I'm hoping I can help change that in the next few months. He needs his grandpa in his life, whether he believes that or not."

"Your brother did the most selfless act known to man, Mitch. I miss him so much, but I am just as grateful to him for stopping the curse." Walter drinks the rest of his coffee, then stands up to leave. "Thanks for having me over, son. I miss you, and your mom does, too." They hug, and he heads for the door, Mitch in tow. As Walter walks across the street to his car, he turns around and says, "You make me so proud, Mitch, and one day soon, you will make a great dad yourself!"

When he turns back around, a car comes barreling down the road at fifty miles per hour and hits him. His body is thrown into the air and he lands on his head, crushing his skull. He is pronounced dead at the scene. The driver is arrested and later booked on vehicular manslaughter. His blood alcohol level is four times the legal limit. He is only seventeen.

A couple months go by and Hunter goes back to school, somber yet playful. He carries a deep guilt with him, knowing the last words he said to his grandpa were of hatred, and he is full of regret. His new girlfriend, though, has helped him through these tough few months. He knows he has to thank her for sticking by him, so he chooses the biggest football game of the season to show her off. This game will decide who goes to state, and he is pulling out all the stops for his date with Gwen. He plans to have a dozen roses sitting on her seat when he picks her up. He will have her favorite coffee in the cup holder, along with a bag of M&M's, also her favorite. Later that night he will give her a gold bracelet with her initials on it. He pulls up in his new truck and the girls go wild, until they see *her* in the front seat. He jumps out and runs to the other side, opening the door for Gwen. He puts his arm around her, and together they go watch the football game, the Indians versus the Panthers.

"Did you want something to drink, Gwen?" he asks politely. "They have a soda machine over here."

"Yeah, um…Sprite, please," Gwen says with a beautiful smile.

"Your wish is my command, my lady." He jumps off the bleachers and walks over to the machine, where a few kids from the opposing school are standing.

"Sweet ride, man, cool truck!" one says to Hunter.

"Oh, thanks, my dad gave it to me for my birthday."

"Man, cool dad! I think I met him before."

"How would you know who he is?"

"He was at the car lot. I was the one who told him about the truck, since it was my mom's. Hi, my name is Andy, and this is my brother, Luke."

"Your mom owned it? So, are you guys from Baltimore, too?" Hunter asks as he puts the money in the machine.

"Yeah, we are. How did you know that?" Luke asks.

Hunter reaches down and grabs his soda from the slot. "Well, that's where the title came from, so I was just asking. That's where I am from. Small world, huh? When did you move here?"

"A while ago…we were only, like, three or something, so I don't remember much."

"I was about three when we moved here, too. How weird is that?"

"If you ever have trouble with the truck, I can help fix it," Andy offers. "I've been under that hood my entire life."

"Thanks, man, I appreciate that. Well, I have to get back to my date, so you guys take it easy!" Hunter walks off, not even knowing who he just met.

About an hour into the game, Mitch calls Hunter. "Hey, how's the game going?" Mitch asks.

"Um…Uncle Mitch, why are you calling me? This is kinda weird, you know, considering I'm on a date!"

"Oh, I know that, Rico Suave. I just wanted you to know that Isabella and I are going to dinner. I was just making sure you had a key."

"Yep, got it," Hunter says.

"Great, then we will see you later. Don't be too late!" Mitch hangs up the phone and checks his watch. "Babe, we are going to be late for dinner. What's taking you so long?"

Isabella emerges from the bathroom with a stunned look on her face. "Um...honey, I think we need to talk."

"Now? Didn't you just hear me about our reservations?"

"Yes, but this is way more important, and I am freaking out a bit." She walks over to him and takes his hand in hers.

"What's wrong, Bella? You don't look good—I mean, you look great, just not in the face. I mean, you always look beautiful to me, even when you look like this. I mean—"

"Okay, you made your point, Cyrano. I think you might want to sit down for this one."

"Are you sick? What's wrong?" He starts to freak out now.

"I am sick...but with a baby."

You could hear a pin drop.

"Babe? Did you hear me?" she asks him as she waves her hand in front of his face.

"Holy shit! We are having a baby! Oh my God, this is incredible! I didn't think we could!" He stands up and starts clapping and hollering.

"I know. This is one hell of a miracle, isn't it? I mean, I thought it was just indigestion at first, and then I chalked it up to stress after your brother died, and that's why I missed my periods," she states.

Mitch stops dead in his tracks and turns around to face Isabella. "Periods? Plural? How many did you miss?" he asks.

"Two. I must have been pregnant before Michael died."

End